Dirty Little Secrets

by

Philip Soletsky

Dirty Little Secrets by Philip Soletsky

Cover Artwork: Rachel Carpenter Artworks

Copyright © 2014 Philip Soletsky

ISBN-10: 1502995859

ISBN-13: 978-1502995858

To Vicki

Who believes in me.

Also by this Author

Embers
A Hard Rain

One

Funerals. Damn but I've been going to a lot of these recently.

I stood with the other Dunboro firefighters, twenty-seven of us in three rows of nine facing the open grave. The white-enameled, flag-draped coffin was suspended above it on heavy canvas straps. We stood at attention; spiffy in our class A uniforms with brass buttons gleaming, as the strains of *Amazing Grace* from the bagpipe corps floated through the air. My dress blues were fresh from the cleaners, the seams sharp and crisp. The department insignia and my rank medallions were polished and perfectly aligned on my collars. My name tag, *Jack Fallon, Firefighter*, was exactly square to the line of the breast shirt pocket. We all took great pride in our appearance, and in full regalia the department made quite a sight.

The rest of the mourners sat on the other side of the grave on folding chairs. They were civilians here, apart from us.

We were burying Ellis Banks, one of our own, a retired Chief no less. Dunboro is a small town in New Hampshire and we have a small fire department. Each death, even of an elderly and long retired member, is an emotional blow.

The widow and her two sons sat under a tent between the two groups at the head of the grave, physically and psychologically belonging to neither.

The town cemetery had an unreal quality about it, the white picket fence too perfect, the grass mown recently and almost too evenly emerald green. The graves lay, not in orderly rows, but in circles and whorls, clustered together by ancient clans and old blood. The physicist half of my brain began to play connect-the-dots, the positions of the markers forming segments which joined and spread creating fractals, molecules, and strands of DNA.

Perhaps the heat was getting to me.

The air was a suffocating blanket of humidity and we were tormented by swarms of mosquitoes. Both were due to an exceptionally rainy spring, one that had burst a dam in our sleepy little town, destroying seven houses and a section of roadway in downtown. Brookline to our south had had even more damage, and Townsend, Massachusetts south of that had been declared a disaster area. I had my own personal reminders of the flood, I thought as I leaned uncomfortably on my cane. I had been caught behind the dam when it blew and was lucky I wasn't dead. My injuries, as bad as they were, could and probably should have been much worse.

Beyond the fact that I sometimes used a cane and often walked with a limp, outwardly my face was the worst of it. What had started as a short line of stitches up near my hairline had become infected. To drain the accumulated pus the cut had been elongated. It now meandered like a strip of N-gauge model railroad track across my forehead and down my right cheek. The antibiotics were still having a hard time getting a handle on it, and the wound felt hot, swollen, and angry.

Amazing Grace ended and I and the other firefighters saluted, twenty-seven white-gloved hands rising as one. I felt the material of my glove snag on the flyaway end of the line of stitches on my forehead. The flag that had been draped over the coffin was folded by an honor guard with precision and presented by John Pederson, the chief of the Dunboro Fire Department. The widow, an ancient and gnarled woman, her hair a frizzy white puff that showed a lot of scalp like a sparse cotton swab, accepted it. She reached out with one quaking hand to take the flag, maneuvering her arm around the oxygen tube clipped to her nose in the way of someone long used to living with it. Her other hand clutched heavily at the handle of a walker with wide tires and a heavy aluminum frame, a cross between an ordinary walker and an SUV, suitable for cemetery off-roading. John returned to the line and snapped back to attention, a thing he was really good at as an ex-marine.

The winch whirred, the arresting gears clicked, and the canvas straps creaked as the coffin was lowered into the patiently waiting earth. The Marshall of the corps shouted "Dis-missed!" broken into two words like a drill instructor would say it. We dropped our salutes and drifted off in small groups, listlessly murmuring bits and pieces of stilted conversation that were quickly smothered by the heat and humidity.

My wife, Valerie, came over from where she had been sitting among the other mourners. She placed her hand lightly on my cheek, what would normally be an intimate touch reduced to a clinical inquiry. Her hand felt cool compared to the heat of the infection. "Does it hurt much?" she asked absently, without really making eye contact.

I shrugged. "Probably not as much as it looks like it should."

When I had caught a glimpse of myself in the bathroom mirror that morning I thought if it hurt nearly as badly as it looked, I would probably be lying in a bed somewhere screaming all the time or blitzed to the moon on Vicodin or Percocet. Personal experience at the supermarket last week had shown me I had a face that quite literally frightened children.

She had paid little or no attention to my response, lowering her hand from my cheek and turning away. I sighed inwardly, probably outwardly too, the distance growing between us already too great to fathom.

I spotted my friend Jonas Gault standing alone in one corner of the cemetery. With the death of Ellis Banks, Jonas was the oldest surviving retired chief of the fire department, perhaps the oldest surviving member of any rank.

I tried to entwine my fingers with Valerie's but she deftly avoided my grasp and we walked separately across the grass past gravestones, some sharp and clean, infused with that new tombstone smell, and some hundreds of years old, reduced by time and acid rain to unreadable shapeless humps of rock.

"Nice funeral ceremony, Jack" Jonas said to me as I approached, "we do a very good job, very respectful."

"We've had a lot of practice," I said somewhat sadly, recalling the funeral last year for Russell Burtran, this funeral for Ellis Banks, and between them the funeral of Althelia Temple, who had been one of the first women to serve in the Dunboro Fire Department.

"Yeah, there is that," he replied and then fell awkwardly silent.

"You OK, Jonas?" I asked him.

He frowned as he shrugged off his class A jacket and hung

it from the tips of two fingers over one shoulder. His dress shirt hung loosely on his age-withered frame as though it was intended for a much larger man, which in a way it was. "Jack," he said with a tired exhale, "growing older is a subtle thing. It seems like just yesterday that I was a young or at least middle aged man. Ellis was Chief, I was a new First Lieutenant, and Russell Burtran and Roger Fiske and John Pederson were as green as new wood. In here," he tapped his temple with his free hand, "I'm still that man."

Valerie stepped forward and gave him a gentle hug. "It must be very hard."

"Growing old? Easy as falling off a log. But it is hard sometimes reconciling those thoughts in my head while standing here at Ellis' funeral." He was silent for a moment after he said that, probably thinking that at eighty-four he was very far from those memories indeed.

I realized that he was standing at the grave of his wife, Elizabeth, when he put his hand lovingly on her headstone. His expression changed, his eyes becoming frightened, haunted. "I've, uh," he began uncomfortably, his eyes looking at everywhere but the two of us, "got a favor to ask of you."

I was concerned for my friend and couldn't imagine what had him so unbalanced. "Shoot." I said.

"It would really be better if I showed you."

"Showed us what?" Valerie asked.

He didn't answer immediately, instead rubbing a hand across the back of his neck. "That's going to take some explaining and a fair amount of time."

"Whatever time you need," Valerie answered for both of us.

"It's also a little bit of a walk, if you're up to it," he said eyeing my cane.

I gave him a small nod, "As long as we go slowly."

His eyes did a sweep of Valerie, assessing her funeral attire, her modest black skirt, black fitted jacket over a white silk blouse, and sensibly-heeled black shoes, "And I think you'll need to change. Meet me at the Bartlett trail cutoff when you're ready, say," he checked his watch, "an hour?"

"Sure," I replied, "But seriously, why all the mystery?"

He frowned, his gaze wandering over the thinning crowd of mourners, and then he looked back at us. He lowered his voice, though there was no one nearby to hear us. "What would you say if I told you I think Ellis was murdered?"

Ghastly as the thought was, I had to choke back a laugh. "I'd say you have a very impatient killer on your hands. Ellis was ninety-two and riddled with bone cancer. The killer might have literally taken him minutes before his time."

"He was murdered," he insisted while nodding, more to himself than us, as if proving some internal point, "and so was Althelia Temple. And the killer has murdered two other people besides them."

"What?" Valerie said loudly, emphasizing and dragging the word out, an elongated explosion of disbelief.

"Meet me at the Bartlett trailhead," was his only reply.

I hesitated, debating telling him that I had no interest in getting involved in whatever mystery he was thinking about, that perhaps I had already bled enough getting tangled up with murderers, but before I could put those thoughts into words Valerie chimed in, "We'll be there."

"Thank you," he said. "Now, if you'll excuse me, I'd like to catch Laura before her kids take her home."

He nodded to me and tipped his hat to Valerie, a pleasantly old-timey gesture, and walked over to the widow who had been transferred to a wheelchair, the flag on her lap. I watched as Jonas lifted one of her hands from the flag and took it in both of his own, kneeling down to speak softly to her.

Her sons stood behind her with slack expressions on their faces. I recalled that both were mentally impaired, the elder borderline functional, the younger able to follow simple instructions and nothing more. Staring into the grave of her husband, no doubt wondering who will care for them after she is gone, the tragedy of her remaining life was wrenching.

"What on earth could he be talking about?" Valerie said softly.

"I have no idea," I replied, squinting in the haze and heat of the bright summer sun as I watched Jonas release the widow's hand and get slowly, painfully to his feet.

He walked out of the graveyard, his head hanging and his shoulders hunched as though he were carrying an enormous weight.

Two

We drove home in separate cars, Valerie in her electric blue Rav 4, me in my new forest green F-150 that was a replacement for the previous one destroyed when a tree, its roots loosened by the spring rains, had fallen on it. My new truck was an automatic and I missed the stick shift, though with the injuries to my left wrist and ankle driving a stick would have been complicated.

The tendons in my ankle, according to the surgeon who had worked on me, had looked like pieces of frayed rope. Sections taken from a cadaver had been spliced in, donated by a twenty-two year old who had been texting while riding his motorcycle, at night, in the rain; a level of recklessness that had stunned even veteran firefighters at the accident scene who had thought they had seen and heard it all. The thirty-eight year old rest of me wondered if I had ever been so young and foolish. My wrist was healing well, though the removal of the cast six weeks ago had been accompanied by the addition of a card to my wallet which explained the complex arrangement of pins and plates that held it together, for when I set off metal detectors at the airport.

We arrived at home and received an exuberant welcome from Tonk, our English bulldog, his blocky body rippling with canine delight. Valerie went upstairs to the master bedroom to change, and I went into the guest bedroom to do the same.

For the record, I'd like to point out that I didn't intentionally move out of the master bedroom.

Initially, innocently, I had switched beds because my injuries caused any motion on Valerie's part during the night to awaken me and discomfort sometimes made it difficult to get back to sleep. My clothing had followed shortly thereafter as it was hard getting around on my ankle, and why go farther to get to my clothing than I needed to when there was a perfectly good empty closet and dresser in the guest bedroom? Then I moved my clock radio so I would know what time it was, and I moved my toothbrush to the guest bathroom because that was closer, and the Robert Parker paperback I was reading, and a stack of woodworking trade magazines that I liked to flip through that I usually kept in a pile on the nightstand. And, and, and.

OK, so I guess I had moved out, and what had started so innocently and practically had eventually taken on a much darker tone.

I marveled at the speed with which we had gone from a loving couple with sort of loose, nebulous desires to have a child, to a fragile couple that desperately wanted one, to a couple crushed by the realization that we couldn't have one. Valerie's infertility devastated our marriage like a blitzkrieg. She felt lessened, roiled by self-loathing at her infertility, and I became uncertain about what our marriage really amounted to without a child. Talks of adoption went nowhere, assuaging neither Valerie's feelings about herself nor my uncertainty. Our relationship deteriorated, awkwardness becoming stony silences accented by brief bursts of anger, fights sought out over the most pointless and insignificant infractions. Despite our best efforts to hold us together, we were coming badly apart.

I spent increasingly more time puttering around in my wood shop, and went to a large number of physical therapy sessions and doctor's appointments alone during which Valerie was off doing I didn't exactly know what. You would think that two adults living in a two thousand square foot house making only a modest attempt to avoid one another would bump into each other from time to time. You'd be wrong. The funeral was literally the first time I had laid eyes on her in a week.

I sat down on the bed to take off the slacks from my class A's and pull on a pair of jeans. It was hot and humid, and I would have preferred to wear shorts, but the Bartlett trail was near a swampy region of Dunboro and while the mosquitoes could bite through denim, I didn't want to make their job any easier than I had to. Pulling on the jeans was an awkward process because the Achilles tendon from the twenty-two year old flexed only grudgingly making it nearly impossible to point my toe down the pant leg, though ongoing physical therapy was improving it slowly. I pulled and shifted and shook the jeans, trying to get my foot to slide in without getting stuck.

Valerie walked by in the hallway and noticed my struggles. She came in and kneeled down, bunching up the cuff and reaching inside to pull my leg through. She had changed into a pair of tight, faded Levis and a Hard Rock Cafe T-shirt that stretched and conformed appealingly in all the right places. It made my heart ache just to look at her, her flow of golden blonde hair, the tilt of her blue-green eyes. She was so beautiful and I loved her so much. Why the fuck couldn't we get past this?

When my leg was through she picked up a sock that was lying on the floor and began working that over my foot. I was capable of doing that myself, but it too was something of a challenge.

"Can I ask you a question?" she said to my foot.

I wanted to shout, 'Yes! Anything! I love you!' but what I said instead was "Sure," some misguided and self-destructive facet of my ego getting in the way.

"How old was Althelia?"

My heart sank a little in my chest at the realization that she didn't want to talk about us at all. "I don't know exactly. She retired from the fire department in 1974." It wasn't that I recalled the retirement date of every firefighter who had ever served in Dunboro, but I recalled hers because we had hung a plaque from the State at the firehouse commemorating her service and the date was on it. "She had probably retired in her fifties or sixties, so she would have been in her late eighties or early nineties when she died."

She had finished with the socks and was fitting on my sneakers, tying the laces. The whole process made me feel like an invalid, which I guess in a lot of ways I still was. "So why would someone kill her and Ellis?"

"Seven months apart," I added.

She shook her head as she finished tying the shoes and stood up, her hands on her hips, "It doesn't make any sense. What could Jonas be thinking?"

"Well," I said, "old people can make enemies just like everyone else. Maybe, crazy as it sounds, someone felt that they just weren't dying fast enough. Maybe someone got tired of waiting for an inheritance. Maybe they were made to suffer somehow before they died. Maybe," I said, a new thought occurring to me, "they were going to suffer as they died, and the killer spared them from that, a Kevorkian kind of thing." I shrugged, "We're just spitballing here; we don't know anything. We don't even know who the other two victims were or if they were nearly as old. Jonas will tell us what he's thinking when he sees us."

I stood up and Valerie didn't step back immediately, placing our bodies very close together. Impulsively, I reached out and wrapped my arms around her. She was stiff at first,

11

unyielding, but then tiredly, almost as if she were exhausted by the whole process, she folded her arms around me. I felt a pull in my chest, a magnetism that wanted to be close to her, and I wondered if she felt the same thing, or anything for that matter. We stood like that, just holding. It was wonderful and awful at the same time.

Her hand lifted from my back, a move that allowed her to glance at her watch over my shoulder. "We need to get going. We told Jonas we'd meet him in an hour."

You said we would meet him in an hour, I thought to myself.

I let my arms drop and we drifted apart, two boats on a vast ocean no longer under their own power, the currents that guided us out of our control. She wouldn't meet my eyes, looking instead at her fingers which she had knotted in front of her. I wanted to grab her and pull her back, mold her against me, and bury my face in the scent of her hair. What I did instead was exhale and say, "OK."

Three

Valerie offered to drive us to the meeting, and I accepted. Just because we're not exactly speaking doesn't mean we can't be civil.

Jonas was waiting for us in the parking lot for the Bartlett trailhead. He had changed into a green T-shirt and jeans he wore the old man way, high up on his waist. There was no vehicle nearby; he must have walked there from his home, no small distance.

After we parked, Valerie got out and went around the back of the car. She opened the hatchback door and Tonk rocketed out. He ran over and sniffed at Jonas carefully, seeing if perhaps there were French fries hidden in his socks.

When Tonk settled down, Valerie clipped a leash onto his collar. If he caught the scent of a chipmunk, or worse yet the sight of one, it might take us hours to get him back.

I took a can of insect repellent from the car and we coated ourselves liberally with the spray. It made the wound on my face sting. When we were done we had so much DEET on us that had Valerie been able to have children, they would likely have been born with webbed toes. I chucked the can onto the passenger seat, hefted my cane, and we were ready to roll.

Jonas eyed my cane. "You going to be alright?"

"Depends on how far we're going," I replied, somewhat humiliated at being pampered by an eighty-four year old.

"A little over a mile."

"I'll be fine," I said, though curious where we were headed because I knew that the Bartlett trail ended in a little less than a mile at the gate of a superfund site, a region completely fenced off and posted by the EPA. The story in town was that a tannery had been down that way in the twenties and it had dumped chemicals everywhere. I wondered briefly if I should have worn a hazmat suit instead of jeans, but trusted Jonas not to lead us to a slow cancerous death.

We set off and almost immediately the trees closed in overhead and the air became still and heavy. Pockets of mist floated here and there as if we were underneath a rainforest canopy. I had never hiked this particular trail before and was surprised at how wide and flat it was, like some narrow roadway. Possibly, I thought, the one that had serviced the tannery.

We walked for a while without anyone speaking, each with our own thoughts, though for my part I didn't really have any. It felt so good just to be out walking, even in the heat and with my ankle already tightening up slightly. The air moving in and out of my lungs, the dapples of sunlight as they fell on my face, the slow, easy beat of my heart inside my chest; it all made me feel alive.

"They went on for a long time before I put anything together," Jonas said as we walked down a shallow slope, the land becoming boggy on either side of the raised trail.

I assumed he was talking about the deaths. "How many?"

"Three over the course of a year," he replied. "Ellis really sealed the deal after that."

"I'm not sure I can do another investigation," I told him. I wasn't sure that I wanted to get involved in any investigation, period. At this point I would have likely let a jaywalker slide. The two murderers I had caught thus far had almost gotten me killed. Besides, I was just a physicist turned carpenter, firefighter, and amateur sleuth.

"Let's hear him out," Valerie said, the steely core of a demand in her voice.

Her tone made me consider the profile of my wife out of the corner of my eye as she walked beside me. Initially highly resistant to the idea of my snooping, believing that I was risking my life, which it had turned out that I was, she had come completely around. While helping me out with the last mystery Valerie seemed to have developed a taste for it. Perhaps she thought that it would fill the wrenching void within her. If so, I could have told her from personal experience that it wouldn't.

"After Althelia, murder number three, I went to the sheriff who handed me off to the State Police," Jonas said bitterly. "I told them what I thought, and they laughed me out of the barracks."

Over the next few steps, my ankle tightened up severely. I hobbled over to a broad flat rock; some chunk dropped off by a glacier a hundred million years ago on its way to upstate New York, and sat down. I knew from experience that a few minutes sitting and working the ankle would loosen it up again.

When they realized I had stopped, Jonas and Valerie came back for me.

"You sure you're OK?" Jonas asked.

"I'm good, just give me a second."

While I worked on my ankle I ruminated. The State Police are sometimes known for being a little stuck up, but it was beyond imagination that they would ignore anyone with a thread that connected three murders. Maybe what Jonas had was just that tenuous.

As if he had read my thoughts, Jonas said, "The connection between the murders was tenuous alright, but it was there. After Ellis I had to do something."

"So you come to us?" I asked, my voice a mix of sarcasm and exasperation.

"I've already been to the cops. I don't know who else I can turn to."

He bent and scooped up a handful of loose pebbles from the trail with his left hand, throwing them off into the woods one at a time with his right. "My friends are dying, Jack. We did some awful things in the past, but no one deserves to die for what we did. I'm just a useless goddamned old man, and I can't just stand by and do nothing, especially knowing that I might be next!" He poured the remaining pebbles from his left hand into his right and threw the whole handful into the woods in disgust. They rattled into the distance, ricocheting off trees and snapping against leaves. He stood with his hands on his hips breathing heavily.

I didn't understand what he was talking about. What had he done, and how had Ellis and Althelia been involved? Whatever it was he was facing, I couldn't let my friend face it alone.

I got up from the rock, testing my ankle gingerly until I was sure that it would hold me. "OK," I said softly, "show us."

We set off again, the trail remaining as broad and flat as

before, just a few inches above the boggy land that surrounded it. Frogs croaked at us loudly from their perches on rotten logs that lay half submerged in the water. The upper faces of the logs had been weathered by the elements to the color of old bones.

The land lifted after that which meant, as I recalled from town survey maps, we were coming to the end of the trail. Shortly a rusty chain link fence blocked our path. It stretched left and right, a slight curvature to the fence line because of the roughly circular area that it enclosed.

Big signs were posted in a color that I've always thought of as 'official warning yellow.' Right at the top they read "Keep Out" in black letters five inches high. They repeated themselves in French and Spanish and then, just in case you didn't happen to speak either of those, there was a skull and crossbones which means keep the fuck away in every language. Underneath that were three paragraphs of government small print naming the responsible government agency (the EPA), the reason for the enclosure (toxic chemical waste), and the penalties for breaking the perimeter (extensive and plentiful, and they didn't even mention the cancer).

There was a gate in the fence directly in front us, a big blocky padlock on it that looked like a museum piece. Jonas fished in his pocket for his key ring and then began sifting through the keys, obviously looking for the one that fit the padlock.

"Uh, Jonas," Valerie began.

"Relax," he replied to her unasked question, "it's not a superfund site."

"Could have fooled me," I said.

"And did," Jonas replied with a tight smile. He found the key he was looking for and opened the lock, leaving it hanging from the chain link next to the gate. He went through first, and Tonk, Valerie, and I followed in his wake.

"Care to explain that?" I asked.

"Ellis and I put the signs and fencing up back in the seventies to keep people away. People ignore simple 'keep out' and 'no trespassing' signs all the time. Though toxic waste seems to get their attention." The smile he gave me was grim.

"Keep people away from what?" Valerie asked.

Jonas didn't answer right away. He kept walking, and we kept following. The air was hot, still, and moist, and since the land was higher, the bogs now behind us, the frogs had fallen silent. It was quiet in their absence, unnaturally so, with most of the noise coming from the crunching of our various shoes and paws on the gravel.

I was just about to repeat Valerie's question when the roadway changed, going from gravel and dirt to cobblestones, closely fitted, with granite curbing blocks. The vegetation along the road held the suggestion that it was no longer quite random but at one time, perhaps a long time ago, had been landscaping. The road turned sharply ahead, whatever lay at the end was beyond the curve and out of sight.

"Cobblestones," I said with wonder.

"They used to go all the way out to main road," Jonas said, "Ellis tore them up. They would have raised too many questions."

Around the bend stood an enormous wrought iron gate, its finials shaped like the points of spears, brick pillars supporting its weight from the left and right. Beyond it was, well, a little hard to believe.

"Oh my God," Valerie breathed.

It was a building, the size and style of an English castle, which had been very badly burned. The roof had mostly fallen in, and charred pieces of roof timber reached up into the sky like blackened skeletal fingers. The windows were high and narrow, almost arrow slits, the glass broken out and soot staining the stonework above them. The front door, at one time a stout construction with thick iron bands at the top and bottom, looked blasted, the wood shattered, the iron twisted. Ivy, its bright green and broad, flat leaves making it seem somehow prehistoric, had blanketed the southern face of the building, its thick tendrils weaving in and out of the window sockets.

"Welcome to Dunboro's dirty little secret," Jonas said.

Four

"This doesn't look like a tannery," I said, my hand wrapped around one of the wrought-iron bars that made up the gate as I considered the building beyond.

"It's not," Jonas replied. "It never was."

"So what was it?" Valerie asked.

"A church," Jonas said.

He lifted the gate latch and bunched up his shoulders, shoving the gate away from him in one motion. It squealed open on its hinges and banged against its stop, a length of pipe that stuck out of the road near the curb. The sound was flat and hard, and echoed back at us a moment later from the stone façade.

We walked through, passing a brick structure on the right. It had a small door and one window, and looked like a guard or information shack of some kind. The mansion was old stone, shaped and tightly fitted using a level of craftsmanship all but lost today, but the shack and gate pillars were standard brick and mortar, built in the last fifty years or less, much later than the mansion. Were they built by the church? Why would a church need a guard shack and gates?

Thirty yards farther on the roadway ended in a circle at the center of which stood a fountain, a stack of four nested concrete bowls. The support for the top bowl had broken and it lay crookedly in the bowl of the tier below it. Off to the left the circle connected to a parking area that looked like it could hold a couple of dozen cars, but contained the burned-out hulk of only one, an early seventies Chevy box truck, the fire damage and rust obliterating any trace of its original color.

"It doesn't feel like a church either," I commented as we stood at the side of the roundabout nearest the building entrance. The interior that I could see through the remains of the front door was so blackened by soot that I couldn't make out anything.

"Church is perhaps the wrong word. It was more like a cult. Before that it was a mansion, the private home of some lumber magnate in the twenties," Jonas replied.

"So I don't get it," Valerie said, "what's the secret?"

"They called themselves the Disciples of the True Path. Hardcore fire and brimstone stuff. They were very secretive, shunning outsiders."

"There are fringe cults all over the country following their own religious dogmas, and they all likely have their own private handshakes. There's no secret in that, dirty or otherwise," I said, shaking my head.

"The guy who ran the place was named Martin Pogue and he was a real piece of work. Magnetic, charismatic. It went from a church to a cult so smoothly hardly anyone noticed. Its transition from a cult to something much darker was equally difficult to pin down."

He paused there and Valerie looked at me, confusion on her face. I shrugged, my own face no doubt holding much the same expression.

"In the fall of 1971 a twelve year old girl escaped from them, scaling the fence at night and running naked to the police station. She was malnourished, showed signs of physical and sexual abuse, and had a brand on her hip, some kind of sigil that said that she was the property of the church. She said that she and half a dozen other girls were being held up here, that some others had died and were buried on the grounds."

Though the sun was still shining and the air was still stifling I nonetheless felt a chill race up my spine and my arms broke out in gooseflesh. I noticed Valerie hug herself. "What did the sheriff do?" I asked.

"He came up here to look into it, but these guys were armed to the teeth and they wouldn't let him in. He called the State and they called the FBI, and they laid siege to the place. Shots were exchanged. Some members of the church were killed in the fire that the church members claimed the FBI started and the FBI said that the church caused. Many fled into the woods and vanished. Pogue and some of his followers went to trial and were sent to prison. The FBI found some graves over there," he said, pointing at an area of scrub brush and weeds off to the west, "all children."

"How many?" Valerie asked, a quaver in her voice.

"I don't think they ever figured it out, but there were quite a few. They had been jumbled all together, dug up and buried again several times for God knows what purpose. Some parts were missing, skulls and some other bones, and there was a theory that maybe members of the cult had taken them or perhaps wild animals. None of the bodies were ever identified as far as I know. It was thought that the church picked up kids, runaways and maybe some kidnappings, and kept them around for a while before killing them."

I saw tears well and glisten in the corner of Valerie's eyes, but she didn't let them fall. In the aftermath of her own infertility, Valerie had become sensitive to the subject of children, all children, and Jonas's revelations of their abuse and murders, even in the distant past, were cutting her deeply.

I regarded the soot-streaked stone and the blasted front door. "What does this have to do with Ellis and Althelia?"

Jonas' hands started to shake and he jammed them into his pockets. His face fell, regaining the haunted aspect it had held in the cemetery earlier.

"Jonas?" Valerie asked uncertainly. She stepped forward and put a steadying hand on his arm.

He made a sound like a bitter laugh or perhaps he was clearing his throat. "When you think about inexcusable things you've done in the past, you always expect the passage of time to soften their impact, make you feel less ashamed about what you've done later." He looked up at her, barely managing to meet her eyes. "But, sometimes at least, the past doesn't let you go that easily."

"I don't understand," Valerie said.

Jonas dropped his eyes again and took a very long time responding. When the admission came, it was like he was smaller afterwards, like he had torn out some important piece of himself to make it. "They were members of the cult. We all were."

For a moment both Valerie and I were too stunned to speak, then I heard Valerie say in a very small voice, "Oh, Jonas, no."

She took her hand off his arm, and Jonas stared long and hard at the place it had been, as though he dearly wanted that support, that human contact, back again.

He nodded sadly. "Don't get the wrong idea. We weren't

23

in on the murders. We had managed to get ourselves out before that started up, don't ask me how. But all the signs were there. When Pogue's true colors came out, it was clear that he was a lunatic, a Charles Manson type. We should have known something was up; we should have done something about it. Instead we ran away and hid, kept our heads down like kids under the blankets hoping the monsters won't find them."

"I still don't get it," I said. "Why did you want to keep people away from it? Sure, the building is structurally unsound and the cult thing is distasteful as hell, but it was forty years ago."

"The town of Dunboro didn't want the reputation as the place with the crazy homicidal pedophile church. Also people knew that there were members of the cult living in town, though most weren't quite sure who we were or what role we had played. They probably wouldn't have cared if we were directly involved or not. With that kind of horror going on in their town they were out for blood. There might have been some lynchings if the church site was sitting here rubbing people's faces in it. So we tried our damnedest to hide it and forget it was ever here."

"So why not just tear it down?" Valerie asked.

"A stone building built in the twenties?" I said, admiring the stonework of the walls. "The fire hardly scratched it. It would cost a small fortune to tear down."

"A lot of money," Jonas agreed. "It just about broke us taking up the cobblestone roadway as far as we did. At least fencing was cheap. Ellis and I put it up and hung the signs. The town didn't forget about it; I don't think that's even possible. But they pretended that they did. No one talks about it, at least not in public, and here it stands."

A wind kicked up and made a hollow moaning sound as it passed through the narrow windows. A fresh crop of goose bumps covered my arms.

"I think I've seen enough. Can we go now?" Valerie turned and started to walk towards the gate without waiting for an answer.

We followed her. Jonas dragged the gate squealing shut behind us. At the chain link fence he carefully snapped the padlock closed, rattling it to make sure that it was locked.

"It would probably be worse if it came to light now," I said. "Just imagine what the media would do with a story about a small town and a radical cult that raped and murdered children."

"They'd probably dedicate a cable channel to it," Jonas nodded, "and the place would be overrun by sightseers, not exactly the leaf peepers that the state is trying to attract, and the real estate market would probably tank even worse than it already has. Believe me, no one wants to dredge all of this up now, which is probably part of the reason that the State Police threw me out."

Valerie had been completely silent since voicing her desire to leave, but she spoke up at that moment, "The other two people who were killed, they were members of the cult too?"

"Yes."

"Fuck them," she said venomously. "They're getting what they deserve."

"But we didn't know," Jonas said.

"You knew," she shouted, the tears she had managed to hold off until then starting to spill. "You said it yourself, that all the signs were there and you cowards hid!"

At the word coward Jonas flinched as though she had struck him.

"Those people, what they did. Oh my God, those poor children!" she cried.

She tugged on Tonk's leash and started a loping jog back towards the car which very quickly became a flat out run, Tonk's short legs a blur as he strained to keep up.

"Valerie!" I called to her back, but she ignored me.

In no condition whatsoever to run, I could only watch her leave.

Jonas looked from me to Valerie's receding shape and back to me uncertainly, "Do you want me to go after her?"

For a moment I tried to envision that, eighty-four year old Jonas chasing after my wife with a full head of steam. "No," I sighed, "Let her go."

Five

I could see that Jonas' humiliation at having been caught so easily in the clutches of the cult was a burden he was finding difficult to bear. On the walk back to the car I tried to convince him that cults created a powerful mix of chemistry and sociology that had trapped many strong people. Their members were fed a diet of fear of the end of the world or a government takeover or an alien invasion, and suffered under the threat of ostracization and isolation. Cults were more prevalent today than forty years ago and their methods had stood the test of time. That it had happened to him was not his fault.

I didn't make much headway.

When we got back to the parking area we unhappily discovered Tonk and Valerie and her car were gone.

"I think I'm sorry for getting you involved already," Jonas said.

I thought about pointing out that I wasn't really involved in anything yet, but what I said instead was, "The problems between Valerie and me run a lot deeper than this. You're not done with your story yet, are you?"

He shook his head, "Hardly started."

"Let's go get a cup of coffee," I suggested.

We headed in the direction of the town's Dunkin' Donuts. Jonas was astonishingly spry for a guy in his mid-eighties and he ambled along at an unhurried but determined pace, one that said, 'I'll get there when I get there, but I will arrive; you can count on that.'

At Dunkin' Donuts we bought a couple of iced coffees and four cinnamon donuts in a little bag, and walked from there to the town common, a small triangular patch of grass surrounded by white split rail fencing mounted in granite fence posts. A cannon that had perhaps played some role in the war against the British was set on a concrete pad at the center of the triangle with a neat welded pyramid of cannonballs piled next to it. We sat on a bench near the cannon and drank our coffee and had one donut apiece in silence, the bag resting on the bench between us.

I sensed Jonas wanted me to begin. He was uncomfortable enough at Valerie's reaction that going forward from here would be entirely my decision. A part of me seriously considered telling him no, I wasn't going to get involved. What I said instead was, "You and Ellis put up the fencing and the sign, but it's not a toxic waste site. Doesn't the EPA care?"

He smiled widely, I thought reliving some funny memory, perhaps of Ellis, that he chose not to share. "I don't think they know. It's not a very popular trail; it doesn't even show up in any of the guides. There are too many mosquitoes and it doesn't really go anywhere. Every so often a hiker probably comes across the sign, and calls their state representative and complains about a toxic waste site in Dunboro. Likely the state rep looks into it, can't find any record of a dump site, and sends back some campaign glossy about being committed to the environment. If it's ever gone any farther than that, I've never heard about it."

Jonas opened the bag and took out another donut.

He fell silent again, and so did I. Jonas likely wanted a more direct invitation to drag me into this mess with him, and again I considered my willingness to do so. My investigations in the past had earned me at least one enemy in the fire department, and smearing the memories of Ellis and Althelia was likely to make me a whole lot more. Throughout the town, and in the court of public opinion if it came to that, people were going to agree with Valerie; the church members were getting exactly what they had coming to them much later than they deserved it. Another part of me was already hooked, the mystery too tantalizing to ignore, the possibilities and permutations unfolding in my mind.

Against my better judgment, I asked, "Who was the first victim?"

Jonas popped the last bite of donut into his mouth and chewed thoughtfully, then swallowed. He dug into his pocket and pulled out several little folded squares of newspaper. He sorted through them for a moment and handed one to me. "Kevin Anderson," he said.

I unfolded the newspaper. The article, from last winter, reported a stabbing death of eighty-three year old parolee Kevin Anderson at what was identified as a halfway house in Lowell, Massachusetts. Seventeen stab wounds to the chest. Newspapers loved to report that kind of number. How many stab wounds, how many gunshots – grist for their mill. I thought it seemed like overkill, that getting stabbed half a dozen times would likely be fatal for many people and for an eighty-three year old more likely still.

"Who was he?"

"Martin Pogue's right hand man in the church. He got a

forty year sentence, but was let out at little early due to budget cuts and good behavior. He had been at the halfway house in Lowell for about three months when someone stabbed him. The police called it a robbery, likely by another resident of the house, though they haven't arrested anyone for it."

"Would he have had anything to steal?"

Jonas shrugged, "I don't know."

"But you think he was killed because of the church?"

"I do now," he replied and handed me another article. "Frederick Teeg, fifty-nine years old -"

"Fifty-nine?" I interrupted him.

"Fifty-nine," he confirmed, "he was eighteen when he was in the church."

I quickly skimmed the article. Teeg has been charged with statutory rape; one of the girls held by the church had testified against him. He had been sentenced to seven years, served them, and by all accounts had turned his life around. Thirty plus years later he was a plumbing contractor living in Milford, married, with a thirteen year old daughter. He had been found five months ago shot to death in his den, once in the chest which the coroner said was fatal, and three more times after that in the face.

"Wow, three in the face," I said.

"Yeah, wow. The daughter was at a swim meet out of state. The wife came home from dinner with some friends and discovered the body."

I remembered when Teeg's murder had hit the news. The violence of it had shocked the small bedroom community. People were afraid it was some kind of drug crime, or maybe a gang killing, in their quiet little town. Neighborhood Watch groups sprouted like dandelions after a spring rain, and burglar alarm companies were swamped with orders. As months went by without an arrest or another murder, the tension had died down some but not gone away completely. An easy way to start an angry and frustrated conversation with a complete stranger was to mention the death while sitting on one of the benches in the Milford town common.

"A shooting is a different level of anger from a multiple stabbing, even with three shots to the face post mortem. It doesn't fit," I said.

"It doesn't seem to, but it does," Jonas was adamant. "Althelia Temple," he announced, with the delivery of the next article.

I didn't even have to read the article; I knew about that one myself. Althelia had never married, had no children, and had been an only child herself. The fire department had been her family for almost forty years, and many of the old timers still spoke warmly of her. I suspected her involvement in the church would come as more of a shock to them than it did to me. She had been found dead in her home in Dunboro, and being sort of a solitary creature it had been a pretty long time between her death and the discovery of her body. Slightly mummified, the cause of death had been uncertain, though I didn't think anyone was talking about murder.

"And lastly Ellis Banks," he handed me the final square of newspaper, a copy of the obituary I had read myself five days earlier while drinking my morning coffee.

"He fell down a staircase at home, didn't he?"

Jonas nodded, "You got one more walk in you?"

My ankle was actually starting to throb a little and we had clocked something like four miles already, but I was going to be damned if an eighty-four year old was going to show me up. "I'm good."

He picked up the bag and silently offered me the last donut which I refused with a wave of my hand. He took it for himself with a mirthful gleam in his eye, "Never turn down a donut. They'll keep you young."

He balled up the empty bag and dropped it into a garbage can along with our coffee cups on our way out of the common. Our last walk was thankfully just a few blocks down Main Street to Ellis Banks' house. Like most of the homes on Main Street, this one was a hundred-plus year old colonial set right up against the road, two stories with white clapboard siding and dark blue shutters.

At the front door Jonas pulled out his key ring. "With Ellis' death, Laura has moved in with her boys. She gave me the key and I told her I'd water her plants until she can get the house packed up." He unlocked the door and we stepped inside.

The front hall was long and narrow with a threadbare oriental runner and a sideboard against one wall, a small stack of mail unopened on top of it. Jonas didn't seem to be anxious to go anywhere in the house so I stood with him waiting in the hall. The air was motionless, far more than simply still. It was as though you could feel that no one lived there anymore, as if the house was settling down in its loneliness.

After several minutes of just standing there I asked, "What are we doing here, Jonas?"

"I was hoping you would look around and tell me what you see."

"A front hall."

"Look around," he said again cryptically.

I shrugged to myself and wandered out of the front hall through an archway into the living room. Two recliners upholstered in olive drab fabric looked out the front windows, a small folding TV tray pretending it was a coffee table between

32

them. On the walls were dried flowers pressed between layers of glass and framed, their petals faded with age. A hallway opened off the end of the living room to the left.

I looked at Jonas who had followed me into the room but he said nothing.

I crossed to the hallway entrance. It was a cramped little passage with a low, uneven ceiling. There was a bathroom to the left with pale pink fixtures and tile and paint, like the entire room had been dipped in Pepto-Bismol. Farther down a swinging door opened into what had likely been a dining room at one time but had been converted into a bedroom. His and hers hospital beds pointed in the general direction of a flat panel television that hung on the wall. Each had a nightstand. His had a clock and a Clive Cussler novel on it, hers a book of Find-A-Word puzzles, a small ivy in a square terra cotta pot, and a box of Kleenex.

"They stayed in this room," I said to Jonas.

"Ever since Laura started using the wheel chair," Jonas confirmed, "a little less than two years ago."

"Where are the stairs Ellis fell down?"

"Through the kitchen, the end of the hall."

I went back out through the swinging door and down to the end of the hallway. The kitchen, like the bathroom, had not been updated in some time. The appliances had seventies-era art deco roundness to them and all were finished in avocado enamel. A stairway led to the second floor from one corner. I went over and stuck my head into it and looked up. The stairway curled sharply to the left and was far steeper than current building code would allow, the risers high, the treads narrow, the whole assembly shoehorned in awkwardly.

"Treacherous," I commented. "What's upstairs?"

"Nothing. When they moved downstairs they had the

upstairs rooms emptied and sealed off to save on heat."

I climbed the stairs, clinging heavily to the railing because my ankle was a little shaky and I had no interest in joining Ellis in the cemetery. The banister was firmly anchored to the wall. At the top I found a sheet of plastic had been taped over the access to the upstairs, the duct tape which held it in place intact all the way around the opening. I leaned on the plastic barrier experimentally. It was ten or twenty mil plastic, thick, tough, and unyielding. I went back down to join Jonas in the kitchen.

"So there would have been no reason for Ellis to go upstairs," I said.

"None," Jonas agreed. "According to Laura he hadn't been upstairs in over a year."

"Was she at home when he fell?"

"She was. She said that she didn't know what had happened. She was watching The Price is Right in their bedroom down the hall and he must have gone upstairs for something. The first thing she heard was the sound of him falling. He was dead on the kitchen floor by the time she got to him."

"But you're saying there was nothing for him to go upstairs for."

Jonas nodded.

"So someone had to come into the house, carry him up the stairs, throw him down, and then get out of the house, all without his wife seeing or hearing anything."

"Unless she was in on it."

I shook my head at the insanity of what he was suggesting. "You're saying Laura murdered her own husband of nearly sixty years, maybe with her sons? They helped carry him up the stairs

34

and throw him down?"

Jonas set his jaw stubbornly, "Maybe."

"And she stabbed Anderson seventeen times? And shot Teeg? Three times in the face? And killed Althelia we don't even know how or why?" My voice had been spiraling upwards with my disbelief, and by the end of my little speech I was cruising in alto territory.

He shook his head angrily in frustration. "Maybe she didn't, but they're connected, all of them, back to that goddamned cult," he insisted, "I can feel it."

"Hold on a second," I pulled the folded newspaper articles from my pocket and looked through them. "Let's say for the sake of argument that someone with a grudge against the cult stabbed Anderson. They had to wait to kill Anderson because he was in prison. But what about Teeg, Ellis, and Althelia? Teeg got out of prison thirty years ago, and Ellis and Althelia didn't go to prison at all. Why wait until now to get revenge?"

Jonas was silent and sullen as I shuffled the articles like large, flimsy, unwieldy playing cards. Then a new thought occurred to me. "The murderer has to be another member of the cult, right? Or how else would they know Ellis and Althelia were in it? How would they have found out?"

He didn't have an answer for those questions either and frowned.

I riffled the articles at random. "Gotta tell you, Jonas, I think you're jumping at ghosts."

"That's what the police told me," he said unhappily.

Why, I asked myself, did I consent to keep getting involved in these things? What was the root of the obsession that drove me, and would I satisfy my need before it killed me? I ran a finger carefully down the line of stitches in my cheek, feeling the heat of the infected and damaged flesh. Prying the lid off this cult was going to expose an unbelievable snake pit, put me at odds with the townspeople who wanted the past to stay in the past, and further strain my marriage which was already stressed near the breaking point. But the fear I saw Jonas' eyes was genuine. He was afraid for his life, and he needed my help whatever the risks. I blew out my breath, "I'll give it a couple of days. Ask some questions and see what I can find out."

A look of relief swept across Jonas' face, as if he was a drowning man and I had just thrown him a lifeline. I thought perhaps when this thing went sideways, and I was almost certain it would, that lifeline would instead drown us both.

Six

Jonas retrieved a watering can from under the kitchen sink and started in on the house plants. I went outside into the sunshine and began hobbling my way down Main Street.

The burden of the investigation was already weighing on me, and the heat seemed leaden, oppressive, the stitches on my face throbbing, a pain that radiated through my jaw and set up residence in my molars. I knew that I should go home, take four aspirin, and lie in bed in a dark room for a couple of days, then tell Jonas I couldn't find anything. It stretched the bounds of imagination to think the four deaths could be connected to either each other or a cult that broke up forty years ago. But I had made a promise to Jonas; I would do what I could.

In little shape to walk for much longer, I decided to see if I could get a lift home from a firefighter at the station house just a little way up Main Street. We're a volunteer department, but often during the day you can find someone there fiddling with their gear or watching a training DVD.

I walked around the construction cones and across the temporary steel plating that was the Main Street Bridge. Standing in the middle of the twelve-foot span I leaned against the railing which had been made of two-by-fours nailed together and looked down into the culvert. Three inches of sluggish water trickled through at the bottom of the cutout, but in my mind I saw myself trapped in the torrent of the flood waters, the raging churn of sticks and rocks and pieces of destroyed houses that had washed out this section of the roadway.

As my path to the fire station took me right past the front door of the police department, I decided to stop in and see what the sheriff, Bobby Dawkins, might have to say about the cult. Initially elected through a bit of chicanery involving his uncle, who was the previous sheriff and was also named Bobby Dawkins, many people in town didn't think much of him. But he kept getting re-elected every four years, and having worked with him I found that beneath his good-old-boy exterior he had a certain New England cleverness about him.

Inside the front door I was greeted by Lurch, an enormous black dog Bobby had adopted that was likely some mix of Mastiff, Newfoundland, and Black Bear. Sort of off balance on my bad ankle, I sat on one of the two long benches that lined the wall in the entryway and gave Lurch's head, which was roughly the size of a basketball, a good scratching. Lurch emitted a contented growling and burbling noise from deep within his machinery that sounded something like whale song. Bobby poked his head around the corner from the office area to see what the commotion was.

"Jack, good to see…" he began, but then cut off when I turned my head and he got a look at my face. He finished with, "ouch." He winced.

"It's not as bad as it looks," I insisted, though really at that moment it felt almost exactly as bad as it looked.

"Well, good to see you up and around." We shook hands;

mine swallowed whole within his.

Like his dog, our sheriff is oversized, somewhere up around six-six or more, and I had a sudden image of Bobby Dawkins at home with Lurch in a comically large house, a recliner the size of a compact car by the fireplace, a dog bed nearby as big as a queen-sized mattress.

He gave my hand a gentle shake, turning the wrist to check the scars.

"It was my left wrist," I reminded him, holding up my left hand so the sleeve of my shirt fell away revealing the patchwork of surgical scars, like a poorly executed suicide attempt.

He looked relieved and gave my hand a more bone rattling shake before releasing it. "So what brings you by? You're not investigating another murder, are you?" he asked with a laugh.

Rather than laugh along with him I frowned, and he stopped laughing and mirrored it back, and then dropped onto the bench across from me with a weary sigh. Lurch went to his master's side, resting his chin on Bobby's knee. "OK," Bobby said, absently ruffling Lurch's ears with one hand, "Let's hear it."

"Well," I began, my eyes drifting towards the upper corners of the room, "I talked to Jonas after Ellis' funeral."

He held up a hand to stop me. "He came to me when Ellis died, told me the whole story."

"And?" I prompted.

"And what? It's nuts. Ellis and Althelia, some plumber in Milford, an ex-con in Lowell. What connection could there be?"

"The Disciples of the True Path," I replied.

Bobby made a face like he had just tasted something very bitter, "Ancient history, long dead. The nutcase who ran it is rotting in prison in Concord, and has been for nearly forty years."

"The plumber and the ex-con were both murdered."

Bobby nodded in agreement, "But not in my jurisdiction, which is why I sent Jonas to the State Police. One was shot, the other stabbed. What makes you think they were even killed by the same guy?"

I didn't have an answer for that, mostly because I had had the same thought, so instead I went with, "What can you tell me about them, the True Pathers?"

He shook his head tiredly, as though a little frustrated that I wasn't going to let this go quickly, "Nothing. It was before my time."

"What about your uncle? He was the sheriff back then."

"He wouldn't talk to me about it, and he sure as shit won't talk to you. If he could have found a way to finish burning that building down or plow it under he would have, and pretended the whole mess never happened."

"Do you have his files from that time?"

Bobby hung his head for a moment and blew out his breath. He took off his uniform cap and ran a hand though his hair, and then resettled the cap on top of his head. When he looked back up at me his eyes had hardened and much of the friendliness was gone, "Forget it. I'm not going to open a bunch of dusty file boxes to you so that you can pick at a scab that the town has pretty well grown over. I know that Jonas is your friend, but he's wrong. There's no one killing off his friends because of some cult forty years ago."

"What about Ellis?"

"What about him? He wasn't killed. He fell down a

staircase."

"Which was sealed off upstairs," I pointed out.

"You think you're the only one who can investigate a murder?" he asked heatedly, more than a little offended. "I talked with his sons, as much as you can with those two. His wife was home at the time. Did Jonas mention that? And she didn't see or hear anything."

"So how did he get upstairs? And why?"

"The how is easy. Ellis wasn't in a wheelchair. His sons say that he got around just fine. As for why, who knows? Maybe he was a little addled and didn't know why he went upstairs himself. I think he just climbed the stairs, forgot the plastic sheeting was there, bounced off, and fell back down again."

I had to admit that his version of Ellis' death had a simplicity to it that was persuasive, though that didn't tell me anything about who had killed Teeg or Anderson or Althelia. Still, I could sense that I had worn out my welcome with Bobby and saw no reason to push it. "You're probably right. Thanks for your time." I stood from the bench, slowly and not without some pain, my ankle having stiffened up considerably while I had sat.

"Hey, protect and serve, right?" he said as he got up, trying to inject a little lightheartedness back into our discussion. "Don't be a stranger."

He gave my hand another bone-rattling shake, then held it in his grasp, "You're not going to let this go, are you?"

In truth, I didn't know what I was going to do, so I gave him a sort of noncommittal shrug.

He scratched at a bit of stubble on his cheek. "I think it's a bad idea, but if you want to know more about all that cult shit, some local author wrote a book about it in the mid-seventies. Like Helter Skelter with Manson. Tried to sensationalize it, make a buck." Bobby's tone made it clear what he thought of that. "I don't know his name, but I'm pretty sure the historical society has a copy. I remember the word death was in the title."

The look on Bobby's face made me want to tell him that I wouldn't dig into it, but Jonas' need for my help outweighed any allegiance I felt I owed Bobby and our burgeoning friendship. Instead when he released my hand I said "Thanks," turned, and left the station.

Seven

Because I was past done walking for the day, I was grateful that the fire department was just next door to the police station. There was only a single car parked in front of it, a green Ford Focus, and I didn't know who it belonged to, but I wasn't worried. I figured any firefighter would be willing to give me a lift home.

I unlocked the side door with the keypad code and stepped into the dark equipment bay. The trucks were parked, silent and hulking, smelling of diesel fuel and cold metal. The uniforms and gear hanging on the rack to my right wafted sweat and smoke. In my three years as a volunteer firefighter I had come to associate that particular comingling of odors with fire stations; in my experience they all pretty much smell the same.

There was a single light on at the rear of the bay, and from that direction I heard a furious rustling noise, clips and snaps being closed, then a female voice call out "Fuck!" in a loud and unembarrassed volume that echoed slightly in the room. This

43

was followed by more clothing sounds and another "Fuck!" which if anything was louder than the first.

I recognized the voice; it was Rachael Woods. I had caught her sister's killer a couple of years ago, and in what I thought then was some kind of misplaced hero worship, she had left college and joined the fire academy in Concord. She had surprised me by sticking with it, and was now living in town and part of the volunteer fire department while she continued to take firefighting classes in the evenings and on weekends with the plan of someday going pro.

At the back of the equipment bay, in the space between the rear of the trucks and the work tables, I found Rachel on her knees adjusting the straps on the suspenders of her bunker pants. The other gear, her jacket and helmet and gloves and hood and respirator tank and mask and a stopwatch, were strewn on the floor around her. She finished adjusting the straps and straightened the boots which were plugged into the scrunched up legs of the pants. Firefighters keep them this way so when a call comes in they can just step out of their own shoes into the boots, pull the pants up, and hang the suspenders over their shoulders. They are effectively almost halfway dressed in seconds.

She turned her head to look up at me. "Seriously, Jack, can you really do this in one minute?"

"In my current condition I probably couldn't do it in half an hour, but yes, at one time I did it in under a minute. Forty one seconds in fact, and with practice you will too."

She swept a strand of red hair that had pulled out of her ponytail away from her face and behind her ear. "This is stupid. I'm not even close," she shook her head.

I agreed with her that it was one of the more stupid things they made you do at the fire academy, what they called donning for time. Could you go from street clothes to fully ready to fight a fire in under sixty seconds? Who cared? Except for a fire call right next door to the station you had more than a minute to get

dressed in the back of the fire truck while it drove to the scene.
And it's not like if you arrived at the scene with your gear half
on that someone was going to throw you into the burning
building anyway. Yet it was what every firefighter did as part of
training.

"Let me see how you're doing so far."

She picked up the stopwatch off the floor and handed it to
me. "Count off fifteen second intervals, OK?"

I familiarized myself with the buttons on the stopwatch.
"Nope, that's not how you do it. If you're concentrating on the
time, you're not focusing on getting dressed. You put your gear
on and I'll let you know how long it took."

She spent some time arranging the gear in a strategic
pattern around her on the floor. This is something they
inexplicably allow you to do during the donning for time test,
though in the fire station your gear is all tucked into your cubby
and hanging on hangers when you come to put it on, and you
have to get dressed crammed in among other firefighters who are
gearing up at the same time. I see this as another indication that
the whole thing is an exercise in pointlessness, like some kind of
gentle hazing. When she was done she looked up at me.

"Ready," I said, the stopwatch held up.

She stood in a slight crouch, her hands loose and open at
her sides like a sprinter at the chocks.

"Set.... Go!" I started the watch.

She kicked off her shoes and jumped into her boots, pulled
up the suspenders, ran the clasps on the pants, shrugged on her
jacket, ran those clasps, pulled the air tank over her head, affixed
the mask to her face, pulled on her hood, then her gloves, then
slammed her helmet onto her head. Finally she attached the tank
regulator to the facemask. "Done!" she shouted.

I looked at the watch. "How long do you think you took?"

She detached the regulator and spoke to me through the hole in the mask, "I don't know. Two minutes?"

"Try sixty-eight seconds. You're almost there."

"Still, I can't see as I can go any faster."

"There are lots of places you can save some time. Put on your gloves last. They slow you down when you're putting on your helmet and attaching the regulator. Get a little more practice with the spring clips on the jacket. Those two things alone will probably save you fifteen seconds."

She finished getting the gear off, pushing the bunker pants down over her boots. As she did so her jeans were dragged down low on her slim hips. Her T-shirt was already rucked up her back, so I got a glimpse of the fuchsia band of her thong before she got her pants yanked up again. I had a few inappropriate thoughts for a thirty-eight year old married man looking at a twenty-two year old woman and fellow firefighter, and then let them pass.

She tried a few more times, integrating my suggestions as she went along. She managed to do it twice in less than sixty seconds and she celebrated, doing a little jig in her fire gear. Then going for three in a row she got her hood twisted around which kept her from attaching the regulator correctly to her mask, and by the time she got it all straightened out ninety-seven seconds had elapsed. With a groan she realized that she had a lot of practicing to do yet.

Still, she was more hopeful than she had been. I helped her clean up her gear and put the tank back on the truck she had taken it from, and afterwards she gave me a little thank you peck on the cheek, which made me think of her thong again. That kind of made everything awkward for me and we stood in a slightly uncomfortable silence at the back of the bay while I searched for either a way to continue the conversation or end it gracefully with more than an "OK then, bye," which would likely have been followed by the peal of burning rubber as I sped out of the parking lot, only I didn't have a car. That's right, I remembered: I still needed a lift, and I was about to ask her for one when the horn on the top of the station sounded.

"No more dress rehearsals," I told her. "This one is for real."

Eight

Given my current condition I was in no shape for firefighting, but I was still capable of driving a truck and operating the pumps. Anxious for a little action I scrambled up into the cab of Engine 3 and pulled it out onto the concrete apron in front of the station to wait for a crew. Rachael geared up and climbed into the back, and though I didn't time her it seemed to me that she had done so in far less than sixty seconds.

In minutes, cars and pickup trucks adorned with a ragtag collection of light bubbles and LED bars and dashboard flashers streamed into the parking lot from every direction. The firefighters ran inside and came out a moment later in various stages of dress, bunker pants up but not clasped, jacket slung over one shoulder, helmet trapped under one arm. They would finish getting dressed on the way to the call. The call was for an oven fire, and everyone was in a rush to get rolling.

Oven fires represent a special opportunity for firefighting because ovens are designed to contain heat if not actual fire. If we can get there quickly, we might be able to keep the fire entirely inside. Even if the fire gets out of the oven, kitchens are often arranged to keep readily flammable objects and furniture away from the cooking areas, and if we can limit the fire to the kitchen we can greatly reduce the damage to the rest of the house.

Three other firefighters, I didn't see who, got into the back, and John, the Chief of the Fire Department, filled the officer's seat next to me. As soon as the dashboard alarm went quiet, indicating that all the passenger doors were closed, I hit the gas. I could see a second truck, Engine 2, pulling out of the bay immediately behind me, a crew climbing inside, and then lost sight of it as I took a right onto Main Street, the truck tires thumping and banging over the steel plates in the road.

The house was a compact garrison, beige vinyl siding with dark brown shutters and trim, set on a small lot right up against Winterberry Road. A family stood in the postage stamp yard, looking uncertainly back towards their house but turning their attention to us when they heard our sirens coming down the road. There were four of them: a couple, which I took to be a husband and wife, a teenage boy, and an older woman, who I figured was a grandmother.

The crew I had with me was a good one. They had all talked out their roles on the drive here and knew what to do the second they hit the ground. While I climbed up onto the back deck of the truck and started the pumps, two of them grabbed a speedlay line, two hundred feet of hose and a nozzle stored next to the pump panel for quick deployment, and raced to the front door. Another took the infrared camera, which would be used to check for leakage of heat from the oven into the walls, to investigate if the fire may have gotten out of some seam in the oven construction and was quietly burning away out of sight. Rachael picked up a portable radio and an axe. Certainly she didn't expect to need the axe for an oven fire, but if you have a free hand it is always a good idea to take some extra tool in. You never know what might come in handy, and in any fire situation it is the unknown that can very quickly bite you in the ass.

John got out of the truck and came around to the family.

"Oh, thank God you're here," the husband said. "We thought it was going to explode!"

At the word explode my whole body tensed. A gas oven on fire raised a whole different set of problems over an electric oven fire. A leak contained in an oven could rapidly achieve a volatile mixture of air and gas and go off with the concussive force of a bomb. A failure of a regulator or a stop valve could demolish the entire house. The town of Dunboro has no distribution line for gas service, and each house has its own propane tank somewhere, often as much as five hundred gallons to stretch through the long winter months when the tank might be buried underneath the snow and difficult to fill. If the fire somehow got past some safety systems and back to the tank the whole neighborhood could be leveled.

"Hold up!" John yelled at the crew, who at that moment was up on the front porch.

Trained and drilled extensively to listen to their Chief the crew froze in place, one guy actually with one foot in the air in mid-step.

"Jack, I'll take the pump panel," John told me, "get in there with a gas meter!"

My throbbing ankle forgotten in a surge of adrenaline, I jumped from the deck and snatched the gas meter from its charger and ran to the front door. Once there I could see the faces of the crew. Besides Rachael there was Robert and Bruce Jonet, twin firefighters. It has taken almost three years for me to tell them apart, and even now I occasionally get it wrong. With them was Roger Fiske, a nearly forty-year veteran firefighter and officer who would have taken the officer's seat had John not been there himself.

Fiske and I have some bad blood between us. At this point the initial cause of it almost doesn't matter, as what began as a simple ground skirmish has rapidly escalated to something close to all-out war. John, for his part, seemed at a loss for a way to defuse the situation. I didn't blame him. As the Chief of a volunteer fire department in a small town with a limited pool of applicants, he was just trying to keep everyone on the crew and give peace a chance. Fiske and I hadn't come to trading blows yet at a fire scene, but it was probably headed for that.

At the sight of me Fiske narrowed his eyes but said nothing. I ignored him and booted up the gas meter, a process which the manufacturer claimed took less than ten seconds but always seemed to take a heck of a lot longer when you thought you might be sitting on a time bomb.

I cracked the front door and stuck the sensor wand through the opening. The meter read zero.

I opened the door wide and stepped into the front hall. The room was square with a flagstone floor and a high ceiling, a swoopy art deco chandelier of brushed aluminum and yellow glass overhead. A gray-carpeted stairway went upstairs directly in front of me. There was a dining room to the left and a living room to the right. A passage continued past the stairway on the right, a bathroom tucked in underneath the stairs.

There was no smoke in the air that I could see. I sniffed. Both natural gas and propane have a chemical additive in them called ethyl mercaptan also known as methanethiol which gives them their distinctive rotten egg smell. It can be detected at incredibly low concentrations by the human nose. I didn't smell anything. The meter showed all clear.

I waved in Bruce and Robert who were holding the hose to follow me and went down the passage. Rachael and Fiske trailed behind them.

The kitchen was dark, the lights off and the windows covered with heavy drapes. I could make out the arc of the countertop and a breakfast table surrounded by four chairs. The oven was an indistinct black square mounted in a wall among the kitchen cabinets. I didn't see any flames or smoke, and the lit display in the gas meter continued to read zero.

We all moved into the room towards the oven. Rachael reached out for the light switch and Fiske slapped her hand down savagely.

"Jesus, bitch, trying to blow us to the moon?"

In the meager light I saw a look of questioning hurt on Rachael's face for a moment but she shoved the emotion down and her expression became impassive. Though I wished Fiske had been more diplomatic in his choice of words, he was right. Deaths and serious injuries have been attributed to errant sparks at gas leaks, such as those that might be caused by flipping a light switch. Rachael had certainly been taught as much in firefighter training, but it must have slipped her mind.

The fire department is no place for the emotionally fragile. Rachael would take the rebuke and carry the lesson with her, a reminder that might one day save her life.

Our flashlights are specially designed not to create sparks, and Roger turned on the one clipped to his jacket. A moment later Bruce and Robert did the same. Rachael must have forgotten her flashlight and I wasn't even wearing a jacket; it was back hanging from one of the grab bars on the truck by the pump deck.

"What do you see?" I asked Roger.

He held up the infrared camera and pointed it at the oven. I got a glimpse of the camera display screen over his shoulder, the oven a white square in the cold, black field of the cabinetry.

"Hot. Three hundred seventy five degrees. You?"

I checked the gas meter, putting the wand right up against

the cracks of the oven door. "Zilch."

"You do know how to use that thing, right Fallon?"

I thought of a bunch of choice responses but kept them to myself. That was a low level dig I could easily ignore.

"Bruce, Robert," Fiske said, "I want you there." He pointed to a spot in front of the oven. "I'm going to open it."

Bruce and Robert stood with the hose pointed directly at the oven door, their face shields down. If Fiske opened it and there was anything bad going on inside, they were going to throw two hundred gallons of water into it in about four seconds flat.

Fiske stood to one side of the oven and I stood to the other. Rachael stood dumbly next to Bruce and Robert and I reached out and snagged the shoulder of her jacket and pulled her to one side. It probably seems like a pretty easy concept to not stand in front of the thing that might explode, but rookies at fire scenes are frequently so overloaded by events that common sense seems to fall by the wayside. Others watch out for them and they learn. Rachael nodded and mouthed a quick, silent thanks to me.

Fiske whipped the door open and everybody tensed, but there was nothing. No smoke. No fire. There wasn't even anything cooking inside the oven.

And it was an electric oven. It's element at the bottom was glowing orange.

We all looked at each other. I checked the oven controls and found that it was on, and actually set to three hundred seventy five degrees.

I turned it off.

Relief washing through us, we gathered ourselves and went back outside. The family was still on the lawn, the Chief with them. Engine 2 had arrived while we were inside and its crew stood next to the truck waiting to see if they were needed.

"What's up?" John asked Fiske.

"It's electric," he said as he brushed past John and climbed back into the truck to put the infrared camera back in its mount.

"Huh?" John said.

"What he means," I said, "is that it isn't a gas oven. It's electric and seems to be operating normally."

John turned to the family, "What made you think it was going to explode?"

The wife looked embarrassed. "I don't cook much. When I turned it on and the metal piece got red I got nervous. And, well..." she trailed off.

I heard Bruce, or maybe it was Robert, start to laugh which he covered with a cough and a clearing of his throat.

I saw John crack the smallest of smiles before he managed to squash it. "That is the way electric elements work," he said. "As they warm up they start to glow, first orange, and then at higher temperatures, red."

The whole family looked at us as if they had never heard of such a thing.

"Engine 2," John called out, "Return to quarters. We'll be off your lawn just as soon as we get packed up," he told the family.

"Thank you for coming," the man said.

"Better you call us and not need us, than need us and not call us," John replied, a stock firefighter reply often used when someone has called us for something stupid.

The crew from Engine 2 got on and the truck drove away, and the family went back into their home. We drained and packed the hose back where it belonged and put the axe, thermal camera, and gas meter back in their places.

No sooner had we boarded the truck then Bruce burst out laughing. "Oh my God, how does someone not know how an electric oven works? I don't cook much," he said, imitating the woman in a falsetto.

"And the grandmother," his brother added, "she was what, seventy? How do you get to be that age and never use an electric oven?"

It was actually worse than that, I realized, because all electrically heated appliances worked that way. Had they never seen a toaster? An electric stove? A space heater? Heck, if you looked down the barrel of a hair dryer it probably became red hot on certain settings.

We really yucked it up on the way back to the station, probably laughing about it more than it was worth but part of that was burning off the adrenaline, the relief that the call had turned out to be nothing instead of the disaster it might have been.

I was sure it was a story that would rattle around in the fire house for some time to come.

Nine

When we got back to the fire house we found that the crew of Engine 2 had already parked the truck and departed. Bruce and Robert put their gear away and walked off, their home not far from the station. John got into his truck and drove towards Massachusetts where he worked as a diesel mechanic. That left me with a choice between Fiske and Rachael to bum a ride; it wasn't a difficult decision to make.

"Can I get a lift?" I asked her.

"Sure."

We turned off the lights and made certain that the fire station was locked; the theft of gear from fire houses is a serious problem even in small towns, believe it or not. She led me to the Ford Focus, unlocking the car with a fob on her key ring.

"I really screwed up today, didn't I?" she asked unhappily as we settled into the seats.

"You're just starting out. It's natural to make mistakes. The important thing is that you learn from them; try not to make the same mistake twice."

"But I could have gotten us all killed."

"Well, it turns out you couldn't have, but I see what you're saying. Anyway, Fiske stopped you. No one can be perfect all the time and we have to work to cover each other's lapses. That's part of the reason we train together in crews. Firefighting is unlike any other activity, except perhaps combat, and you need to learn a whole new way to approach and solve problems. You're smart, you'll get it, but it will take some time."

"Thanks," she said, putting her hand on mine.

The contact sent a surprising flush through me, an uncomfortable feeling not unlike the experience of a teenager on a first date. I realized there were conflicting forces in play; the distance and friction that overshadowed the relationship between Valerie and me, against Rachael who was vibrant and engaging and enthusiastic. It was a mix every bit as volatile as an infusion of fuel and air, and I didn't want to fool around and see if it would explode. On the other hand simple female companionship, not sex, not love, but just the thereness of friendship that Rachael could provide was something that I ached for as Valerie became increasingly cold and remote.

"Hello?" Rachael said, snapping her fingers in front of my face. "Earth to Jack? You in there?"

I came back from my thoughts to find I had been so deep inside myself that I had lost a little time. Rachael's hand was off mine, but I still felt the heat of her touch as if I held it near a candle.

"I'm sorry, I was thinking about something else."

"Obviously," she smiled. "I asked if I was driving you to your house."

"Yes, but could we make one other stop first? I need to go by the Historical Society. It should only take a few minutes."

"Yearning for some moldy old town records? Sounds like fun."

The Ford Focus turned out to be a sporty little car and she drove it energetically, jack rabbiting away from stop signs, taking corners short and hard, swaying the suspension back and forth. The motion caused our shoulders to bump from time to time which made my heart feel like it was being jarred in my chest.

The Dunboro Historical Society occupied one large room sectioned off from the town hall basement. It had its own parking area around the back. Rachael glided the car into one of the many available spaces in the lot, the Historical Society not really being one of the hot destinations in town.

She shifted the car into park. "Do you want me to wait here or should I come inside?"

"You're welcome to come, but you were probably right about the moldy old town records part."

"Wow," she rolled her eyes dramatically, "you really know how to sell it." She paused as if giving the matter great thought. "Ah, what the hell. Live dangerously, I say." She undid her seatbelt and got out of the car.

I had never before visited the Historical Society, probably like ninety-nine percent of the people in town, but it was more or less what I had expected it to be: deserted, with creaky wood floors, rows of dusty filing cabinets, and some framed stuff on the walls like the original town charter and front pages from among the first editions of the town newspaper, the Dunboro Daily. The Daily is only printed twice a month, and I think has been so since its inception. Perhaps the original publisher who picked the name had grandiose plans, though we were hardly a town that generated news on a daily basis. Maybe he had just liked the alliteration.

The center of the room was dominated by a table on which was built a topographic map of the town out of Paper Mache or maybe plaster, the hills painted gray and black, small twigs trimmed to look like trees poked into the surface. A few of the early town buildings were rendered in the model. I noticed the town hall and the lumber mill, and some of the houses along Main Street that still stood more or less unchanged to this day. Out at the end of the Bartlett trail, which did look a little like a road in the plaster, there was no model of the stone mansion, though there was a peculiar unpainted flat spot indicating where one might have been.

"Can I help you?" Emmy Farmer said as she shuffled over to greet us.

The Historical Society was just the one room, but I hadn't noticed Emmy when we had entered. I couldn't imagine where she had come from. I thought, though not exactly kindly, that maybe she had climbed out of one of the filing cabinets like the crypt keeper. Emmy was, just to throw a number at it, one hundred and forty three years old, but she could probably pass for one twenty in the right light. She was short, hunched over, with a pinched face. Her yellowed hair was done up a massive beehive that added a good six inches to her height.

The fire department had responded to her house dozens of times in just my meager three years of volunteering. Wired up about the time of the Civil War and rewired during World War II, her home's electrical service was an arcing and sparking collection of aluminum-core conductors and crumbling canvas insulation. The place was a frigging tinderbox in which Emmy lay in bed at night smoking filterless Camels about as fast as she could light them. There wasn't a firefighter on the department who didn't know her address by heart.

"I'm looking for information on the Disciples of the True Path," I told her.

Emmy's pinched face became even more pinched – if that were possible. "At the historical society we have chosen not to focus on the town's darker events."

It had never even occurred to me that the historical society might be a group that censored the pieces of town history that it collected. Then I reconsidered. The historical society wasn't an official town function at all; it was just a bunch of people who gathered up town mementos and displayed them, like scrapbooking on a large scale, and they naturally focused on the things that interested them and ignored the things that didn't. It was more like the selective amnesia that Jonas had mentioned than any particularly malicious intent to censor the past.

Perhaps feeling she was not adequately serving her only customers in what I had to imagine was quite some time, her face relaxed somewhat and she said, "I have some pictures from the night their church burned, if you would like to see those."

"I would, thank you."

She crossed to one of the filing cabinets and opened the top drawer, then after a few moments of riffling through the file tabs closed that drawer and opened the next drawer down. More riffling, then she found the one she was looking for, pulling it out of the drawer and opening it on top of the cabinet. Rachael and I walked over to look at the pictures.

There were only three of them, and they showed roughly the same thing, the focus of the shot being the burning mansion, the flames leaping high into the night sky, the collection of police and fire trucks gathered in the roundabout parking area. I had half been expecting to see black and white photos, or perhaps something in a sepia tone, like old shots of Eliot Ness arresting gangsters during prohibition. These pictures had of course been taken in the early seventies, and the color film paper and developing pigments were of high quality. Most of the colors had held true, though some of the brilliance of the reds had faded.

The contrast of the images was good; the cameraman had had some talent and set the f-stop correctly to get the halo of the fire, the strobing of the lights on top of the emergency vehicles, while the shadowed outlines of the people in the foreground remained sharp and crisp. The firelight had illuminated the sides of many of the cars and I saw emblems of the FBI and the State Police. There was a SWAT van. There was a lone Dunboro police cruiser pushed into the periphery of both the shot and the activity, a solitary figure standing next to the car leaning on the hood. The figure was large and at first I thought it was Bobby Dawkins, the town sheriff, and then realized it must have been his uncle. Big must run in that family.

I laid the three of them side-by-side across the tops of several adjacent filing cabinets. In the correct order I grasped that they were sequential pictures taken over a span of just a few seconds, most of the people more or less unmoved from shot to shot. The last one in the series showed the moment that the roof had collapsed, a pillar of fire and released heat towering over the building, warped and stressed roof timbers crumbling inwards. Studying them carefully I could see the sag of the roof line as it had prepared for collapse, what the photographer must have noticed that caused him or her to fire off the three pictures in rapid succession hoping to catch it.

If there was something the images had to tell me about the murders of church members occurring today, I couldn't see it. "I heard that there was someone who wrote a book about Disciples of the True Path, like a true crime thing. Do you know anything about that?"

Emmy abruptly gathered up the photos which she squared together with a sharp crack against the top of the filing cabinet. "Scandalous! Completely unnecessary muckraking of the worst kind." She jammed them back into the file folder and jammed the file folder back into the drawer. "Whatever prurient interests you may have in all of that, the historical society cannot help you." She slid the drawer closed with a bang. "Dunboro is a respectable town, and I'm sure none of our fine citizens had any interactions with that man."

"Pogue?" I offered.

"That man," she emphasized, "and his lunatics. If that is the kind of dirt you wish to dig up, Elmer Branch is more likely to help you than I. Good day." She left us.

"Elmer Branch wrote the book?" I asked her departing back, but she ignored me, steaming away from us towards the end of the room where another row of filing cabinets, these slightly taller, blocked her from view entirely, and was likely where she had been hiding when we had first come in. Perhaps that was where she kept her crypt.

"I guess we're done here," I told Rachael, and she followed me outside.

Once back in the car, Rachael asked, "That stuff about the Disciples of the True Path; you're investigating something, aren't you?"

"Maybe," I replied, "maybe not. I'm just poking around as a favor to Jonas. I'm not even sure there is anything to investigate."

"Tell me about it."

So I did. It didn't really take very long as I knew little more than the articles had told me. Rachael was a very receptive audience, and the banter, her making observations and shooting comments back at me, reminded me of Valerie and I investigating the murder of Lorraine Watson four months ago. Rachael was easy to talk to, effervescent, with a quick mind.

"So are we going to talk to the book guy now?" she asked when I had finished with the story.

"Well, I don't know that we're going anywhere," I replied, emphasizing the 'we're' part.

"Oh, come on! You can't just tell me that story and expect me to go away. I want to hear what he has to say. Besides, you still need a ride."

I had my truck at home and considered having her drop me at it. I was perfectly capable of driving myself. Besides, I could see clearly that I was headed into an emotional minefield. Warning signs were flashing everywhere, ironically almost the least of which was the concern that investigating a series of possible murders could be dangerous for Rachael, for both of us, and by what right could I ask her to get involved in that?

"See?" she said, holding her phone up in front of my face, the screen displaying a little Google map with a destination marked. "He lives in Milford, some nursing home, less than five miles from here. So are we going?"

I knew that I should tell her no, that undoubtedly one of any number of disasters lay down this path, but for reasons I wasn't quite sure of I stalled on my answer and she launched into the conversational gap.

"We're going," she said decisively, giving her car key a joyous twist.

Ten

Elmer Branch lived in a building that fell somewhere into the ever more complicated category of senior living facilities. Each resident had an efficiency apartment, but the facility also contained a common cafeteria and extensive meeting areas and social centers, a small movie theater, and there was a twenty-four hour nurse on duty. Beyond the nurse and movie theater, the flow and floor plan of the place reminded me more than anything of the dorm apartments I had lived in as a grad student.

A concierge of sorts buzzed his room from the front desk, announced our arrival, and then directed us to the elevators when Elmer agreed to see us. I was relieved there were elevators, as I was near the point my cane was all that was keeping me from dragging myself along the floor.

The upstairs hallway looked much like that in any mid-level hotel but with a whiff of an antiseptic or medicinal odor drifting through the air. Elmer's doorway was extra-wide and had the peephole down around bellybutton height, so I wasn't surprised when he answered the door in a wheelchair which he rolled backwards allowing us to enter.

He began to hold out his hand to shake mine after he had opened the door, but stopped short. "Tarnation, son, what happened to your face?"

"Long story," I replied.

"I'll bet it is," he said, his hand held out to me cautiously. "Elmer Branch, failed author, and you are Jack?"

"Fallon," I completed for him, "I'm a volunteer firefighter."

"Thank you for your service," he said sincerely.

"You're welcome," I replied self-consciously. I always feel weird when people say that to me, which happens more often than you would think.

Elmer was lean but didn't have the stringiness that you so often see in the elderly. He had a full head of dark hair, and bright, inquisitive blue-grey eyes in a cherub's face. I noticed that his legs looked adequately muscled, not wasted at all, like he didn't really need the wheelchair or at least hadn't been in it that long.

"And you are?" he turned his head to Rachael, a swift, darting motion like a bird.

"Rachael," she paused as she shook his hand. "Rachael Woods. I guess I'm also a firefighter."

He widened his eyes brightly. "Really now? And so lovely. Tell me, Rachael Woods, are you trained in CPR?"

"I am."

"Would you care to indulge me in some practice doing mouth to mouth?"

Rachael blushed mightily but said nothing, the spray of freckles across her cheeks glowing like beacons. I had no idea she was so easily embarrassed.

"I'm sorry. You have to forgive me," Elmer said, though the way he said it made it clear that he was anything but sorry; he had loved making Rachael blush and she had just revealed herself as an easy target. "I seem to be losing my world filter in my old age. Whatever goes through my head just comes out my mouth." He abruptly spun his wheelchair around and rolled off farther into the apartment past an open bathroom door on the left and a bedroom on the right. "Come in. Please. I don't get very many visitors."

We followed to where the hallway widened into a small living room. There was a recliner with an ottoman and a small love seat upholstered in a fabric that looked like gold burlap, and an old pine coffee table between them that had been painted white. He flipped himself out of the wheelchair and into the recliner with little difficulty, lifting his legs up onto the ottoman.

"Ahh," he settled in, "much more comfortable than the wheelchair. Do either of you run?"

Without even considering my reply I gave him the old standup comedy standard, "Only when chased."

In response to that Valerie would have given me an eye roll, but Rachael chuckled and Elmer smiled with his eyes gleaming. The wonders of a new audience with old material.

"I ran for thirty years," Elmer said, "marathons, iron man competitions, the whole malarkey. My knees are done, shot, kaput. And these aren't even my knees, they're the second set of rebuilds and they're shot too. Go easy on your body," he said, eying my cane, "it's the only one you're going to get."

"I'll keep that in mind," I told him.

"But you didn't come all this way to get orthopedic advice

from old Elmer. What can I do for you?"

"I understand you wrote a book about a cult that was discovered in Dunboro in the early seventies."

"The Disciples of the True Path. Great story. Couldn't sell it. You sure you're not a movie producer?"

"No, sorry," I said.

"Damn," he frowned, "it would have made a great film. Pogue was the spitting image of David Carradine. He'd be perfect for the role."

"Um, David Carradine is dead." I thought it had been autoerotic asphyxiation or something like that, a fact I chose not to share.

"Damn," he said again, "the man was a fine actor. Creepy as hell. Dead in the eyes." He used his index finger to point out his own eyes. "Say," his attention darted back to Rachael, "if the front desk could find a Wonder Woman costume and send it up, would you put it on for me?"

Rachael, who had just about gotten her last blush under control, flushed afresh and looked down into her lap, "I don't think so."

"Oops, sorry again!" he exclaimed with a smile. "Damned filter."

His speech pattern was frenetic, disconnected. I wondered if what I had taken for a bright look in his eyes was instead a kind of desperate energy, as if he was using the chain of rapid fire speech to cover up some dementia. I had had a maternal aunt with Alzheimer's who had behaved very similarly. Or maybe he was just toying with Rachael and me.

"Do you remember Lynda Carter?" he asked me. "Statuesque, dignified and half-naked at the same time." His eyes took on a wistful glaze.

"Mr. Branch, you wrote a book," I prompted.

His eyes came back to mine. "I wrote a lot of damned books. Couldn't sell them though. The publishing industry is locked up tight. You can only get a book out there by knowing someone."

"On the cult in Dunboro," I added.

"The Disciples of the True Path. Great story. Couldn't sell it."

"Martin Pogue, looked like David Carradine, we got that part," I said, trying to forestall what I saw as an oncoming loop in his dialog, feeling that there was likely some kind of dementia involved.

"Then you've met Pogue," he said with wonder. "Did you visit him in prison? What did he tell you?"

"I haven't seen Pogue," I replied.

"Amazing. Spitting image of David Carradine."

I heard Rachael sigh next to me. I was beginning to wonder if it was possible to keep him on a single train of thought long enough to reach the station, any station. "Mr. Branch, do you have any copies of your book, the one on the Disciples of the True Path?"

"Of course. I have them all. Box in my bedroom closet. Why don't you go get it while I chat with the lady?"

I looked at Rachael and she beaconed an SOS at me with her eyes, but then gave a resigned shrug. Elmer was harmless. It wasn't like he was going to chase her around the apartment in his wheelchair. Or he very well might, but I was pretty sure she could outrun him.

I got up from the couch and went back up the hallway to the bedroom. When I opened the closet door I was greeted by the odors of old leather shoes and mothballs, a smell that instantly transported me back to my own father's closet when I was a small boy. I read somewhere that the sense of smell is most strongly linked to memories and I don't doubt it for an instant. In that moment I was maybe all of seven years old, remembering the way that my small feet slid around inside the enormous expanse of my father's brown dress shoes.

Shaking off the memories, I looked up at the top shelf. There were a number of sweaters vacuum packed inside clear plastic bags, a few mothballs visible in each package through the plastic. There was a dusty felt fedora, the fabric worn shiny in spots. There was also a cardboard box, the size ten reams of paper come in.

I took the box down; it was heavy. I folded back the flaps. It was full of hardback books, the covers in garish colors, the name Elmer Branch along the spines. The publishers were companies I had never heard of. It didn't take me long digging through them to locate one entitled Cult of Death, the cover picture a blackened silhouette of the stone mansion blown slightly out of proportion making it foreboding and sinister, the sky behind it the color of blood. Cheesy.

I flipped through it a little bit. There were pages of black and white photos clumped together in the center of the book. One was a picture of the mansion during the fire, similar to if not the same as the one we had seen at the historical society. There were several more after the fire had been put out. I also noticed one that looked like Pogue's booking photo with his name and prisoner number held on a card in front of him. Elmer was right; Pogue did look like David Carradine.

The book was over four hundred pages long and would take me some time to read. I considered asking Elmer to summarize it for me, but given his uncertain mental state I couldn't be sure that he wouldn't leave something out or get some of the facts wrong. After reading it, if I had any questions, I could come back and see what answers I might get out of him.

I put the book aside and closed the box, returned it to the shelf, and shut the closet door. On my way up the hallway carrying the book I heard Elmer say, "Come on, it's not a hard question. Are you wearing a thong?"

"Found it," I announced loudly as I came into the room holding up the book.

Rachael's face was scarlet, a flush that traveled all the way down her neck to the collar of her T-shirt. Elmer's eyes gleamed mirthfully.

Upon seeing the book cover he held out his hands, and I gave it to him, "Ahh. I remember this one." He rested the book in his lap, his hands caressing the cover. "This story had it all. Sex. Violence. A small town. Deep, dark secrets. But Helter Skelter had just come out. I couldn't compete with that: Charles Mansion, Sharon Tate, the Hollywood jet set. Damn," he said unhappily.

"I'd like to read it. Can I buy a copy?"

"This," he held the book up and waved it, "is all vanity press. The printing company is long gone. This is probably the last copy in the whole world." He said this like the world was really missing out on a fine treasure, the planet somehow lacking because of it.

"Could I borrow that copy?"

He pursed his lips, tapping the spine of book against his thigh, "Sorry, it's the only one I have."

"I promise I'll take good care of it and get it right back to you."

He shook his head, "Can't risk losing it."

"What if I had the book scanned and had more copies printed? Then you could have as many as you want."

He was tempted by the offer. "OK, I'll need fifty copies."

"Fine, sure," I held out my hand for the book, though I couldn't imagine what he might want fifty copies of it for, and I realized as I said it that fifty copies of a hardcover limited printing might cost me a thousand dollars, maybe more.

He offered the book, and then pulled it back at the last second, just out of reach, "And I'm going to want a peek."

"What?" I asked.

"No!" Rachael said.

"Come on," Elmer prodded, "one peek and the book is yours."

"A peek of what?" I asked.

Rachael blew out her breath and folded her arms across her chest. "No," she repeated.

Elmer waggled the book in the air.

"Seriously?" she said.

Elmer tilted his head and raised his eyebrows.

"Fine," she said exasperatedly. She turned her backside to him, lifted the back of her shirt and tugged the waistband of her jeans down a few inches giving him a view of the top of her thong.

Gentleman that I am I averted my eyes almost instantly.

She let her shirt drop back into place and turned to him with her hand out, the other on her waist with her hip cocked.

He placed the book gently into her outstretched hand, "A thing of beauty," he said.

She slapped the book into my stomach, knocking some of the wind from me which left my mouth with an oof. "Come on, Jack, let's go." She stalked from the apartment.

"You're a sick man, you know that?" I told Elmer.

"And if you're a smart one, you won't let that slip away," he replied, his face radiant.

I trailed Rachael out of the apartment.

Eleven

Back at the car I had been expecting Rachael to be upset, humiliated at having sunk to Elmer's level. Instead, as soon as she closed the door, she shocked me by laughing.

"I can't believe I just did that! Is this what investigating is like? Such a crazy rush?"

"Not for me," I answered cautiously. "Mostly I find it's asking a lot of questions of people who would just as soon not answer them."

"But it's exciting," she insisted, "and crazy," she repeated. "Have you ever done anything like that?"

"I kind of don't have the right equipment, so no," I replied. Her jubilation surprised me. Though I did understand her excitement at having found a piece of the puzzle, unearthed a clue, and I suppose I might have been willing to do what she had done if the clue was a good one. It was likely that I would never know, however, unless I came across a middle-aged Fruit of the Loom fetishist.

"So where to now?" she asked, her eyes positively glowing.

"Uh, my home, I guess. I need to read the book. I'll let you know what it says when I'm done."

She snatched the book from me, "Uh-uh. Flash your thong and get your own copy. This one's mine." She fanned the book, stopping at the pack of pictures in the middle, saying "huh, he does look like Carradine," to herself when she looked at Pogue's picture.

"Rachael," I began, but she cut me off.

She closed the book with a snap. "I'll tell you what, we can go back to my place and look at it together. Flip through it, hit some of the highlights."

My gut told me right away this was a bad idea. This was followed by the feeling that I was blowing it way out of proportion. I was a grown married man, not a love-sick teenager. My wife and I were having problems, and the attraction of a young, vivacious woman was strong, but that didn't mean I had to act on it. Moreover, I was slightly disgusted at myself for objectifying Rachael so completely, for thinking she would be so overwhelmed by my magnificence there was no other outcome than we would fall into bed together. Also, Valerie and I were going to have a confrontation when I got home about me investigating the cult for Jonas, some fresh take-no-emotions-prisoner knock down drag out, and I was looking for any way to delay that as long as possible.

"Sure," I swallowed, "that sounds like a good idea."

Given the green light, she raced over to her place like a competitor in a NASCAR event, dodging, bobbing, and weaving the twisty roads of Dunboro as if there was a trophy at stake.

Her place was a small cabin tucked back into the woods that appeared to have no official driveway. She just pulled off the road past a mailbox and navigated the gaps between the trees, the ground a whispering cushion of long pine needles beneath her wheels, and stopped in front of the home. I had a little trouble getting the door open wide enough to climb out with the press of branches on all sides.

It was only late midday, late midday on a summer's day at that, and there was still plenty of sunshine left, but here the light came down in sharply defined shafts, patches of darkness lurking everywhere. I would have thought the effect would be lonely, perhaps sinister, but instead it felt enchanted like a Disney movie, the air filled with birdsong and the pungent odors of forest growth.

The cabin's siding was dark green, the shutters white. It was difficult to tell what the roof material was, asphalt or cedar shingle or metal; because it was uniformly layered with the same long pine needles as the ground.

"Cute," I said.

"I like it. Might be kind of difficult keeping some kind of driveway open in the winter, though," she said as she opened the front door. I noticed that she didn't use a key, that she had left the door unlocked. Dunboro remains one in the dwindling list of small towns across the US where you can still get away with that, but I wondered about the wisdom of a single woman living alone doing so in an isolated house a good half mile from her nearest neighbor. I followed her in without making any comment on it, however.

The inside smelled faintly of potpourri, something like cloves and nutmeg. She flipped a wall switch and a floor lamp with a blown glass globe threw light across the room and projected a big oval of light on the ceiling. The living room at the front of the house was painted pale green with an arc of sectional couch in dark blue. There was framed poster art on the walls, Cezanne, Van Gogh, Rembrandt etchings. Through open doors to my left I could see a bathroom and the bedroom.

She tossed the book onto the corner piece of the sectional couch. "I'm going to change. I stink like my fire gear. I can't believe you didn't say anything about it in the car."

"I don't think you smell too bad."

"Why you little flatterer you," she laughed at me as she headed into the bedroom. She kicked the bedroom door closed with her heel and it bounced against the jam and then swung back open about ten inches. "I'll be out in the minute," she called, "There's a bottle of wine in the fridge. Why don't you open it?"

"Sure, wine's a great idea," I mumbled to myself.

The kitchen was simply an area off to the right delineated by the flooring changing from the mid-depth carpeting to linoleum which curled up a little at the edges. A peninsula of Formica countertop enclosed the narrow galley span of the kitchen appliances. I picked up the book on the way by the couch and put it on the countertop while I opened the refrigerator. There were two bottles of wine on their sides on one of the shelves, one white, and one red. I spent an inordinate amount of time debating the unintentional romantic impact of one versus the other, in the end inanely deciding that the color red was somewhat more passionate and so grabbed the bottle of white by its neck and drew it off the shelf. As I turned to place it on the countertop I saw a flash of motion through the partially open bedroom door. One of Rachael's sneakers fell onto the floor in my field of view, followed by the crumpled ball of her jeans.

I quickly felt myself blush; probably a blush that would have competed with Rachael's earlier, and I busied myself by opening cupboards looking for glasses. I found a pair of crystal wine goblets on a top shelf, slender with a twisted stem and a delicate bowl. They looked expensive and a little out of place, like a graduation gift. I passed on them and instead took out two ordinary drinking glasses, simple cylinders with a thick, heavy base.

Grasping the cork which was half jammed into the bottle I worked it out with a pop just as Rachael came out of the bedroom. She had changed into gray yoga pants, like sweatpants except that they were completely form fitting and dipped down in a low V in the front, and a short white T-shirt that didn't quite cover her stomach. No bra was in evidence. She was barefoot.

She saw me preparing to pour the wine into the glasses and said, "Don't use those. I've got really nice glasses that I never get to use." She crossed the room and shimmied past me in the narrow kitchen, her back to my front, a lot of contact there, and opened the cupboard. She returned the two glasses to their shelf and reached up, way up, to retrieve the goblets. Her shirt rode high, exposing the bottom curve of her ribcage, the stretch of skin over the bones, shadows in the hollows between.

Some guys are ass men, some like breasts, some are into legs or feet, but for some reason I have always been enticed by the female ribcage, and I had a strong surge of desire to run my tongue along those hollows, taste the secret sheen of sweat visible there.

She came down off her toes holding the glasses and bumped my groin with her backside, a slide of friction as her heels approached and then reached the floor.

I felt another flush, but this time of something approaching anger. I was certain she was manipulating me, the little brushes of contact, leaving the bedroom door open, not wearing a bra, perhaps even all the way back to the glimpse of her thong earlier in the firehouse. That conclusion was instantly shouted down by another part of me which said that I was being ridiculous. She had not put on a thong that morning on the off chance that she was going to run into me at the firehouse today. Everything she was doing indicated that she was a woman comfortable in her body and our friendship, unaware of my marital problems and the impact her sexuality was having upon me. She was not coming on to me. I should, this other voice inside me counseled, get over myself.

I tried to cool off as she offered me a glass of wine. I took it and she rang her glass against the one I held in numb fingers. "To catching a murderer," she toasted.

It was an odd toast that probably deserved some witty retort. The one that I delivered sounded something like, "Urm."

She picked up the book and passed by without touching me, though something in my jeans was straining a little to bridge the distance. In the living room she folded herself onto the corner section of the couch under the lamp.

Conscious that I wanted to be close enough to see the book, but not too close, I strategically placed myself on her left, a meticulously maintained gap of air between us. She defeated this plan by handing the book to me and then leaning in. My air gap was history.

I flipped open the book to the pictures, the first one of the fire.

"How did the fire start?" she asked me.

"I don't know," I said. My mouth dry, I took a quick sip of wine. "The cult members claim the FBI started it, while the FBI claimed the cult started it so that some of the members could get away in the confusion."

"How many got away?"

"I don't know that either. That's one of the things that I was hoping Elmer could shed some light on. Maybe he could even tell us who some of them were."

I turned the page and we were greeted by a full-page picture of Pogue's mug shot. The caption read, 'Martin Pogue was sentenced in 1972 to forty years in prison for murder and attempted murder.'

The facing page was split in half, the upper picture of a man in blue jeans and a flannel shirt out in the woods somewhere, a rifle propped on one shoulder. He looked cocky, the way he stood with his weight on one foot with one hip thrust forward, one arm casually draped over the stock of the rifle. He had a lot of brown hair, a loose shag of it around his face, a big droopy moustache, a thick shapeless beard. There was also an energy somehow visible about him, like a tightly coiled spring ready to sproing. 'Kevin Anderson was Pogue's right-hand man in the cult. He was sentenced to prison for murder, attempted murder, rape, sexual assault, and other charges.'

"Nice guy," Rachael said.

"Salt of the earth," I replied.

The bottom half of the page showed a similarly dressed man, jeans and flannel shirt, though the sleeves were torn off ragged at the shoulder. Unlike Anderson, this man was clean shaven; his hair was a military buzz cut. He had a boney brow that overhung dark, mean eyes and a forehead so flattened that it had to indicate a reduced brain pan volume. His arms were long and rangy and sported a number of tattoos that couldn't be made out in the photograph. 'Paul Rhodes was the cult's enforcer, responsible for making Pogue's word law. He was sentenced for murder, attempted murder, rape, sexual assault, assault with a deadly weapon, and battery.'

I felt Rachael shiver beside me, "What a Neanderthal. I'd hate to run into him in a dark alley."

"I think today he's around seventy years old."

She shook her head, "I'm not sure that matters."

I considered the photo again, noticing as I did so that, although he was smiling, Rhodes' hands were clenched into tight fists, as if in the photo he was about to enjoy hitting someone or had recently done so. "Point taken," I said, and turned the page.

The next photo was a mug shot of a teenager, his eyes about as big as tea saucers and beads of sweat visible on his face. He looked to be about six seconds shy of a stress-induced heart attack.

"Who's the kid?" she asked.

I read the caption out loud. "Martin Teeg, 17, was tried as an adult and sentenced to 7 years in prison for rape and attempted rape."

"That's it? Those are the only four who were charged?"

"I guess so." I flipped forwards through other pictures, but they didn't show any more cultists. There was a picture of the building after the fire was out, some interior shots with sensationalist captions like 'the dungeon in which victims were likely kept before sacrifice,' and a portrait of the guy who had built the mansion in the twenties. There was also a picture of a SWAT van with the pathetic caption, 'A van of this type was used in the siege of the cultist headquarters.' Elmer had really been padding out his book there.

Rachael took a sip of her wine then asked me, "Are you hungry?"

"I'm OK"

"I'm starving. I haven't eaten since breakfast." She got up off the couch and went into the kitchen. "I thawed out some chicken for dinner. It should be enough for two."

"I wouldn't want to be a bother," I said. I also thought to myself that I should call Valerie and discuss my dinner plans with her, but we had been eating separately without any plans as a couple for so long that I didn't hold onto that thought for more than a few moments.

"No bother," she insisted, "and it will go perfectly with this wine."

Great, I reflected, perhaps I should have chosen the red.

She took a package of chicken breasts out of the refrigerator and retrieved a cutting board and got to work. She really knew her way around a kitchen, first pounding the breasts thin with firm, even strikes from a tenderizing hammer that caused her own breasts to move about in fascinating ways underneath her brief shirt, then sautéing the chicken in a pan with wine, garlic, butter, and mushrooms.

"Read to me," she said as she cooked.

If for no other reason than to keep my eyes off her, I cracked the book open to the space past the pictures and started reading. It was tough going, not only because I was feeling awkward but because Elmer's sentence structure could best be described as shattered. His prose was all fragments and it was hugely redundant. He also frequently started a sentence with one train of thought and ended at another. Reconsidering my earlier belief that he was suffering from some age-related dementia, in the light of his writing style I wondered if perhaps Elmer had just always been like that, some kind of scatterbrain.

The section I was reading was a lengthy and adjective-laden exploration into supposed undiscovered cult members living in Dunboro. Elmer had shied away from specifics, either because he was afraid of being slammed with a libel suit or because he just didn't know for a fact who any of the undiscovered cult members were, but there were several enticing hints dropped here and there. One was described as "a well-respected member of the community with a long history of service to the town." Ellis had been fire chief about a decade when the cult came to light, so perhaps that passage referred to him. Another description read, "A high-ranking member of the school board," and another "A respected businessman and Rotarian." Would it be possible to narrow such general descriptions down to specific people after so many years? What purpose would identifying ex-cult members serve now, unless I had some other way to winnow that list down further and find the murderer? If, I reminded myself, there was any murderer to find.

She served the chicken with baby asparagus and thick, crusty bread and we ate sitting on stools side-by-side at the counter. We started talked about the cult and skimmed lightly through more of the book, but then branched off into firefighting, and novels, and plays that were coming up by the local theater groups, and we polished off most of the bottle of wine. We ate slowly and passed a lot of time, and afterwards we agreed that she should drive me home.

She gave me the book to read, claiming that she had too much studying to do. I recalled my own stint at the firefighting academy and there had been little reading or studying involved. I thought she was doing it partly as a kindness because she knew how much I wanted to read it, and partly because the small sample I had read to her while she had been cooking had convinced her it was very nearly unreadable.

On the ride home I considered my feelings for Rachael, the suddenness and strength of them. Valerie and I were rapidly approaching a critical juncture for our marriage. Not talking about our problems, not discussing where we were going, was not, and likely had never been, a solution. When we arrived at my house I got out of the car, waving goodbye to Rachael absentmindedly as I closed the door softly behind me. I was determined that Valerie and I would have that conversation, as unpleasant as it might be.

The sound of Rachael's car fading behind me, I noticed the house was dark; Valerie wasn't home. Not only was Valerie not at home, but the way that Tonk raced out to do his business when I opened the front door told me that she probably hadn't been home other than to drop him off since we had met Jonas earlier in the day.

Where was she?

Twelve

Valerie is a grown woman, I reminded myself. In our marriage I am not jealous or controlling, and Valerie most certainly did not have to account for her whereabouts or activities during the day with me or anyone else. Still, she had been upset when she had left Jonas and me, and I was concerned about her.

I settled for doing the parent thing – waiting up without appearing as though I was waiting up. I fed Tonk dinner and then sat down to read in the kitchen with a cup of citrus green tea. I started at the beginning this time and it was clear that Elmer had front loaded the book with a bunch of action scenes to try and hook the reader. He recounted the story of the girl escaping from the cult and fleeing to the police station. Sheriff Bobby Dawkins, the first, was portrayed as a cross between Buford Pusser, the bat-wielding sheriff from Tennessee who was the subject of the Walking Tall movies and TV series, and Wyatt Earp. Elmer described in rich and gory detail the confrontation between the sheriff and the cult members when he came to investigate the girl's allegations, the subsequent siege by the state and FBI, and the fire. Even these action sequences were nigh unreadable as Elmer used a choppy sentence structure which made it difficult to figure out who was shooting at whom.

When I started getting drowsy I found myself again wondering where Valerie might be. My cell phone sitting on the surface of the kitchen bar silently mocked me. I could easily pick it up and call her, know where she was in an instant, but a part of me maybe didn't want to know. Perhaps I was projecting my own feelings about Rachael earlier, but I was certain Valerie was with someone else.

I dumped out the rest of my tea, now cold, and gave Tonk a last opportunity to do his business, then left the porch light on for Valerie when we went inside. Upstairs in bed, I took another crack at reading and promptly fell asleep with the book on my face.

I awoke the next morning with the bedside lamp still on, the book on the floor by the bed, and Tonk resting his head on mine. Tonk may have been warmer and softer than the book, but he also had very bad breath, and when I pushed him away a long string of saliva tethered us together. I don't drool that much, so it had to be his.

I went down the hall to the master bedroom but Valerie wasn't there and the bed was made. Valerie is one of those people who make the bed as soon as she gets out of it, so I couldn't tell if she had slept in it at all. I stood in the upstairs hallway listening to the normal sounds of the house, the hum and click of the various systems doing their thing, and I could tell she wasn't at home. Detective that I am I went to the kitchen and looked for a mug that might have been used that morning, one perhaps damp with coffee residue or recently washed and sitting in the drying rack next to the sink. No dice.

Finally, out the front window, I noticed the porch light still shining brightly.

So she either hadn't come home last night, or she came

home, hadn't turned off the porch light, and this morning had gotten up, made the bed, and left without having any coffee or waking Tonk, and Tonk is a very light sleeper. Though not exactly damning evidence, I was pretty sure the former was true.

Like all people do when a family member is missing, I had a momentary flash of her helpless and injured somewhere, her car lying undiscovered in a ditch, or perhaps she was unconscious in an emergency room with no way to tell the staff to contact me. However as a firefighter I knew the statistics; car accidents that go unreported for twenty four hours were incredibly rare. Similarly, the police and hospital staff would have an enormous number of tools including Valerie's driver's license, her fingerprints, her car's license plate, the VIN, and her dental records to identify her and know to contact me. I could, without the slightest hesitancy on my part, put any fear of her possible harm aside.

Wherever she was, she was there by choice, and sadly I didn't really know where she would go or who she would turn to if she were upset. This was followed by the more disturbing thought that I couldn't remember the last time I knew for a fact she had slept at home. We were that disconnected.

As I saw it, I had exactly two choices. One, I could confront Valerie, talk about us, get all the unpleasantness out, and perhaps like lancing a particularly nasty boil, get us on the path to healing. That was assuming getting it all out would lead to a new beginning and not our end. Two, I could do nothing, we could go on as we were going, and just hope this patch would pass, scab over, drain on its own, and not rot our marriage from the inside out.

Doing nothing, especially in the light of the understanding that I didn't know what doing something would lead to, was tempting. That thought was followed by the bitter realization that, as active and take charge as I was in so many facets of my life, where Valerie and I were concerned I was such a passive fuck.

As a distraction from the state of my marriage which was depressing the crap out of me, I picked up the book and riffled the pages. It again fell open to the pictures in the middle, and I found myself looking at Pogue, wondering about the thoughts that went on behind his dead eyes. I recalled that Elmer had asked if I had visited Pogue in prison. Was such a thing possible? For what reason would he agree to talk to me, and what would I ask him if he did?

Perhaps before I hauled myself to the state prison in Concord for an attempted chat with Pogue, I should question people a little closer to home. I could, for example, see what John Pederson, the Chief of the Dunboro fire department had to say. He had been a firefighter back then, had likely been at the church fire, and had known both Ellis Banks and Althelia Temple personally. I could also talk with Laura Banks about Ellis, or see what I could find out about the stabbing of Kevin Anderson at the halfway house in Lowell or the shooting death of Martin Teeg in Milford. My investigative dance card was full.

I snapped a leash on Tonk and headed out. There was no reason for the poor dog to stay at home all day alone, and I had no idea what time Valerie might be back.

The temperature was warm, but the humidity had fallen a few percent so it was more comfortable. Despite all of the walking of the previous day my ankle felt loose and easy which I took as a sign that it was getting better. I loaded Tonk into my truck, climbed inside, and considered my options.

Tempting as a talk with John seemed, because I was fairly certain he would be open and candid with me about what he knew, the chances of finding him at the fire station were slim. The fire department in Dunboro is a volunteer company from the lowliest firefighter all the way up to its Chief. During the day John worked as a diesel mechanic at a garage in Townsend, Massachusetts, and I didn't see my questions as any reason to disturb him at work. I furthermore didn't want to intrude on

Laura's grief, approach her with a bunch of half-baked – and that was putting it kindly – theories about her husband's death so soon after the funeral.

I contemplated which way to turn as I sat in my truck at the end of the driveway, Tonk positively rapturous in the passenger seat with his head out the window. My process of elimination seemed to have left me with only two choices, Anderson or Teeg, and therein lay a conundrum.

Up until this moment my detective activities had remained strictly amateur. I had avoided direct interactions with the police, either investigating things in which they were not interested or exploring from such a different direction it was unlikely our paths would cross. Yet now I was planning to walk into a police station and ask questions about a murder they were actively working. Granted, probably not too actively in the case of Anderson, given that he was an elderly ex-felon likely stabbed by another felon, but the murder of Teeg, the plumber and father shot in Milford, had inflamed the entire town. I had no idea how I would be received by the police, but the chances were good that it would not be kindly, perhaps bordering on open hostility.

I reached over and rubbed Tonk's head for luck.

I was doing this all for Jonas, I reminded myself. Ultimately that was all that mattered. Besides, what was the worst that could possibly happen? I would ask my questions, they would refuse to answer them, and I would leave. No harm, no foul.

I poked the address for the Lowell Police Department into the GPS, waited while it calculated a route, and followed the yellow brick road.

Thirteen

I had been expecting the homicide division of the Lowell police department to look like the set of Barney Miller, scarred wooden desks and mounds of paper, blackboards scrawled with notes in chalk. Of course, that television series had been made in the seventies, and even the Dunboro police department had modernized since then. I was nonetheless surprised by a space that felt more suitable for worker bees at a large company, perhaps an engineering firm or an HMO, than a police department. The room was a small array of cubicles, walls of blue-gray fabric panels edged in gray metal strips, matching modular filing cabinets and desks with wood-grained laminate tops. The cube walls were low, maybe only four feet or so and barely provided the illusion of privacy. There was shockingly little paper in evidence, most desks having nothing more than a phone and computer terminal with a flat panel screen on their pristine surfaces. There was a general hum of activity, the click of keyboards, some people on the phones, the occasional bang and rattle of a desk drawer being opened or closed, but on the whole the place was eerily quiet.

I had been standing in the entranceway taking in the scene for no more than a few moments when a man at a desk just to my left, one without a surrounding cube structure, asked me who I was there to see, looking at me like I didn't have six inches of stitching in my face. He was paunchy and soft. His head was entirely hairless except for eyebrows and was almost the exact shape and smoothness of an egg. He wore glasses with lenses about as thick as possible under the laws of physics, and behind them his eyes floated, heavily distorted.

"I'd like to talk with someone about the murder of Kevin Anderson."

"And you are?" the man asked.

"Jack Fallon. I'm a firefighter from Dunboro, New Hampshire." I had worn my fire department jacket to bolster my identity. It had my name and the name of the department stitched on it and everything.

"Wait here," he told me, and got up and went off into the cube farm.

He zigged and zagged his way down the aisles, stopping to lean over to talk to a man at one of the desks, then pointing back my way. The man nodded. Egghead returned and took a seat behind his desk without a word to me.

"Should I go talk to him?" I asked.

The man looked up and blinked, no expression upon his face that I could read. "He knows you're here. He'll come get you when he's ready."

That seemed like an insulting attitude to me, but I had no prior experience to base that on and so let it go. The man out in the cube farm typed on his computer, looking up at me every so often, though I could tell that he too was not giving my stitches a second glance. Maybe that's a cop thing. Egghead ignored me completely.

While I waited, I considered what it might mean that Egghead knew the name Kevin Anderson. I didn't believe that Lowell was such a small city with so few murders committed that it would be possible to know the names of every one. Was it a hot case for them? Or was the city broken up into police divisions, and this one had just a few open murders on their books? I didn't know.

The wait felt long to me, though I resisted checking my watch and didn't see any clocks within my line of sight. I wondered what would happen if I just walked out. Would they let me leave? Follow me? Arrest me? I'm sure Valerie would be thrilled to pieces to receive my one phone call from the Lowell lockup.

Eventually the guy stood up from his computer, but rather than come to me, he beckoned me over with a curl of one finger. I found that more insulting still – calling me over like I was a dog – and I was starting to consider the trip down here to be ill-conceived. I walked over anyway, lowering my expectations with every step.

I took in the man's appearance as I approached. He was fit, wearing a charcoal suit. He was shorter than I was but broader, but not overly enhanced like a body builder. His skin was swarthy, and his black hair was short and thick. His cheeks were darkened by the beginnings of a five o'clock shadow at nine thirty in the morning. He wore a gold badge on a leather flip out threaded through his belt, but no identification card that I could see.

"Jack Fallon," I introduced myself, holding out my hand.

He regarded me with dark eyes that transmitted a low level hostility. He ignored my outstretched hand. "I know who you are," he said. He grasped the corner of his computer monitor and turned it so I could see the screen. There was a picture of me in my class A uniform below the banner headline "Volunteer firefighter solves triple homicide." I remembered the article; I believe Valerie had it scrapbooked somewhere.

"What brings you to Lowell?" he asked. "Dunboro run out of murders and you figured you'd come here and help us out?"

In the spectrum of responses that I had thought I might experience, this was down about as far on the negative end as I had allowed my ruminations to go. The cop was already brimming with anger, and I had yet to even open my mouth.

"I can see that coming down here was a mistake, so I'll leave you to it." I turned to go.

"Whoa. Whoa. Not so fast, sport" he said. "You have something to tell me about Kevin Anderson, I'm going to hear it." He dragged open the bottom drawer of his desk and pulled out a slim buff-colored folder. Kicking the drawer closed with his heel, he gestured with the hand holding the folder down the aisle towards the back of the room. He followed me, sort of border collied me in truth, and at the end of the aisle opened one of the doorways along the wall and ushered me inside.

It was a nothing room, a big closet, forty square feet, with plain sheetrock walls painted off-white without adornment of any kind. A small rectangular table and four chairs, doubtlessly dredged from the same office supply company that had sold the cubical parts, were shoehorned inside.

He slapped the folder down on the tabletop, but remained standing. Normally I would have remained standing too, keeping us on similar psychological ground, but my ankle was sore and I couldn't see anything to be gained by a chest-thumping competition. I squeezed around the table and slouched into one of the two chairs on that side.

"So," he said, once he had closed the door, "what do you know about the murder of Kevin Anderson." He opened the file and slid out a picture which he placed in front of me.

It was of a narrow, dingy room with peeling paint on the walls. A lumpy, stained mattress on a rusty metal frame was pushed to one side. There was a small fridge in the corner, a hot plate on top with blots and crumbs of food scattered around it. Kevin Anderson, at least I figured it was Kevin Anderson, was lying face up in the space between the bed and the wall, one leg flung over the bed frame railing. His T-shirt was sodden with blood, pierced a dozen times. There were two wounds in the right leg of his jeans, both up high on the thigh, blood soaking the pants leg around the holes. There was one more in his throat above the collar of the shirt that gaped like a second mouth. The killer had stabbed Anderson in the side of his neck last, the knife still stuck there. I recognized from the distinctive handle that it was a Wusthof eight inch Ikon cook's knife, just like the one Valerie and I had in the knife block in our kitchen. It wholesaled at over a hundred and fifty dollars, and fit in at Anderson's flop house room like a diamond in a McDonald's Happy Meal box.

Blood had bubbled out of his nose and stained his chin and teeth. His eyes were wide open and dulled. Blood had pooled on the floor, and there was a big red handprint smeared low down on the wall, likely Anderson's because his hand was nearby. It was a color photograph, and the dominant color was a dark red, almost red-black.

The edge of the door frame was visible in the corner of the picture. Anderson had opened the door and the killer had struck immediately and in a frenzy, without words, without warning. If there had been any warning, Anderson would have backed up, ended up farther away from the door.

I sensed the cop watching me closely as I looked at the picture. If he was hoping that I would be shocked, I was going to be a great disappointment to him. Somewhere along the line in the fire department I had gotten past that response to human bodies in almost any condition.

I had once been on an ambulance call to a suicide attempt. A young girl had sawed away at her wrists with a dull steak knife until they were pulped, looking astonishingly like hamburger meat. I had also been on a call for a man hit by a log-hauling truck; his body crushed and rolled by all eighteen, deep-tread tires. We had hosed his remains off the blacktop after picking up what we could. If this cop wanted to whip out and compare death scene photographs, I could play that game all day.

"I'm afraid that I don't know anything," I said putting the book down on top of the photograph as if it wasn't even there. "Just what I've read in the article." I pulled the article out of the book and unfolded it, and put it on the table in front of him.

He barely glanced at it. He had probably already seen it.

"But," I continued, "I think it might be linked to a cult that was up in Dunboro in the seventies, and there have been other deaths in New Hampshire that I believe are connected."

I laid it all out for him, showing him the book and the other articles. I gave him Jonas' name; I couldn't see any harm in doing so, though he didn't bother to write it down. It took a while to tell it all, and while I did so he leaned his hands on the table but never took a seat.

When I was done, he shook his head. "What is it with guys like you?"

"Excuse me?" I asked.

"Did you watch too much Starsky and Hutch as a kid? Did you want to be a cop but couldn't get into the academy? Or do you just think with your PhD that you're smarter than everyone else?"

"Look," I said, "I'm just trying to help."

He stood up and placed a hand over his heart and gave me a slight bow, "The police department of Lowell deeply appreciates your expertise, Firefighter Fallon. I'm sure we'd have no idea how to find Kevin Anderson's murderer without your help."

"Fine," I said, gathering up the book and articles, getting up from the chair and coming around the table, feeling really angry, at him for wasting my time, and at myself for thinking this could have resulted in anything else. "I thought maybe some of this might be news to you, that it might give you some new angle to look at that could lead to Anderson's killer. I guess you don't see it that way, so fuck you very much for your time, and I'll be going."

I moved to the door, but he didn't step aside. Instead his eyes narrowed, and what had been simmering hostility in them boiled over. "Let me give you some advice," he began.

"No thanks," I said, shouldering him out of my way, cutting

off whatever piece of his mind he had no doubt been aching to give me from the very second I had walked into the squad room.

Getting physical with a cop had not been a smart move on my part, but he didn't follow me, he didn't taze my ass. He remained in the doorway to the interview room and shouted at my back. "You stay out of my investigation and out of my way, or so help me I will flatten you!"

I got many looks from other cube dwellers as I went by. Egghead at the front desk positively glared at me which, coming through those monster glasses of his, had a bizarre funhouse surrealism to it.

It occurred to me as I left the police station that I had never even gotten the detective's name.

Fourteen

On the way home I called Jonas and asked him to meet me for lunch at Norma's, the only restaurant in town. It occupied a renovated colonial on a stretch of Route 13 that the locals laughingly referred to as bustling downtown Dunboro. Our entire commercial base consisted of Norma's, a bank, a Dunkin Donuts, a gas station, and one of those stores that mysteriously can't seem to hold onto a business, though not for any lack of trying. In my four years living in town, it had already housed a florist, a consignment store, a horse dressier, and a custom mountain bike shop. On this day it stood empty, a sign on the front excitedly proclaiming 'Coming soon! The Cobbler's Daughter!' I wondered, as I sat at a table for two with Jonas by the window, if it was going to be a shoe store.

Norma delivered our lunches herself. She had been busy when we came into the restaurant and took the opportunity to greet us. After hugging Jonas, she turned to me and looked at my face with concern. She didn't need to ask how it had happened; she knew the story about my getting caught in the

97

collapse of Baxter Dam. Instead she offered me an encouraging, "I think it's getting better."

I thought it was getting worse, with a sort of fiery itch to it, like my face was being stung by bees, but I was pretty sure it wouldn't kill me, and I had a doctor's appointment later in the week. "Day by day," I replied to her, and she wrapped her arms around me and hugged me gently to her bosom. Norma was what would euphemistically be described as a woman of size, and my face pressed into her ample chest was an experience not entirely unlike being gently smothered with warm pillows. She released me, and left us to enjoy our lunch.

Jonas was having chicken-fried steak and mashed potatoes, with fried corn on the cob, for Pete's sake. I was having a triple-decker turkey club on multigrain bread, and I tossed aside the middle slice of bread.

He wore a sort of dreamy smile as he poured gravy from a boat onto the expanse of steak, something roughly a quarter the size of a doormat, and the heap of mashed potatoes. I hoped that someday I lived long enough not to give a shit about what I ate. There was a small pile of French fries next to my sandwich, but I couldn't help but think of each one as five minutes on the treadmill.

I didn't want to spoil the lunch, but questions about the cult had come up that Jonas needed to answer for me. I waited until we had settled into eating before asking my first one. "I have a copy of a book written about the cult and the subsequent trials. It says that only four people went to prison over what went on out there."

Jonas stopped eating and rested his elbows on the table, his fork in one hand and his knife in the other, "It's possible. I seem to remember that there were a lot of arrests the night of the fire, but I don't know what happened to them all. I do remember there were four big trials. I went to all of them. How could I not? If you dig back into the newspaper archives, I'm sure there is a lot of material to find. Pogue, Anderson, and a gorilla named Rhodes. Pogue introduced Rhodes to the congregation as a man of God from some church out west, but I knew that he was bad news from the first time I laid eyes on him. It was only a short time later that Althelia, Ellis, Laura, and I talked about getting out. I don't know where Rhodes is now. And there was the kid, Teeg."

"The plumber in Milford. He was charged with raping one of the girls," I noted.

Jonas shook his head, moving the knife in front of him with a slashing motion as he did so, "The story at the time was that he had raped a lot of girls, but the girls were so afraid, or maybe so under Pogue's thrall, that they wouldn't testify." Jonas kept his voice low, his eyes alert for eavesdroppers. "In the end the prosecutor managed to get one rape charge to stand up."

He put the knife and fork aside, wiped his mouth with his napkin, and pushed his plate away, his appetite gone. "Teeg's rape trial was the worst. There was a whole bunch of commotion about whether or not the girl would have to testify. She was only sixteen, a runaway who had been living at the church for years. I remember when she took the stand. A pudgy little girl, stringy hair. Her name was Alice. Alice," he tapped his fingertips on the tabletop as he searched his memory, "Lahey. She was completely dispassionate, like she was on autopilot, as she told a story that made me want to vomit. Teeg didn't serve much time, not for what he did. If she killed him, I wouldn't blame her."

Jonas' thoughts were not that far from my own. If Alice had shot Teeg, was she also responsible for the others? I looked at Jonas' steak knife abandoned on the table and I tried to picture a grown up Alice Lahey using a hundred-and-fifty-dollar knife to kill an eighty year-old felon in a flop house in Lowell. "Maybe. But that brings me back to Ellis and Althelia. Why them?" I asked.

The corners of his mouth turned down, "I don't know."

"Let me ask you this," I said, "you said you and Ellis and Laura Banks and Althelia were all in the church, but left before the craziness started."

He swallowed, "Well, it was all crazy in retrospect, but yeah."

"Who else was in it?"

. "I can't tell you that," he said, his eyes downcast. "Those people still have families in this town. Some of them are still living here themselves. I'm not going to start smearing them or their reputations and memories."

"But you're willing to talk about Ellis and Althelia?"

"They're dead. Someone murdered them. I figured you had to know that to find the killer."

"So that's what this is? Need to know?" I clenched my jaw, exasperated. "Jonas, did it ever occur to you that the killer, if there is one, was probably a member of the cult?"

He picked up and toyed with his fork, made little tracks in the potatoes on his plate, "A lot of those people were my friends."

"I'm not going to go all bull in a china shop on you," I said gently, "but I've got to ask some questions. I'm trying to solve a jigsaw puzzle here and I don't have even half of the pieces."

Jonas sighed, "This was forty years ago, Jack. So many of them are dead."

"OK, let's skip the dead people for the time being. Who's still alive?"

He leaned forward across the table, looked left, looked

right, full on clandestine spy, "There are only three others," he whispered.

I was relieved to hear it. Three didn't seem like an insurmountable number to investigate. Of course if I included family members and heirs of people who had died, the list would get longer quite quickly and people in New Hampshire really knew how to carry a grudge, across generations if necessary to even the score. The Hatfields and McCoys had nothing on us. "OK," I whispered back, feeling ridiculous. If it weren't summer, we'd both be wearing trench coats.

"Emmy Farmer."

That was a surprise, and cast her responses to my questions at the historical society in a whole new light. She had likely been the one who had removed the church building from the town model. So Emmy had a secret to hide. Still, I couldn't see her as the killer. Firing the handgun that had killed Teeg would likely have put her flat on her back. "OK," I said.

Jonas crooked a finger at me and I leaned forward. He barely breathed the next name directly into my ear. "Edward Knox."

I fell back into my chair. "Holy crap, Jonas!" I said in a loud voice that drew stares from many other diners in the restaurant. I leaned forward again and whispered fiercely. "Seriously? Edward Knox? As in town selectman Edward Knox? As in longest serving town selectmen in town history Edward Knox?"

Jonas nodded minutely.

I quickly scanned the room. Edward Knox was known to often have lunch at Norma's, but thankfully I didn't see him. "And you're just telling me now? Are you trying to make me a pariah in this town?" Edward Knox played Santa Claus in the town parade every Christmas. He was responsible for starting the town food bank. He served Thanksgiving turkey and

Christmas ham at missions all over the state. He had been sponsoring the elementary school baseball team longer than I had been alive. Half the people in town thought he walked on water, and the other half would be willing to swear in a court of law that they had seen him do it.

"Forget I said anything about him," Jonas whispered quickly, "He's not involved."

"How can you say that? How can you know?" If I even considered walking into the selectmen's office and asking the town's most beloved figure what he knew about a cult in Dunboro and how he might be linked to murders today, I needed to get my head examined. If I brought it up at a town meeting, I'd likely get lynched.

Jonas picked up his fork and pushed the food around on his plate. I ate a few French fries, treadmill be damned. I thought I deserved a little comfort food.

There was no way I was going to go on a fishing expedition over Edward Knox. It just wasn't going to happen. I did however wonder if knowing what I now knew about Emmy Farmer, if I could force her to open up a little more. Maybe she had some materials squirreled away in the historical society or in some personal collection that she could be persuaded to divulge. Still, Emmy was nowhere near as stupid as Richard Nixon; if there ever had been tapes, Emmy would have burned them long ago.

The skin on my face felt stretched tight, as if my skull was about to burst through. I rubbed the back of my neck with one hand. "OK, OK," I whispered, trying to regain some semblance of control over my racing thoughts, "Emmy Farmer and Edward Knox. Super. Just super. You said there were three others. Who's the last one?"

Jonas licked his lips and leaned forward again. He inhaled, paused, then exhaled and leaned back, no name uttered. His eyes darted around the room, looking at absolutely anyone but me.

His behavior was making me crazy. I was certain I had been through the worst of the revelations. No name could possibly pass his lips that would shock or surprise me any more than Knox. "OK, Jonas, let me have it. Who are we talking about here? Gandhi? The Pope? Oprah?"

He said the name. Actually, he didn't say the name, but his lips formed the words, carefully and distinctly, and I read them easily. I blinked at him, my gaze wary. I must have misread him, somehow, though that didn't seem likely.

His lips formed the name again, even more slowly. My second read matched the first.

I felt my jaw drop open. My breath left me in one big woof. I must have looked like I was having a heart attack.

Jonas nodded and mouthed the name one more time.

Bobby Dawkins.

Fifteen

I left Jonas with the check, I think. Maybe. Perhaps I dropped some cash on the table. I can't be certain. I'm not even sure how I got out of the restaurant. All I know was I found myself back in my idling truck in the parking lot, Tonk's paws on my chest and his face about two inches from my own, the nub of his tail batting the rearview mirror every which way.

The sheriff, the chief of the fire department, the town selectman! Back in 1971 had Emmy Farmer held some position in town, perhaps secretary or treasurer? And today Knox was still a selectman, and Emmy Farmer ran the historical society, and Bobby Dawkins the first had been replaced by Bobby Dawkins the second as sheriff. Was the cult somehow reconstituting itself? Could I trust John Pederson, the current chief of the fire department, or did he now hold the same role as his predecessor? That kind of thinking, I cautioned myself, was starting to sound dangerously like some lunatic conspiracy theory. Before this thing was over I would need to get myself fitted for a tinfoil hat.

Where could I go? Who could I talk to?

I drove home in a daze, with no more idea in my head than to climb into bed, or perhaps under it, and stay there. I could order a pizza, rent a movie, and hide until... Until. I didn't know until what. A week passed, or a month. Maybe until winter started, or ended. Or until the sun went dark.

Valerie's car was in the driveway. I found her inside having a microwave meal, an irradiated conglomeration of tomato sauce and bubbling cheese and some unidentified medallion of meat in a shallow black plastic bowl that served as shipping container, cooking vessel, and serving dish. Afterwards it could be recycled. Tidy. Efficient.

She was frowning, a thinking frown. Valerie had some whole speech ready to go, something she had been working on for a long time. I watched her abandon it when she saw the look on my face. My fried brain wondered only briefly what that speech might have been about before letting the thought drop.

"Tell me," she said, nothing more than that.

So I did. I laid out what I had done, what I had found out, what I thought, what I knew, what I feared. How it seemed like everyone in town was somehow involved; everyone had a secret to hide. Valerie was brilliant and engaging, everything I loved about her and everything I needed her to be. My earlier feelings about Rachael, my suspicions that Valerie had been with someone else last night, seemed like the vilest sort of betrayal on my part.

When I was done I felt drained, but calm. Valerie would

help. She was the person I could always turn to. She would know what to do.

"You have to stop, Jack. This isn't your responsibility and you need to give it up."

Her response was like a slap in the face. Everything we had done, everything we had been through together, and she hadn't learned anything about me, about what drove me, about what I needed from her. Her answers were no answers at all, just a retreading of old ground we had worn bare long ago. And what about Jonas?

I was irritated with myself at thinking for even a fleeting second that anything had changed between us. Our frictions remained right where they had been all along. Our marriage was like a minefield. No, strike that; it was a stupid metaphor. If our marriage was like a minefield, why did we keep hitting the same mines over and over again? Why did they seem to surprise us every time we stepped on them? How had we failed to recognize the dangers before we even wandered in here? And why, though it pierced my heart to even consider this idea, would anyone in their right mind choose to live in one?

I turned to go.

"Wait, Jack, what are you going to do?" she asked, real concern in her voice.

I turned back. "I'll tell you what I'm not going to do. I'm not going to give up. I'm going to solve this thing."

I realized as I said it that I had no plan. I knew I wasn't going anywhere near Edward Knox. And I was going to stay away from the Lowell PD, and the Milford PD by extension. And I certainly was not going to involve Laura Banks in any of this. What did that leave?

Valerie pushed away her meal unfinished. It seemed I was ruining a lot of appetites today.

I reached across the counter and took her right hand in both of my own. "We can't go on like this," I told her.

"No," she agreed softly, "we can't."

"I'm worried about us. I worry about us every hour of every day. But I have to do this for Jonas. I believe him now. I don't understand how or why, but he's in real trouble. There's something very dark buried in this town, and I think it's coming to the surface. I don't have enough to convince the State Police to get involved, and I'm not sure I can trust Bobby Dawkins."

Her eyes downcast, I felt her hand shift within my grasp. "I know," she said, even more softly, so softly that I almost lost what she said in the hum of the refrigerator compressor.

"Teeg," I said. "I need to go talk to his widow."

"Why?" she asked. Her eyes lifted, and all I saw in them was pain and confusion and loneliness, pretty much everything awful, and I was the one who had put it there.

"His murder feels wrong, like it doesn't fit. He was just a kid back when the cult was active, and he had been by all appearances out of it for forty years. He was a father and businessman and popular in town. If I can figure out why he was killed, I think it will tell me why they all were."

She pulled and her hand slid from between mine, effortlessly, like breaking a link in a particularly flimsy chain. "Have a good time," she said.

"I need you to come with me."

"Why?" She dragged her fingers through her hair, and I thought she might tighten her hands into fists and tear it out in clumps. "For what earthly reason?"

"Look at my stitches. She's a widow living alone with her daughter. If you're not there, she probably won't even open the door." It occurred to me that Rachael would be just as good for that purpose, perhaps better as she would be more enthusiastic. That thought made me a little disoriented, like someone had just given my internal gyroscope a good, hard shove. Hopefully without letting any of that show on my face I pressed on, "More importantly, you're good at this. You can read people. If it weren't for you helping me back in the spring, Lorraine's killer would never have been caught."

The lines of her face and along the curve of her jaw hardened, and a flush stained her cheeks. "Do you understand how much I hate you doing this, how much I hate the risks you're taking? Do you realize how much it hurts me to open myself up to the pain these people are experiencing? Did you see Lorraine's mother, Arlette, at the funeral? She was devastated."

"We helped her," I insisted, "You helped her. You found her daughter's killer."

She shook her head angrily, "We didn't help her, Jack. She thought her daughter was missing and we proved she was dead. We just exchanged one kind of pain for another. I still write to her and call her on the phone. Did you know that?"

I hadn't, and it surprised me. I realized that Arlette, having lost a child, and Valerie, unable to have any, had forged a bond, but I had not appreciated how strong or enduring that bond had become. Arlette's grief at the funeral I had believed was transitory, part of the process of healing. Perhaps I had been fooling myself, thinking that by riding in on my white horse and solving the mystery I had made everything right, but I had never considered the aftermath. Surely she was better off knowing what had happened to her daughter, right?

"Arlette's not better," she said, as if reading my thoughts. "She doesn't sleep at night. She lost her job. She's drinking again after fifteen years of AA. And there's nothing I can do but listen to her, fat load of good that does."

We had caused that? I had caused that?

In past investigations I had revealed an affair and destroyed a marriage. I had ruined friendships and smeared reputations. Who had gone and appointed me Grand Inquisitor?

Yet I realized, even as I had those thoughts, I wasn't going to stop, at least not now. Jonas would be killed if someone didn't do something, and at the moment I didn't see anyone else willing or able to do so.

I would expose the past of a popular town selectman and a beloved former fire chief. I was likely going to make an enemy out of the town sheriff as I revealed the activities of his uncle. I would dig into Teeg's life with no idea what impact it might have upon his widow and daughter. And it looked like I was prepared to risk destroying my marriage to do it.

Piled up like that, the scales of my value system seemed appallingly out of balance. If the road to hell was paved with good intentions, I was carefully and conscientiously shaping and fitting each and every stone along the way.

"I need to go talk with Teeg's widow," I said, "and I'd like you to come with me."

I had just thrown that last bit out for the heck of it. I had no serious expectation that she would agree after all she had said. Her feelings for me at that moment probably resided somewhere between simple dislike and outright loathing. When she refused me, would I call Rachael to fill her role? I considered sliding back to that betrayal with an ease that I found disgusting.

Instead, as she often did, Valerie surprised me. She threw up her hands and said "Fuck it. Why not?"

Sixteen

The Teeg residence was located not far from downtown Milford, on a street lined with identical row houses. The buildings were all three stories tall and narrow, packed tightly side by side on small lots. They were so close together that it was possible to stand in the alleyway between any two and touch both of them with arms outstretched.

Teeg's home was all in white: siding, trim, shutters. Even the curtains in the windows were white. Illuminated brightly by the afternoon sun, the effect was neither blinding nor even particularly cheery, but tired. Much of the siding was stained with mildew and asphalt runoff from the shingles on the roof. There were tufts of sickly green up on the soffits where water intrusion was allowing moss to grow. The house lacked gutters, and back splatter from rainfall had stained the foundation skirt brown.

I parked in the street and Valerie and I got out and traversed the cracked concrete walkway. Laurel bushes had once flanked it both left and right, but some disease had wiped them out and all that remained were skeletal branches. The lawn was thin and weedy, and hadn't seen a mower since the spring thaw.

No doorbell in evidence, I knocked.

The door opened a short time later about three inches, the total distance allowed by a chain that spanned the gap from door to jam. I realized immediately that this was a serious security chain, not tin plated cast iron, but real forged steel. If installed properly, a set of two or perhaps four wood screws penetrated the door and frame to considerable depth at each end. It would take my truck to break through it.

The wedge of face that appeared in the space looked far less substantial. The woman's skin was pale and papery thin, the bones of the cheeks and the orbits of the eyes plainly visible. The eyes themselves were red and raw, and they slid away from me whenever I tried to catch their attention.

"Mrs. Teeg? Melissa Teeg?" I inquired.

"Yes."

"I'm Jack Fallon, and this is my wife, Valerie. I'm a firefighter from Dunboro."

· "I know who you are," she said. "I've seen you in the paper. The flood in Dunboro last spring, that poor girl in the car."

I nodded encouragingly, I hoped soothingly, though

the stitches in my face probably made me look downright scary, "I think I know something about your husband's murder. If I can ask you a few questions, I may be able to find his killer."

Her wandering eyes latched onto Valerie. Melissa Teeg looked to her, silently pleading with her, though for what I couldn't imagine. "Please," she said to me, her focus remaining on my wife, "talk to the police. I've told them everything I can."

I hoped that Valerie, as the target of her attention, would add something useful, something that would make her want to talk to us. She remained mute, squirming uncomfortably under Melissa's gaze.

"Mrs. Teeg," I tried, "if you're in any kind of danger, if someone has threatened you, I can help."

"I don't need any help," she replied. She wasn't getting whatever it was she had been seeking from Valerie, and her head dropped, her vision settling somewhere down around our knees.

"Mrs. Teeg. I…"

"Please," she cut me off, "Talk to the police. Just leave me alone." She closed the door with her shoulder, using the weight of her whole body, as if I was trying to force my way inside and it took all of her strength to stop me. After the door was closed I could still feel her there on the other side, leaning into it, making sure that it stayed shut.

"Are we done here?" Valerie asked.

I thought of a number of abrasive responses on my

part, such as 'You were a lot of help,' or perhaps in a more Ralph Kramden state of mind something along the lines of 'Bang! Zoom! Right to the moon, Alice!' Instead I sighed. "Yeah, we're done here."

Seventeen

As soon as we returned home, Valerie got out of my truck and into her car and sped off without a word. She didn't leave any rubber behind, but she came pretty close. I thought about calling after her, trying to get her to come back and talk, but saved my breath instead. Seen from her point of view, I wouldn't have stopped and talked to me either. I mean, seriously, what was left to say?

I parked and let Tonk out of the house. He galumphed around the yard a little, stretching his legs and snapping at butterflies, and then came and sat by my side on the front porch steps. I ruffled his ears and he licked my cheek. That simple gesture of affection almost brought me to tears, an empty, hollow feeling in my stomach.

No more games, no more jokes. This moment, this exact sliver of time, could be the point at which my marriage ended, where the woman I loved more than anything else drove out of my life forever.

I went inside and onto the internet, trying to distract myself by looking up articles about Knox. Know thy enemy, right? He cut a wide swath through the local papers – charities, benefits, local causes – in every way the perfect selectman.

Outside of town his reputation was less sterling. He came from old family money, a big construction firm started by his great grandfather. It did major public works projects in Boston, and there had been allegations of bribery and kickbacks over the years, but nothing ever seemed to stick. That came as no surprise. The public works department in Boston was an ocean of corruption and scandal and billions of dollars were involved. Indeed, I would have been surprised to find a construction company within a fifty mile radius of Boston that had never been accused of bribing someone; it was just the way contracts happened in the big city.

I did find that back in 1972 Knox's construction firm had just about gone out of business. Articles in the business section of the Boston Globe described work stoppages at a number of construction sites which a company spokesman described as a temporary cash flow problem. Further articles discussed the transfer of several of those contracts to his competitors who had finished the work. That was happening at the nearly same time as the cult was being broken up. Coincidence? Cause and effect? It was an interesting factoid certainly, but I couldn't seem to make it fit anywhere, and I was having a lot of trouble getting my head in the game.

I shut off the computer and rubbed at my forehead, carefully avoiding the stitches which felt hot to the touch and pulsed with their own heartbeat against my fingertips.

Valerie leaving was, I fully realized, all my doing, but it was also worse than that.

The reasoning I had asserted until now: I was doing this for Jonas, someone had to help Jonas, Jonas was in trouble, was a lie. John Pederson, the Chief of the fire department and a fine and honorable man, knew Jonas better than I and had more of a personal connection with him. Was he overturning his life to help? No, he was not. And Bobby Dawkins, he was the Sheriff of this town, and he too was doing nothing. These men did not want to see Jonas come to harm, and neither were they shirking their duties. They were being reasonable about what should be done. I alone, driven by some restlessness, some defect within myself, went beyond all reason. I dug and prodded and twisted and wrecked, collateral damage on the way to some goal even I could not clearly define. I laid waste to all the best parts of my life with a single-mindedness that was breathtaking. I was Sisyphus expending all my energy rolling a boulder up a hill, knowing full well it would crush me when it rolled back down.

And the worst part of all was that I knew I wasn't going to stop.

My mind was working the mystery like a Rubik's Cube. It rotated the axes this way and that, examining the permutations, seeing what the cube faces ended up looking like. I had no more control over it than I had control over the weather. That part of me, it insisted, it demanded; the problem was an obsession for it. Nothing mattered more; no price was too high.

How had I become like this? Had there been some event which transformed me from a thinking man, a scientist, a physicist, who guided his life with careful judgments and facts, into someone as completely out of control as any drug addict? Or had I always been this way? Even in this moment of introspection, it was not a question I felt secure enough to look at too closely. Perhaps my whole self-image was a lie as well, my motivations seeming suddenly unclear to me.

I wondered who I could talk to about this. My natural choice, Valerie, was out. Such a conversation with Rachael was fraught with risk on so many levels that I was almost embarrassed the idea had come to mind at all. I considered talking to Bobby, but given his uncle's involvement with the cult, I wasn't sure I how much I could trust him, and how much his conflicting allegiances might color his responses. John

Pederson? What, if anything, did he feel he owed to the memory of Ellis Banks?

I then had a new thought, one so absurd that it made me laugh out loud, a peculiar and desperate sound. Tonk looked up at me from his bed in the corner of the kitchen and cocked his head; one of those looks that made me think he and all of dogkind were far smarter and more insightful than they were letting on; they were playing dumb for the free room and board. He didn't like the sound of it, but the more I examined the idea, the more right it seemed. Oh, it was plenty crazy, don't get me wrong, but it had a brilliance to it, a certain cosmic balance, that appealed to me.

There was, I had realized, one individual who understood all about obsession, and he certainly knew everything there was to know about the cult. The real question was would he talk to me.

I didn't know, but it was time to go see Martin Pogue.

Eighteen

Gaining entry into the Concord State Prison required passage through an astonishing number of checkpoints: an outer outer gate, an inner outer gate, an outer inner gate, an inner inner gate, and etcetera. Even so, I found the experience more pleasant than getting onboard an aircraft in post 9-11 America. The guys manning the metal detectors at the prison were professionals, as opposed to the untrained stooges at the TSA, and I got to keep my shoes and belt. Personnel at each level conscientiously checked my ID and took down my visitor information.

The final barrier to entry was guarded by a kid, or at least he looked like a kid to me. As I get older, that seems to happen more and more often. He was probably all of twenty-two or three, and floated inside his uniform like a boy wearing his father's clothes. I noticed there was a Spiderman comic book on the desk in front of him as he slid the visitor log, a thick three-ring binder with the NH State seal on the cover, through the slot in the bulletproof glass between us.

I used the pen chained to the binder to write my name, address, date and time of my visit, and the person I was visiting in the appropriate slots on the page. The kid checked the information I had written against my driver's license. They still do this kind of thing on paper and not computer?

A second guard appeared and escorted me through a locked door and down a hallway. The walls were concrete blocks painted pale yellow, the floor linoleum tile squares the color of raw liver sprinkled with white and gray speckles. I knew from the prison website that it had been built in the late 1800s and renovated in bits and pieces several times since then. I wondered what era had spawned this particularly joyous color scheme.

Formidable doors lined the hallway, their faces flat metal sheets studded with rivets, each sporting an old-fashioned keyhole that you could stick an index finger into. Overhead were banks of harsh fluorescent lighting, but at the end of the hall, through a thick wire mesh, a large window let in a bright golden ray of sunlight like the promise of a better tomorrow. Down that way an orderly unenthusiastically shoved a mop around on the floor. Against the blinding corona from the window his shape was fuzzy and indistinct, but even so obviously top heavy with muscles.

I was expecting to hear a lot of noise, the raucous shouting of inmates echoing down the concrete corridors, the clang of metal cell doors rolling open and slamming shut, the crackle of the PA system announcing shift changes or prisoner activities. Instead, the place was quieter than my high school library used to be. I could hear the swish and slap of the mop as it moved. My escort's shoes, some kind of work boot with heavy upper construction and a non-skid sole, squeaked and squicked against the tile.

We stopped at one of the doors and he unlocked it with a comically large key, a serious chuck of brass that would have fetched five bucks at a recycling place. He swung the door open against the squealing protest of a pneumatic cylinder and ushered

120

me inside.

"Wait here," he told me. "I'll bring Pogue to you."

He left, a rattle and solid thock from the door telling me that he had used the comically large key to lock it behind him.

The interior of the room continued the decorating scheme of the hallway; the bare walls were the same bland color, the tile floor still reminiscent of entrails. A round table with a wood grain top sat in the middle of the room with four scoopy orange fiberglass chairs around it that looked like they had been stolen from the set of That Seventies Show. The air was stale. Still, on the whole, the place was nicer and roomier than the interview room in Lowell.

I pulled out one of the chairs and sat down and tried to organize my thoughts which were racing around in my head at about a hundred miles an hour. I couldn't do it. I couldn't even imagine what my first question should be. My initial instinct had been to shake his hand when I met him, try and adopt a business-like, civil, attitude. I had discarded that idea when I had been told by a guard it was not permitted to pass anything to the prisoner or make physical contact. But nothing had as yet come to mind to replace it.

I looked at the locked door and wondered what to do if I needed to piss which, frankly, a little nervous about meeting Pogue, I felt like I might need to. There were four cameras looking down at me from high up in the corners of the room, so I could communicate my need with some kind of signal, but couldn't think of a universal sign that I needed to piss, short of cupping my groin and dancing around nervously like a five year old. For the time being, I was pretty sure I could hold it. I paused in my thinking and shifted uncomfortably in my seat. How many cups of coffee had I drunk that morning?

The rattle and thock of the deadbolt being withdrawn announced Pogue's arrival, and as the door swung open I was expecting him to be wheeled in strapped to a hand truck a la

Hannibal Lector, or perhaps swathed in chains like a penitent
Jacob Marley, or frothing at the mouth with four strong guards
restraining him. Instead Pogue walked in calmly, no fetters in
evidence. The solitary guard remained in the hallway and locked
the door again behind him.

At somewhere in his mid to high seventies, Pogue looked
old, but by no means decrepit. He also no longer looked
anything like David Carradine. Time had rounded his face and
softened his features, and he had grown a narrow moustache.
His gray hair, almost white, had been cut longish and was parted
and neatly combed. He wore a blue work shirt that was too large
for him so he had rolled the cuffs several turns to keep the
sleeves from hanging down over his hands, and a pair of blue
jeans, the waist just below his sternum. He had no socks, and his
pale ankles, threaded with varicose veins, ended in shoes a cross
between sneakers and slippers on his feet.

He pulled out a chair and sat down opposite me, his hands
folded on the table in front of him.

My first impression was of a man at peace, but I rapidly
revised that. He looked, I thought, like a man resigned to his
fate; a man who, whatever plans he may have had for his life,
they haven't panned out; there was nothing remaining to salvage
and no battles left to fight.

At a loss for how to begin the conversation, I decided on
the direct route and waded right in. "My name is Jack Fallon
and I'm a firefighter from Dunboro. I'd like to talk with you
about your cult."

"Church," he corrected me. "I know why you're here."

"You do? How?"

"That's all anyone has ever visited me about." He shrugged
his shoulders as if to say it was obvious, which I supposed, now
that he had pointed it out to me, it was.

"I believe that someone is killing people who were associated with the cult."

"My church," he said again firmly, his face stony.

"Your church," I allowed.

He seemed dissatisfied by my response, and said nothing.

"Kevin Anderson was stabbed to death in a halfway house in Lowell," I told him.

"I know," he replied, "I have television privileges here."

I leaned forward in my chair, closing the distance between us, trying to assert myself physically, "Do you know who did it?"

"No," he replied, his eyes fixed on mine.

"Do you know why he was killed?"

"No."

"Fred Teeg was shot to death in his home in Milford. Can you tell me anything about that?"

"I've been in here for almost forty years. What do you think I can tell you about it?"

"What about Althelia Temple? Ellis Banks?"

He was silent, but there had been a small glimmer of something in his eyes at my mention of Althelia Temple. What did it mean? I was still trying to come up with a way to probe further when he spoke.

"Are you a righteous man, Mr. Fallon?" This question was not accompanied by a malevolent or penetrating glare, but was said with great contemplation and purpose.

I didn't answer him immediately, instead giving the question the level of consideration with which he had delivered it. "I like to believe that I am," was my eventual reply.

He nodded, though I'm not sure if it was to me or to himself. "I suppose we all like to believe ourselves to be righteous, even while doing great harm. The road to Hell…"

"Is paved with good intentions," I completed for him softly, this conversation eerily like the one I had been having with myself a short time ago. To what great harm was he referring?

He nodded again and allowed himself a wistful smile. "Often," he said, and then fell silent.

What I was sensing from him now was sadness, but sadness at what? That he had been caught? That his nutball cult hadn't killed more children? Perhaps I was misreading him, and I found myself wishing that Valerie were there. She was so much better at this human stuff than I was.

I decided to try a different approach. "You were their leader, the founder of the church."

"I was, a long time ago."

"Don't you care about these people? Don't you care about what is happening to them?"

He took a deep breath and spent a long time composing his answer. He looked up at the ceiling as though trying to catch a glimpse of God, and as he did so he fingered the stubble of whiskers on his Adam's apple. He hadn't shaved that morning, but it hadn't been a long time since he had. Perhaps it had been yesterday. When he brought his eyes down to mine they were clouded as though weighted with unshed tears. He blew the breath out through pursed lips which made a faint whistling sound. "More than you can imagine."

Despite what I had been told about Pogue, I found it

difficult to envision him as the maniacal leader of a homicidal cult. He was pleasantly innocuous, and was no more threatening than my father's brother, a bespeckled and bow-tied gentleman who was an associate professor of sociology at NYU. I reminded myself, however, that charm and personal warmth are often characteristics attributed to sociopaths and serial killers.

Pogue seemed suddenly angry, though with me or himself or his circumstance I couldn't be sure. He made an abrupt slashing motion across his throat, which at first I thought was an overt threat. Then I realized that it wasn't meant for me, but instead for the camera over my shoulder. He was ending the meeting, cutting me off, and I was just getting started.

He got up and stood by the door. I desperately tried to think of some way to draw him back to the table, but came up empty.

A guard retrieved him a minute later, and I struggled with the feeling there had been something important he had to tell me if only I had asked the right questions, though I had no idea what those might be.

I was disappointed. It was not like I had been expecting him to confess to any of the murders. He couldn't have committed them anyway; prison is an excellent alibi. Nor had I thought he would reveal to me a conspiracy he was masterminding from within prison to purge his cult roster of previous members for some unknown reason. I had however been hoping that he would give me something, some new avenue to explore, because everything I had been looking at so far had led me to nothing but dead ends, and I had nowhere else to go.

The one fact that kept sticking in my craw was the timing of the murders. The cult arrests had occurred forty years ago. Why kill these people now? What event or events was precipitating the murders today?

Having returned Pogue to whatever hole he had been pulled from, the guard came back for me. He squicked his way down the hallway at my side and deposited me back in the anteroom. The kid behind the glass was still reading Spiderman, and he glanced up only momentarily as he shoved the visitor log at me through the slot.

While I had been inside, someone else had come to visit another prisoner, and the page was flipped over to a fresh sheet. I turned it back and marked the time I was leaving in the appropriate column. The padding of papers underneath the one I was writing on was thick, maybe as much as a couple of hundred pages. This wing of the prison held only elderly prisoners, those serving long sentences, and they received few visitors. Some days only a couple, some days not even that. Looking at the dates, I could see gaps lasting weeks during which no one had logged in at all. I fanned the sheets and saw the recorded visits stretching back years.

"Do you ever throw these out?" I asked the guard.

He looked up at me, marking the spot on his page with a finger. Right underneath the tip Spiderman was delivering a knockout punch to Doc Oc, the word KA-POW in red with three exclamation points delineating the mightiness of the blow. "Not as long as I've been here," he said.

Uncertain if he would allow me to do so, but figuring it would be easier to beg forgiveness than ask permission, I quickly flipped the sheets back to the date of Ellis Banks' death and then scanned backwards. It was right there in front of me in black and white, or rather blue pen.

Seven days before he had died, Ellis Banks had visited Martin Pogue in prison.

Feeling like I was on a roll, I flipped back farther still to the date of Althelia Temple's death.

She had visited Pogue only five days prior to her death.

I had no idea of the date on which Teeg had died, and didn't think I could spend an hour standing there thumbing through the log looking for his name, but thought he would turn up in it as well.

I closed the book slowly and slid it back through the slot to the guard who accepted it without looking at it or me.

I had found a concrete connection between Ellis and Althelia, the dates of their deaths, and Pogue, but what the hell did it mean? Why would they come visit him? Would it be worth my time to go back and ask Pogue? After a little consideration, I decided I wanted to ask Jonas what he thought about them first. I could always come back; Pogue wasn't going anywhere.

Nineteen

"That's ludicrous!" Jonas said heatedly.

He had been standing in his kitchen opening a can of something for dinner, but he abandoned it, the opener still stuck in the can, and paced around his home. It didn't involve much pacing; Jonas lived in a single room shack deep in a parcel of land known as Wexler's Forest in the town of Dunboro. I had driven over to his place directly from the prison.

Out of curiosity a couple of years ago, I had done a parcel search down at the town hall and found that Wexler's was entirely owned by the State; Jonas' shack was squatting on State land. Not that I had any plans to turn him in for it. I suspected many people in town already knew it; the location of Jonas' home wasn't exactly kept secret.

"I saw it with my own eyes, Jonas." I was seated at a square table made of splined birds-eye maple. Jonas had built it himself, as he had all of the furniture in the shack, and I was pretty sure the shack itself as well. His world-class carpentry skills put my meager sawdust making ability to shame.

"Why would they go see him? For what reason?" He stopped at the shack's lone window and stared out at unspoiled acres of woodland.

"I don't know. I thought maybe you would have some idea." I tried to keep my voice even and relaxed. Whatever Jonas' blood pressure was, at his age extreme stress couldn't be good.

"I do have an idea: that it is complete and utter horse shit!" He spun away from the window and resumed his pacing, past the bed in the corner, past the wood stove in one wall, past the door leading outside, past the corner unit and Coleman camping stove and cabinets that was his kitchen. It was probably twenty steps all the way around. The cabin had no electricity. The bathroom was a detached outhouse. If his shack had been made out of bamboo and bundles of palm fronds, it would have fit right in on Gilligan's Island.

"It's not horse shit. It's true. The guards at the prison checked my driver's license half a dozen times. There's no way someone else went in with fake Ellis and Althelia IDs. They were really there. So I need you to calm down and help me out."

"Ellis didn't have a driver's license; he gave up driving years ago," Jonas muttered.

"So he signed in with a passport or something," I sighed. "Jonas, you're missing the point. Their IDs were checked. They visited Pogue."

He dragged another chair out from the table and dropped into it. "And I'm telling you that doesn't make any goddamned sense." He rapped the tip of one gnarled finger against the table, emphasizing each word. "We gave up the church when Rhodes showed up. We met and we talked about it and we were done,

129

kaput, finished. None of us had anything to do with Pogue and his group after that."

I leaned my elbows on the table and dropped my face into my hands, rubbing at my temples. Why did nothing in this mystery seem to connect properly? "OK, let's try this. Tell me about the church."

"What's to tell?" Jonas slumped back in the chair, his arms crossed on his chest.

I shrugged, "I don't know. What was it like? What went on there?"

"Initially it was like every other church I ever went to, perhaps a little more strict in its interpretation of the scripture, but otherwise the same."

"I never went to church, so humor me."

He took a breath and let it out in a huff, "It was a church. There were sermons. There were masses. There were sometimes religious study classes for the kids. One of the rooms was like a dormitory and some homeless people and runaways would live there off and on. I built some of the bunk beds. They would work the grounds; there was a vegetable garden around back. Between that and donations they would get fed."

"Did Pogue live there?"

"Yeah. You've seen the building; there was a lot of space. Essentially anyone who wanted to could stay there. I slept there a few nights myself, and I think Althelia did as well. We thought those people were our friends, our community, and you could find great spiritual peace and shelter within those walls."

"Were there ever any events away from the church, at other locations, like your homes maybe?"

"Some congregations need to hold events away from their church because the building isn't big enough. We didn't have that problem."

"OK," I said, trying to see if anything he was telling me changed the picture I had started to put together in my mind, "so when did Rhodes show up? How?"

"I don't know the how of it, and I couldn't tell you the exact date, but he came in fast and hard. One day he was a stranger sitting in one of the pews among the homeless and the runaways, and the next he was virtually running the place. He brought in some rough-looking men. The guard shack and the gate were built, and some of them starting manning it. They wouldn't exactly stop you from coming and going, but they would ask you uncomfortable questions, forceful questions, whenever you tried to leave. I had no doubts in my mind that the day was coming when I wouldn't be able to just walk out, and I wasn't going to wait around for it to happen."

I could see the pain that just remembering those days was causing him, the humiliation at having been almost sucked into the cult like a small asteroid helpless in the grip of a black hole. "You got out, Jonas. You stopped it. How did you do it?"

"Not alone," he gave a hollow, graveyard chuckle. "Althelia and Ellis, Laura and I. We met at the fire station, huddled in the back of the lower bay like fugitives, like members of the French resistance during the war. We had a feeling that if we went back through those gates, we wouldn't be coming out again."

"They weren't armed, were they?"

"Later, when the FBI showed up they were, but at that time?" he gave a shrug. "Look, Jack, it wasn't like that. It wasn't exactly that they were going to *bodily* keep us from leaving."

His emphasis of the word bodily confused me, and he must have seen that on my face.

"Spiritually, Jack." His chair was far back from the table and he leaned forward with his elbows on his knees, looking down at his hands, cleaning underneath one thumbnail with the edge of the other. "I know you're not a religious man, but you must feel a sense of community from the fire department."

He paused there and I nodded, I knew about that sense of belonging, that feeling of being a part of something larger than yourself.

"The church was like that for us. More so. And deciding to leave, deciding to break away from it, was harder than you can imagine. Those people had become our world, our friends, our spiritual leaders, everything. Althelia cried that night."

Jonas looked up at me with his head lowered, uncertainly, trying to see if I understood. I suppose that I did, on an intellectual level, but emotionally I couldn't quite connect. If overnight the fire department changed into a mob of arsonists, I didn't think I'd have any trouble walking away. But this talk with Jonas had accomplished one goal. I thought that I now understood something that Jonas himself had been missing all these years. Something crucial.

"So you decided that night that you were done. You stopped going to the church?" I asked.

He nodded vigorously, "We all stopped going."

"But you," I pointed at him specifically, "you, Jonas. You stopped going."

"Right, I stopped going," he looked at me like someone had just hit me with a shovel and struck me stupid.

He still didn't get it.

"If you stopped going, how do you know the rest of them did?"

When he finally got it, his jaw dropped. The look on Jonas' face was of a shock so pure it was almost like a caricature.

Twenty

I was sitting on the steps of my front porch trying to teach Tonk to fetch a tennis ball. This was a mostly fruitless endeavor in which I threw the ball and Tonk watched it go. Then, after several minutes of me trying to encourage him to go pick it up, I went and picked it up and put it in his mouth, then I praised him and gave him a cookie. In all likelihood what Tonk was learning was how little work he could do and still get a cookie out of the deal, but as long as he was learning something I felt like it was time well spent.

Today's paper lay face down on the porch at my side, just where I had pitched it in disgust. I had gotten up that morning intending to go talk to Laura Banks. As the last surviving member of that group, beyond Jonas, she could confirm to me that only Jonas had stopped going to the church and the rest of them, for whatever reasons, had continued. That would lead to more unpleasant questions, such as if they were still involved when the child murders were happening. Then the newspaper had come along and blown that plan to hell.

All the investigating I had done, all the questions I had asked, and I had missed the most fundamental linkage between the present and the past, the reason the cultists were dying now, and I had had to read about it in the goddamned paper.

Every so often I sensed Valerie watching me from one of the upstairs windows, and once I caught a glimpse of her silhouette out of the corner of my eye. She didn't come out to talk with me, and I didn't go inside to talk with her. Where she had been, what I was doing looking into the murders for Jonas; we weren't discussing any of it. Yeah, we were doing just swell.

I reached out intending to grab the paper, but instead let my hand lay flat on top of it. How had I missed it? Pogue had more or less told me, and still I had missed it completely. I was the living embodiment of the amateur detective, heavy on the amateur.

I picked up and threw the ball again and was surprised when Tonk actually bounded after it. Then he veered off and ran into the woods at the far side of the yard. It had likely been a squirrel that had caught his interest and not the ball at all. I got up and retrieved it, and then, tossing it from hand to hand, returned to my seat. Tonk thrashed around in the brush and low weeds at the edge of the yard.

Forty years. Pogue had been sentenced to forty years in prison.

That sentence ended on Monday, three days away.

And while the address he was planning to live at was something of a closely guarded secret, the general consensus was he was coming back to Dunboro. I had been thinking of going to visit Pogue again in prison, ask him some more questions, and here he was coming to me. Like the old Saturday Night Live skit tag line, how conveeenient.

The lazy silence of the day was suddenly shattered by the blatting of a pack of motorcycles out on Route 13. As the major

North-South thoroughfare in this part of New Hampshire, motorcycle traffic on Route 13 was not exactly an unusual occurrence on warm, sunny days. What was unusual was these motorcycles turning onto my street, and then appearing a short time later beside my mailbox.

They rolled down the driveway rumbling and roaring, flushing Tonk from the bushes and sending him sprinting across the yard and up the steps to hide behind me on the porch. I counted nine bikes in all; big, angry, road-worn Harleys covered in a lot of chrome and glossy black paint. The riders were doing the biker stereotype proud in stained denim jackets or T-shirts and jeans, some with leather chaps, and they wore matte black round helmets without decals or adornment. The nine of them were all men, scruffy, with mean, flat faces.

They came to a stop at the end of the walk, no more than ten feet away, and raced their engines with a bone-rattling sound that shook leaves from the trees and quite possibly was heard in Concord. Then as one they shut their bikes off, and in the sudden quiet I thought maybe I had gone deaf. Without having the slightest idea of what they were doing here, the message of their threat was transmitted loud and clear.

Both Ellis and Althelia had died shortly after their visit to Pogue in prison. With the smell of hot metal and rubber in my nose, my ears ringing, I suddenly realized that, with my visit, my life might now be at risk as well. The fear instinctively tightened the muscles in my stomach and across my shoulders. I felt my heart rate increase.

I saw Valerie's silhouette appear in the window again for a moment and then disappear.

A guy who looked like their leader knocked out his kickstand and got off his bike. The other eight remained straddling their machines. He moseyed up the walk on worn combat boots with rounded heels, probably in his head envisioning John Wayne in some kind of standoff. He had the look of an athlete gone to fat, a lot of fat, with short, wiry legs leading up to a stomach that hung hugely out over the waist of his jeans, and a broad chest. His thick, meaty arms below the cut off sleeves of his denim jacket were scrawled with blurry blue-green tattoos. I noticed a smudged scorpion and a streaky stallion. He had a bushy beard, unruly eyebrows over his small, dark eyes and greasy hair that stuck out from under his helmet in clumps. Wrapped around his right fist, already clenched in preparation for forthcoming violence, was a strap of leather studded with metal points. If he hit me in the face with that, which I thought was perhaps his intent, I would probably lose at least an eye.

As he approached I got up slowly from the porch steps. I leaned heavily on the cane, far more heavily than I had to, to try and show them how frail I was. Nine on one, I was frankly hoping that they wouldn't hit a cripple. If they decided to attack me anyway I was planning to lull them with my infirmity and use the cane as a weapon. With eight of them still on their bikes I thought maybe I could take the leader down fast before they could even come to his aid, leaving only the eight of them remaining to beat me to death. You're inside dialing 911, right Val? Tonk growled from his spot on the porch behind me. That was an absolute first; I had never heard him growl at anyone before.

The biker stepped close, way inside my personal space. His position gave me no room to swing the cane if I wanted to, but left him plenty to drive his fist into me. Backing up would have meant climbing up the steps to the porch backwards, an awkward undertaking on my bad ankle. I held the cane in my right hand, and realized that I would have to drop it to throw a punch. If I threw a left, the collection of pins and healing bones in my wrist would probably explode like shrapnel on contact. I was a couple of inches taller than he was and probably had some reach on him as well. Small comfort.

His voice was just what I had thought it would be, a deep bass rumble like the rubbing together of large boulders. "You've been asking a lot of questions about Martin Pogue," he said. Expecting his breath to wash over me in a fetid wave I was surprised to find myself suffused in a wintergreen cloud, as though he had just scarfed down a breath mint. Considerate.

The first wiseass response that came to mind, the one that Jim Rockford would have given, was something to the effect of "I wouldn't call it a lot." I prudently kept that to myself figuring it would only lead to blood being spilled, pretty much all of it mine.

He put his hands on his hips and the front of his jacket gapped open. Jammed into his belt was a big gun. It looked bigger than a handgun, with a blocky body that made me think it was some kind of submachine gun, but what the fuck do I know about guns? My heart skipped a few beats as I envisioned myself lying on the front walk punched full of holes.

"Stay away from Pogue," he rumbled, "It's none of your business."

"What isn't?" I asked, my mouth in gear before my brain was engaged.

The question seemed to confuse him for a second and he turned his head to look back at the other bikers. I considered throwing a punch then. If he had a glass jaw, a punch to his neck or the side of this head might put him down in one shot. Maybe I could get his gun before his posse unloaded on me. I didn't because, though they were undoubtedly threatening, they didn't seem to be right on the verge of attacking and I didn't want things to escalate to a confrontation that would likely go badly for me.

He turned back. "Any of it!" he barked.

"OK," I said. "I'll stay away from Pogue."

"The fuck right you will," he said menacingly.

His eyes narrowed as he studied me, trying to figure out if I was lying to him. I attempted to convey sincerity, but probably what my face mostly showed was confusion. I truly had no idea what was going on. What did they think Pogue had to tell me that they wanted kept secret? Had Pogue told Ellis and Althelia something or had he not told them and they had died anyway over a secret they never knew? Would I be the next? I promised myself, if I were still alive in the next ninety seconds or so, I would go over what Pogue had told me with a fine-tooth comb, see if there was some hidden message there that I had been too dense to understand when he had said it.

Without another word, the biker turned away from me and headed down the walk and I let out the sour breath I had been holding for what seemed like the last two minutes. A small breeze kicked up from somewhere and a line of sweat on the back of my shirt chilled my spine.

He then spun back and closed the distance quickly, far too fast for me to even get my hands up. His right fist drove into my stomach with a force that both lifted me up on my toes and doubled me over, the studs on the leather strap digging into my flesh and muscle. As I bent, he slammed his left into the side of my head, very much like the punch I had been thinking of delivering to him a few moments earlier.

I fell bonelessly to the walkway. There was a burning line in my stomach where the studs had punctured the skin. I felt stitches in my cheek pop as my head hit the ground. I heard Tonk barking from somewhere that sounded very far away. Then there was nothing.

Twenty-One

I don't know exactly how long I was out, but it didn't seem like very long. The sun had not traversed any great distance in the sky. The grass of the lawn looked no longer. I wasn't cover in fallen leaves or snow. On the other hand, the bikers were gone, and far enough away that they were not so much as an angry rumble in the distance. I had also lost enough time that Valerie had come outside.

My head was cradled in her lap, a towel pressed against the side of my face. The pain in my cheek was a sort of distant heat, not at all unmanageable. The blow to my stomach throbbed, but in a slow, blunted kind of way. It felt good, my head in her lap, her hand caressing my brow; the most intimate contact we had had in a month.

There was a horrible wailing sound in my ears that turned out to be the siren on Bobby's cruiser which pulled into the driveway and screeched to a stop. So after Valerie had called him, Bobby had had enough time to drive over from wherever he was. I was pretty sure that if I estimated the time those activities took and figured I had been unconscious at least that long, that I wouldn't like the result one bit.

Bobby jumped out of the car before it had fully settled on its springs. "Is he alright?" he asked Valerie.

"I'm fine," I groaned. I felt Valerie startle beneath me; she must not have been aware that I was conscious.

It took both my hands to lever myself into a sitting position and when I got there the world seesawed sickeningly. The towel fell off my face and Valerie retrieved it and handed it to me. There was a fair sized spot of blood and pus soaked into its fibers. I thought about putting my hand to my face, getting some idea of how bad the damage was, but decided that I was better off not knowing and pressed the towel back in place. I could hear the siren of an approaching ambulance in any case.

Tonk came over and sat down next to me, concern in his doggy eyes.

"Valerie called and said there was a motorcycle gang here threatening you," Bobby said.

"If nine constitutes a gang, she was right. More than threatening it seems," I replied, using my tongue to prod what felt like a loose tooth on one side of my mouth.

"Any idea who they were? What they wanted?"

"They told me to stay away from Pogue."

I heard Valerie sigh behind me. Given my injury it was probably about as far as she would allow herself to go towards saying 'I told you so.'

"The cult leader?" Bobby pulled out his trusty notebook and flipped back the black cover. He began taking notes.

"I went and visited him in prison. He wasn't at all what I was expecting him to be. He was calm and behaved rationally."

"What did he tell you?"

"Nothing. At least nothing that meant anything to me. But if I had to guess I'd say they were worried that Pogue had told me something."

"The bikers?"

I nodded. That had been a bad idea as the world, which had just about settled down, swayed again, and I swallowed a quick twist of nausea. This was accompanied by an echoing pounding that began deep in my brain, like someone hammering on a kettle drum. I was starting to wonder if I had a serious concussion.

"So who are they? What did they think he told you? What's their interest in Pogue?"

"I don't know," I said as the ambulance arrived. I held out a hand and Bobby helped me to my feet. My knees didn't seem to have the ability to hold me up exactly and I clung to him unsteadily. The pain in my cheek was getting worse, an electric burning that somehow amplified itself in the muscles of my face and the bones of my skull.

"Anderson, Ellis, Teeg, these bikers. Jonas is right; something is going on and it all links back to that cult," I said through gritted teeth.

"What?"

"I don't know," I said again, "but Pogue gets out of prison on Monday, and I suspect whatever is going on, it's about to hit the fan."

The ambulance crew raced over with a gurney and with Bobby's help they laid me down on it. As my head fell back onto the thin pillow I felt my brains slosh ominously. Agony exploded behind my eyes and for a moment the world went white, a blinding white that was painful to look at. A whimper escaped my throat that sounded like it came from a beaten dog.

One of the ambulance attendants, a woman, leaned over me. I knew most of their names through common calls the fire department and ambulance crews had worked, and I was pretty sure I knew hers as well, but I was hard pressed to come up with it. I was, at that moment, finding it difficult to come up with my own name without a hint, which she was good enough to provide.

"Jack? Jack? Are you in pain?" she asked.

I was way beyond spoken words, and getting farther away by the second. I made the whimpering sound again hoping to get my point across, which I did. She gave me an injection. I hurt so much from so many injuries; I couldn't even tell you where the needle went in. Whatever she gave me opened a doorway to a wonderful place. A peaceful place, a place of liquid darkness, a place without pain. I eagerly dove through it.

Twenty-Two

In the emergency room a doctor who reminded me of Jed Clampett without the overalls had examined me and pronounced that "I had had my bell rung pretty good," which I had known without a medical degree. He surprised me by pointing out that I had two cracked ribs, which meant the biker had likely kicked me a few times while I was down, though considering Valerie's state of mind I couldn't completely rule out the possibility that she had done it before Bobby had arrived.

This diagnosis was followed by a little vomiting (me, not him), some dizziness (me again), some thoughtful and concerned frowns (him), and an extended period of double vision that Jed told me was due to a slight bruising of one eye socket. The fact that it was slight was of little comfort as the images slowly, queasily diverged as the swelling increased, and then began to converge again as it subsided several days later.

While I lay in the hospital with my eyes crossed I was visited by two Rachaels, both of whom expressed great concern at my injuries simultaneously. I showed them the little clumps of stitches in a line on my stomach from the puncture wounds caused by the studded strap. Both Rachaels hugged me, which felt nice at first and then felt somehow smothering and then had me making a quick lunge for the puke bucket by my bed all in the span of just a few seconds. My equilibrium was all fucked up.

I was visited twice by Bobby Dawkins, which from my point of view counted for four visits. The second time he came into the room I asked him if he was considering starting his own barbershop quartet. He didn't get the joke and I didn't have the energy to explain it to him, so half nauseous and giggling to myself I blamed it on the meds.

I saw neither hide nor hair of so much as a single Valerie.

I watched Frederick Pogue get out of prison from the comfort of an inpatient bed at St. Joes Hospital in Nashua. In the past year I had spent so much time there, they should probably consider naming a wing after me.

The State Police attempted to play a kind of shell game with Pogue, sending out four government sedans with darkened windows all at once which scattered as soon as they hit the highway. The police underestimated the resourcefulness of the local media, who diverted traffic helicopters to follow the vehicles, and a whole convoy of reporters who joined the parade. While a small percentage of the media presence was lured away by cars which headed east, towards the seacoast, and one which headed south into Massachusetts, the smart money was on Dunboro as the destination. With the line of news vans that rolled into town and four helicopters swarming in the air, the people of Dunboro must have thought they were being invaded. In a way they were right.

The overhead view showed the sedan pulling into the driveway of a house on Deer Run Lane. Bobby Dawkins was there waiting for it, and he leaned over and spoke to the driver who rolled down the window. The downwash from the helicopter was whipping the bushes into a frenzy and Bobby had to clamp his hat down on his head to keep it from blowing off. He pulled something from his pocket which turned out to be a remote control, which he pointed at the garage and the door trundled up. The sedan drove inside and Bobby Dawkins joined it, the door closing again at his heels.

The cameraman on the helicopter panned way out showing more of the street. Neighbors could be seen coming out of adjacent houses and looking up, their hands shielding their eyes from the sun and wind. News vans parked along the road and extended their uplink dishes. Reporters and camera crews scrambled to record stand ups.

I recognized one of the logos on the vans and, after a little squinting and a few wrong buttons, managed to change channels on the television. This station was interrupting its regular programming with a breaking news report. The camera swept back and forth across the windows on the front of the house. Not all of the blinds were drawn, but most of them were, and no motion could be seen within. The newscaster did a voiceover, recounting the story of the cult and the murders. The camera pointed up the street showing the other news crews and cameras. For one instant it showed a camera that was pointed directly back at it, the two cameras filming each other as if that was somehow itself newsworthy. I held my breath, but fortunately the world didn't explode from the collective irony and a moment later the cameras moved on.

Neighbors and others were starting to gather in the street. There was a lone protester, or at least I think he was a protester. The man, dressed in jeans and a plain blue T-shirt, held a hastily assembled sign of white poster board and blue Sharpie which read 'Matthew 7:15.' There was a bible in the top drawer of the bedside nightstand and, with one eye closed, I looked it up.

Beware of false prophets,
who come to you in sheep's clothing
but inwardly they are ravening wolves.

Whoever wrote the bible certainly foresaw every contingency.

One of the Dunboro deputies along with two State Police cruisers showed up and began some semblance of crowd control. If the town selectmen had been hoping that Pogue's release and move back to Dunboro would go unnoticed or that the circus would fade quickly, I suspected they were going to be disappointed. Another protester arrived, this one carrying a sign which read simply 'Pogue.' The letters were in black and kind of jagged, so perhaps it was meant to be hostile, but it was honestly quite hard to tell what he wanted, and he wasn't shouting anything, just standing there silently holding his sign. Perhaps as time went by Dunboro would get a better class of protesters.

The cameraman appeared to become bored, sliding the image across the home's gutters, around the flowerbeds planted by the front door stoop, and zooming in on a small defect in the siding.

The image then snapped over to the front door as it opened and Bobby Dawkins came out. He walked down the steps and was instantly surrounded by microphones. Dozens of questions were shouted at once in an incomprehensible clamor. Bobby bulled his way through saying "No comment," over and over again, not in response to the questions, but in his own paced delivery. He got into his squad car still saying it, I could read his lips through the windshield, and drove away. A few minutes later the door to the garage rolled up and the government sedan backed out. It was impossible to tell through the darkened windows if Pogue, or even a driver, were inside. Cameras pressed right up against the car, catching their own reflections in the silvered glass.

Pogue was presumably still inside the house, but if so he was sitting in the dark well away from the windows. No lights went on. None of the opened blinds were closed, nor the closed blinds opened. Some reporters tried to approach the house and were rebuffed by the police.

As more time passed and more nothing happened, the crowd thinned. Some of the news crews packed up and left. At some point the two protesters wandered off, possibly to get a cup of coffee together.

I found it all gripping and couldn't look away. I watched it through dinner, which was a thin piece of white meat that was either chicken or pork, or perhaps a particularly bloodless piece of beef. Whatever animal it had been in life, I suspected from the taste that it had died of boredom. It was served with grayish green beans and rehydrated mashed potatoes. Emeril Legasse, eat your heart out. And lime Jell-O! Joy!

I kept right on watching even as I had to change channels to continue to get video, and then later was reduced to reading the text crawl along the bottom of the CNN screen.

The evening passed without a single sighting of Pogue, or in my case I suppose that would be a double sighting, but everyone knew he was in that house. Pogue had returned to Dunboro, like a particularly sinister swallow returning to burn Capistrano to the ground. And while I didn't know what it was he had planned, I was pretty sure I wasn't going to like it.

Twenty-Three

"Get your ass down here."

That certainly had not been what I was expecting to hear when I answered my phone two days after checking out of the hospital. The number reported by caller ID meant nothing to me, just some Massachusetts area code.

I was sitting at the counter in the kitchen, CNN on the television turned down low. The North Koreans were rattling their sabers again. Tonk was grinding his way through his morning kibble, making slightly less noise and mess than a wood chipper in the process. Valerie was home for a change. The floor joists over my head creaked and shifted with her movement around the bedroom upstairs, and there was the gurgle and splash of water in the bathroom drain line in the wall behind me.

"Are you hearing me, Fallon?" the man on the other end inquired. His voice was familiar, but I couldn't place it.

I took the cell phone away from my ear and checked the number on the display again. It still rang no bells. I put the phone back against my ear.

"Yeah," I ran a finger along the new line of stitches in my cheek. When the old stitches had burst, the wound had drained, and it felt much better today. Maybe I should send the biker who had hit me a thank you note.

The man said, "I just Googled the trip from your place to here, and it says forty-three minutes. I'll expect to see you in forty-five." Then he hung up.

I took the phone with me to my laptop and looked up the number online. It was for the Lowell Police Department. Like Alice said, curiouser and curiouser.

As I got ready to leave, it never even occurred to me to tell Valerie where I was headed. We were detached, like two ships passing in the night. Or perhaps more distant than that, like a ship and plane. A very, very high plane. I also didn't take Tonk with me. Without any idea what I was headed down to Lowell for, I didn't know if I would be able to take care of him. I just had to trust that Valerie, whatever her plans for the day, would do so.

Down in Lowell, the police detective, I still didn't know his name, was outside the door waiting for me. He was leaning against the railing for the wheelchair ramp wearing either the same or a very similar black suit to the one I had seen him in last time.

I was still ten feet away when he lurched himself off the railing and said simply, "Follow me," as he took the walkway that went across the front of the building and around the side. Obediently, at least for the time being, I followed. At a gated parking lot in back I waited while he stopped and filled out a page on a clipboard and then returned it to the attendant in the small guard booth. He got a set of keys in return.

We walked to one of the patrol cars, a black and white with the number 423 stenciled on the roof and high up on the fenders. He held open the rear door on the passenger side. "Get in."

"Am I under arrest?" I asked.

"Get in," he repeated without any change of tone or inflection.

I shrugged to myself and got in. If I were under arrest, I figured, he would have handcuffed me and stuffed me into the car, or taken me into the police station. Something else was going on, and I wanted to know what.

He went around the car, climbed inside, started it up, and drove out of the lot.

"Where are we going?" I asked him through the ten small holes drilled in a circular pattern into the Plexiglas sheet that separated us. Perhaps it was Lexan. That would have made more sense. Bulletproof.

He ignored me.

I tried, "Humid weather we're having."

That also got me nothing.

"In Moby Dick, do you think the whale is a Christ figure, or do you subscribe to the school of thought that the whale represents man's unattainable goal of life fulfillment?"

"Shut up," he said tiredly.

So, he wasn't a fan of the classics.

I leaned back in my seat and watched the city of Lowell roll by outside the window. Lowell is an old mill town, built a long time ago. The buildings we passed along the main drag were made of bricks that were rounded and pitted by two hundred years of wear and tear. The facades showed real craftsmanship, creative stacking and orienting of the brickwork to spell out the year the building had been erected, or arranged in an expanse of concrete which read "L.R. Mason Building" or "Chatham Insurance Company." Incidentally, the Chatham Insurance Company, at least at the ground level, was inhabited by a lingerie store named *Dangerous Liaisons*, the mannequin in the display window wearing a leatherette teddy and holding a riding crop. I wondered if Mr. Chatham had considered that future when his building was being constructed.

I played the lazy tourist, surveying Lowell from the comfort of a chauffeured police car, until we pulled into the driveway of the Lowell Memorial Hospital. We parked under the ambulance portcullis near the emergency room doors. As the detective got out he flipped on the roof strobes and left the engine running. He opened the door for me – there was no handle on the inside – and led me in through the automatic doors.

He stopped me a fair distance from the admitting desk with the palm of one hand against my chest, then went and had low words with a nurse behind the counter. He lifted his badge away from his belt and showed it to her. They exchanged some more words. The nurse shook her head, I thought sadly. The detective clenched on hand into a fist and banged it on the desktop. They exchanged some more words and then she pointed off down one of the hallways. He nodded to her and came back to me.

"Come on."

We hiked a serpentine trail through the treatment areas of the emergency room. It was a quiet day at Lowell emergency, and most of the partitioning curtains were rolled back against the walls. Examination tables waited with clean, crisp sheets. There were glass jars filled with gauze pads and tongue depressors, and trays of gleaming instruments.

We approached a bed that had the curtains closed around it. Two uniformed Lowell cops flanked the divide in the curtain, and they moved aside when they saw the badge on my escort's belt. He swept the fabric aside with his arm and stepped through the gap, and I followed him.

The sheet on the gurney inside the partition was bloodstained and pulled up over a body. It had been yanked up somewhat hastily, and a single foot clad in a sneaker stuck out the bottom. The sneaker was beat to shit, the tread held to the body with a loop of duct tape around the toe, and there was a hole the size of a silver dollar in the sole that had been packed with black plastic, like a piece of a Hefty garbage bag.

Without preamble he uncovered the body to the waist. If he was still trying to shock me, he was doing a better job of it.

Underneath the sheet was a woman, fiftyish, doughy. Her skin was bad, pockmarked by merciless adolescent and adult acne. Her face was sagging, her hair limp, around her eyes were bags and folds like a basset hound. She was wearing stained and threadbare gray sweatshirt and pants, the sweatshirt sliced up the middle so the doctors could work on her.

She had been stabbed many, many times with a knife with a narrow blade, much narrower than the chef knife used on Anderson. An incision had been made in her abdomen. Clamps and other instruments still hung out of the wound. She hadn't been dead long; it was still wet in there.

Bloody gauze pads and bandages littered the bed around her and were scattered on the floor. Three IV bags hung from the post at the head of the bed, two fed lines into her right arm, and one into her left.

When I spoke I found my voice rough and unsteady. "Who is," I began, then swallowed and amended, "was she."

"Her ID says Alice Lahey."

I recognized the name immediately. "She testified against Teeg."

He nodded, "Yep. And shot him. And stabbed Anderson."

"I don't understand. Who stabbed her?"

"Paul Rhodes. When you mentioned your little cult, I decided to find out what I could about the other members. Pogue got out of prison and moved to New Hampshire; there's no easy way for me to keep track of him up there. But Rhodes went right into the same halfway house Anderson did when he got out. I decided to just wait and see what would happen to him. At about six o'clock this morning Rhodes says she knocked on his door and attacked him with this." He picked up a plastic evidence bag from the instrument tray containing a bloody knife. Not just any bloody knife, but a Wusthof Ikon steak knife, $419.99 for a set of six at Amazon.com. "Spryer than Anderson, he apparently got it away from her and used it."

I regarded the woman on the table sadly. That fucking cult had set her on a trajectory for destruction; she had never had a chance.

Pleased at my discomfort, I'm sure the detective considered his bringing me down here as a success. He smiled cockily and rubbed in a little salt, "So I just wanted to say congratulations, sport. You were right; the cult was at the center of it all. It didn't do anyone any good, least of all this poor woman, but if you spin it right you can probably get your name in the paper again, something else for your hero scrapbook."

I really, really wanted to hit him, give the Lowell emergency room staff something to do on this quiet morning. Even as riled up as I was, I wasn't that stupid. But I did dearly want to wipe that smile off his face, and thought I had an angle to do so. "So what you're saying is she shot Teeg, but then stabbed Anderson and tried to stab Rhodes?"

"Yeah," he nodded, "that works for me."

"With that knife?" I pointed to the evidence bag he still held in one hand.

"Yeah," he said, but there was perhaps the hint of a question in his voice.

"That eighty dollar piece of imported German stainless steel cutlery."

"That what?" he asked, his smile faltering.

"And the knife used on Anderson," I continued, "retails at over a hundred and fifty. Not only that, but they're usually sold as part of the Wusthof Classic Ikon Knife Block set, which sells for more than eight hundred dollars."

He turned the bag this way and that, examining the knife from different angles. "What are you saying?"

"I'm saying that if you think this poor woman, who jammed garbage bags into the holes in the soles of her shoes, used more than two hundred dollars' worth of knives from a set worth almost a thousand bucks to attack Anderson and Rhodes and was working alone, you're dumber than you look, and you look pretty fucking dumb from where I'm standing." Then I left.

The cops stationed outside the divide in the curtains didn't try and stop me as I pushed past them, and I kept going all the way through the emergency room and into the parking lot. There my plans were spoiled, because when I got outside I remembered my truck was back at the police station. I would have called a taxi, but frankly didn't even know if Lowell was a large enough city to have its own taxi service. Maybe one would have to come from Worcester. With few options available to me, I climbed into the back of the police car and waited.

The detective came out to the car, chastened, with his head down. He flipped off the roof lights and saddled up and began driving back to the police station. On the return trip he was the one asking the questions, and I was the one ignoring them. He asked me if I knew more about Teeg's murder than I was telling him. Did I have any ideas who Alice Lahey might have been working with? Did I know what Pogue was up to in New

Hampshire? He almost had me when he asked if I thought the trip downriver in Conrad's Heart of Darkness represented an insight into the evil in all men's hearts, or the inherent tendency of man towards moral ambiguity in a vacuum of societal norms. Quite a surprise, a cop with a classical education.

When we reached the station I became concerned he wouldn't open the door and let me out, or that he would have me arrested. Sure, he didn't actually have anything to hold me on, but he could run me through the system. I'd have to get a lawyer, and then maybe try to sue him for wrongful arrest, which would cost me a lot of money and time and energy and ultimately get me nothing. It didn't come up, however, because once he had parked he came around and opened the door. Perhaps he had run through the same math I had, and realized it would gain him nothing more than being a pain in my ass, and he was too worn out to play such games.

Once I had climbed out he regarded me with tired eyes. For the first time I thought I was seeing the real him, not the cocky exterior shell he assiduously maintained. This job was killing him. He asked, "You know who set her up, don't you? You've got it all figured out."

"Me?" I said, "I'm just a firefighter."

I left him and went back to my truck.

Twenty-Four

By and large, as a society, we have staggeringly short attention spans. One day's fascination is often rapidly supplanted by tomorrow's shiny new bauble. That appeared to be true even in the case of Martin Pogue.

He remained inside the house on Deer Run Lane, not venturing out to so much as collect his mail, the bulk of which seemed to be junk and was building up in the box at the end of the driveway steadily. If the blue glow that could be seen filtering through the living room drapes was any indication, he appeared to spend a great deal of his time watching television.

The thought of all the wonderful shows he had missed during his forty years in prison where they had no doubt restricted what he could watch, the multiple seasons of Jersey Shore and American Idol to catch up on, made me woozy. I considered it fairly likely that, exposed suddenly and without warning to a concentrated dose of The Kardashians, he might realize the futility of human existence and kill himself, thereby saving us all a lot of anguish.

Recently a second layer, likely a heavy blanket, had been tacked up over the windows behind the drapes. After that no light escaped the house at all.

He had his meals delivered, and for a brief time the public was captivated by grainy telephoto images of Pogue shrouded in almost complete shadow as he leaned out the door just far enough to collect his dinner. His pale arm, as he fished out the doorway into the light to take the bag from the deliveryman, gave him more than a passing similarity to a vampire reaching out from a coffin.

Days passed with no more riveting entertainment in the offering, and people eventually wandered off in other pursuits. The neighbors went back to their lives, no doubt breathing a sigh of relief that their home values had not been severely and adversely impacted. The State Police, initially planning to hang around for a couple of weeks, found their presence was no longer necessary and were reassigned to other duties.

The last guy to leave was the one holding the 'Pogue' sign. He never elaborated on his message, never updated his sign, and never spoke. He just stood there, peacefully, out on the sidewalk in front of the house with as blank an expression on his face as I have ever seen from someone not in a persistent coma. Then one day he looked up at the house, gave a mighty sigh, and departed, leaving his 'Pogue' sign leaning against a tree stump. In his absence, the tree stump did an equally admirable job of conveying his message, until later that same day when a neighbor came and took the sign, folding it over several times as he returned to his home, presumably to throw it in the trash, or perhaps try and sell it on EBay.

How did I know all of this, you might ask? Because I remained sitting in my truck parked in front of an empty lot down the block. Don't ask me what I was doing there. Stake out was probably too grand a phrase to describe it, as most of the day

I wasn't there and no one else was filling in my gaps. I vacillated between the certainty that there was a second shoe yet to drop regarding the cult and that it would start with Pogue, and believing that I was completely and utterly wasting my time.

I had been there daily since being discharged from the hospital, and in an odd kind of way I was obeying Jed Clampett's orders to "take it easy for a while." There were very few activities I could have undertaken, perhaps including the aforementioned coma, that would have been less taxing than sitting in my truck six or seven hours a day watching the still life diorama that was Pogue's residence.

It was not, however, a vigil that I sat alone. From time to time Rachael would join me, and she sat slouched down in the passenger seat now, her shins up on the dashboard, a plastic bottle of Pepsi trapped between her knees and the palm of one hand. She wore a baggy Nike T-shirt over a pair of black spandex leggings, liquid and shiny, like she had poured hot wax down her thighs.

"What do you think he's doing in there?" she asked me, neat little black Adidas sneakers on her dangling feet.

"Cloning Hitler using a nose hair retrieved from the bunker in Berlin," I replied matter of factly.

She lolled her head in my direction, leaning it against the headrest, to give me a lazy eye roll. It was a pretty good one, conveying loud and clear that she didn't find me nearly as amusing as I found myself, yet she had a long way to go to achieve Valerie's eye rolling prowess. Living with me, Valerie had had years of nearly continual practice. Rachael returned her attention to the house. "He's probably watching more television," she answered her own question based upon my earlier reports of his activities. "If he accidentally turns on the Kardashians, his head will probably explode."

I chuckled at the parallels between her thought processes and my own, then got a little stab of pain in my stomach that I could have blamed on the stitches but knew was due to the abyss that had formed between Valerie and me. I had not seen her in days. "We should be so lucky," I muttered.

"Do you think Jonas is really in danger?"

"I do since the bikers took a crack at me."

After the attack Bobby had thrown an APB onto the police network, though my description of them: nine guys, scruffy, black Harleys, bad tattoos, had been unhelpful. It probably narrowed the suspect list down to a scant two hundred thousand across the state.

"While I suspect they enjoyed doing it, they had another motive as well, some secret that they thought Pogue was keeping," I said.

"Any idea what secret he could have kept in prison for forty years?"

"None."

"Huh," she grunted, then sat up and put the soda bottle in the center console cup holder. "Welp, gotta go drain the lizard," she opened the door and hopped to the ground.

"The fire department has really corrupted you, you know that?" I said.

"I'm so glad you noticed," she smirked over her shoulder as she closed the door and scooted off behind some bushes in the empty lot.

What secret had the bikers been afraid Pogue would tell me? I tried looking at it from their point of view. What were bikers interested in? The answer, when it came to me, seemed so simple it had to be right. Money. Or drugs. Something of value.

If Pogue told someone about the whatever-it-was in prison, and that person told his biker buddies outside the prison, the entire chain of murders could be blamed on them trying to get information. Though if that were the case, how then did the nine bikers sneak into Ellis' house and kill him while his wife was at home without her knowing? And why shoot some and stab others and throw Ellis down a flight of stairs? And how did Knox fit in, if he did at all? OK, so it wasn't the whole answer, but perhaps it was a start.

It also went part of the way towards answering a question that had been nagging me since Pogue came back to Dunboro. Where was his money coming from? All his meals were being delivered; that wasn't cheap. The house he was living in was a nice one. Was it rented or did he buy it? Come to think of it, the church building had been a frigging mansion. Who had owned it?

All of those little mysteries started and ended with Pogue, which made me feel good about sitting in my truck watching his house.

Could I, I wondered, just walk up and ring the doorbell? With what I knew, perhaps I could get some answers out of him. That was followed by the chilling realization that if the bikers thought Pogue knew the location of what they were looking for, how long before they came and tried to pry it out of the horse's mouth, so to speak? I most definitely was not looking for round two with those guys.

A sudden desire to slouch down in my seat and maybe take a tarp out of the bed of the pickup truck and hide under it was interrupted by my fire department pager. The first tone set had not even completed when Rachael came running back to the truck adjusting her clothing.

I reached down to flip on my fire department lights, my fingers fumbling over an unfamiliar piece of tape. I had figured that a pickup truck with a big light package on the roof would stand out too much parked on the side of the road near Pogue's house for days on end, so I had removed them, and taped over the power switches when I had done so. For some reason my brain seemed unable to process that piece of information at that moment, and I continued to probe at the tape's edges in confusion.

"Go!' Rachael said, jarring me out of my stupor.

"Going," I replied, shifting the truck into gear and hitting the gas.

Twenty-Five

Daytime volunteer fire department coverage in small towns can be spotty to say the least. Once primarily populated by farmers and local craftsmen, many towns, like Dunboro, have become little more than bedroom communities with white collar workers commuting to Nashua, Manchester, Concord, and, for the particularly masochistic among us, Boston. What remains is a dwindling pool of retirees and kids, the bulk of the firefighters attending to their normal day jobs far from town when the call comes. I was therefore disappointed but not particularly surprised to find only one other car in the parking lot when we reached the station.

Max Deaks, the assistant fire chief, was waiting in the silent truck still parked in the garage with the bay door open. Max was more than capable of driving a fire truck, but the town insurance company had recently balked at the idea of people without official training and a CDL license behind the wheel. Though he had been driving large trucks since he was fourteen, and was far better at it than I, Max had never gotten the license. The lawyers had spoken and Max's driving days were over. I thought bitterly that, had only Rachael and Max been available, neither would have been permitted behind the wheel, and the call would have had to go out for mutual aid from an adjacent town in the hopes that their daytime coverage was better. That's lawyers for you.

As an added black irony, Max, though an extremely knowledgeable firefighter, has a bad back and had squeaked past his last physical with an iffy EKG. No one was expecting him to don seventy-five pounds of gear and traipse into a burning building. Putting him in the driver's seat was absolutely the best place for him where he could contribute without jeopardizing his health, but with a four hundred thousand dollar truck on the line, even a minor fender bender could bankrupt us all when the insurance company refused coverage because he had not been properly licensed.

So I drove, with my bad ankle, and Max filled the officer's seat about as effectively as a two hundred pound sack of grain. Rachael sat alone in the back, essentially untrained and of slight build and not terrifically strong. Let's just say that we were not exactly bringing our A game.

The call was for a motor vehicle accident on Route 13, a car and a propane truck, with entrapment. We had no sooner rolled out of the stationhouse than Max was on the radio calling in a first alarm for mutual aid. He had yet to see the accident, but he already knew we were seriously outclassed.

My first glimpse of the scene convinced me he was right.

The propane truck lay on its side, the oblong bulbous tank leaning precariously against and partially crushing a much smaller vehicle, maybe a Hyundai Elantra or a Honda Civic. A woman was trapped in the car, reaching over from the driver's seat and pounding ineffectually on the passenger window with her fists. I couldn't see the driver of the truck at all. The propane tank had a wrinkle and a crack in it, propane venting from it in a vaporous jet ten feet long.

Max leapfrogged over the second alarm and called in a third, also requesting police assistance to evacuate nearby homes and businesses.

The southbound lanes of Route 13 were blocked by the accident and traffic from the north was backing up. In the northbound lanes cars continued to sneak by, driving within arm's reach of a visibly leaking propane truck. People lacking any semblance of basic survival instincts fucking amaze me sometimes.

I hauled the steering wheel to the left and then the right, slewing the truck sideways to block the northbound lane. This earned me an angry honk from the motorist at the front of the line. Unbelievable.

We came to rest a hundred yards from the accident.

Rachael leaned into the gap between the front seats. "Pull up closer, Jack."

"I'm close enough already."

"Too close," Max said, "propane expands in volume by a factor of three hundred from liquid to gas. If that tank is full and it explodes, the crater is going to be a quarter of a mile across."

The actual number I knew is more like two hundred seventy, but he was close enough for government work. "We have to get that woman out of the car. We'll use the deck gun to hose it all down and disperse the gas."

Max shook his head, "We don't have enough water for that. The deck gun would run our water tank dry in three minutes flat. It's going to take you longer than that to get her out. Rachael, get on a hose. Jack, I'll run the pumps."

He didn't say it, but that left me with the fun job. I was going to get up close and personal with thousands of gallons of leaking propane.

I jumped down from the cab and took a Halligan bar from its bracket. Something like the Swiss Army Knife of crowbars, a Halligan has a spike and a wedge and a prying tool all mounted on a forged steel handle two feet long and weighing twenty pounds. My ankle chose that moment to tighten up, but I ignored the pain as best I could and lurched towards the accident. I wasn't up to this, but given a choice between Max, Rachael, and myself, I was the best of a set of bad options.

Close to the car, the temperature dropped fifty degrees. The expanding gas was sucking up heat in a process similar to how an air conditioner works. My breath plumed in front of my face. Everything reeked of methanethiol, and the propane was displacing the oxygen and making me lightheaded.

The woman's eyes were wild with desperation and tears streamed down her cheeks. "Help! Help me, please!"

"Get back!" I shouted to her. "Cover your face and look away."

She crouched back towards the driver's side of the car, which wasn't easy to do because the truck had pushed in the roof on that side. She covered her head with her arms and pressed her face down into the seat.

I slammed the end of the Halligan into the window. Pebbles of safety glass flew everywhere. I reached through and tried to open the door but it was jammed.

Behind me Rachael and Max got the hose going. Water pattered on my helmet and back, fell onto the roof of the car, and sprayed against the propane tank near the rupture where it ricocheted into a rainbow mist, some of it falling back to earth as sleety snow.

"Give me your hand." I stretched towards her through the broken window.

"I can't," she sobbed, "My foot. It's trapped."

I noticed her left leg disappeared into the space under the dashboard which had crushed down against her thighs. Nothing is ever easy.

This was taking too long. There were so many other people around. All it would take was one stray spark...

I turned away and moved towards the front of the propane truck.

"Wait!" she shrieked, "Don't leave me here!"

"I'll be right back."

She either didn't hear me or didn't understand and kept yelling.

Around the far side traffic had come to a stop less than twenty feet away. The front car was a silver Audi, the driver a man in a really great suit standing in the open door talking on his cell phone. Cell phones are excellent sources of static electricity sparks.

"Hang up your phone and get back!" I shouted at him.

"I need to get through here. I have a very important appointment."

"I need you to get in your car and back it up," I said firmly. "You do realize this is a leaking propane truck, right?" I hooked a thumb at it over my shoulder.

"Can I drive around?"

He just wasn't getting it. I realized that I still held the Halligan in my hand. I approached him, the bar held up like a weapon. "GET – THE – FUCK – BACK!"

The look on my face, the bar in my hands, he thought maybe I was going to bludgeon him with it. I didn't think I was going to, probably not, almost certainly not. He didn't give either of us the opportunity to find out as he gasped and then quickly jumped into his car. The two cars behind him made screeching U-turns and raced up the road. He started the car moving without closing his door, the force of the turn slamming it shut as he too sped off. The fourth car left a U of smoking rubber on the asphalt and slalomed its rear end as it turned. More cars reversed up the road.

I scrambled onto the propane truck, climbing from the wheel to the fender to the driver's door of the cab, everything precarious and slick with ice from the water spray. The truck was nearly on its side, and I had to haul the door open and prop it with my shoulder as I balanced straddling the opening. The driver was inside. He had either already popped his seatbelt loose or hadn't been wearing one because he lay in a heap at the bottom against the passenger door. He was about my age and thankfully skinny. There was a cut over one eye and he was shaking his head to clear it, but he appeared not to be seriously injured.

I reached down to him. "Come on. Let's get you out of here."

He stretched up an arm which swayed a little uncertainly before steadying. Getting to his feet, he turned his head and spat some blood onto the inside of the windshield. "The car came right across the centerline. I had nowhere to go." He grasped my hand and planted one foot against the base of the stick shift for leverage. He hooked his other foot into the rim of the steering wheel as he climbed with my help.

"How full is your tank?"

"Full boat," he said unhappily, his free hand grabbing the edge of the door jam. "Only two deliveries this morning. Three thousand gallons plus."

I got him out and we clambered to the ground.

I pointed up the road, "Start running and don't stop."

"What about the people in the car?"

"They're my problem. I want you clear."

"You got it." He threw me a thanks and a salute and ran. It's always great when people can follow directions.

The road in front of me was empty for a couple of hundred feet. Beyond that, cars lingered, far closer than I would have liked. I hoped it was far enough.

Back around the truck the woman was still sobbing and screaming. Rachael and Max were still throwing water. There was an inch of slushy snow layering the ground and the car. Where the hell was mutual aid? Then I realized that we had been on the scene for maybe all of six or seven minutes, though I was exhausted and it felt like much longer. Time did that sometimes at a fire scene.

The woman gasped when she saw me again. "Oh, thank God!"

I debated going back for the Jaws of Life to cut her out, but they weigh more than sixty pounds; I wasn't sure I could lug it all the way back here, not in a reasonable length of time. I had to try something else.

I took off my helmet and threw it aside. I shucked my jacket next. I dove in through the window and wormed my way into the space under the dashboard. Icy water soaked through my T-shirt and my teeth immediately started chattering. My shoulders got pinned between the seat and the edge of the console for a moment. Smaller and thinner, Rachael would probably have been a better choice for this. I shifted and managed to keep moving forward.

The propane fumes were thick. My head was swimming.

The emergency brake pedal had come down against the side of her foot and broken it but it appeared to be the ankle strap on her sandal snagged on the side of the accelerator that was keeping her from getting free. I tried to work the buckle but it was a frigging tiny thing. I pulled off one glove with my teeth and spat it into the foot well. The buckle was open seconds later.

Freed from the shoe, her foot shifted and she howled in pain.

I wormed myself backwards. "You're loose. Come on." I took her by the shoulders, pulling her out of the car window after me.

Outside I tried to set her on her feet, hoping we could three-leg it away from there. Her good ankle turned badly on the remaining high heel and the broken foot was completely useless. She almost fell down.

I scooped her up and made my best possible shambling run back towards the truck. She wrapped her arms tightly across my shoulders and buried her face in my neck.

Rachael had extended a hose line half the distance to the accident. "She's the last one," I said to her as I went by, "there's no one else over there and the gas is thick, so back it up."

Rachael backpedaled at my side, like a bodyguard protecting my retreat, the hose spraying towards the propane truck.

I saw an ambulance approaching, coming north in the empty southbound lane. I wanted to hold onto the woman until I could put her right onto a gurney, but I just couldn't manage it. Slumping to my knees, I laid her carefully out on the pavement around the far side of the fire truck. It took both of my hands braced on the road to get back to my feet. I stood over her waving my arms to signal the ambulance driver. Once I was sure I had their attention, I stumbled off to help Rachael.

She stood by the front bumper fighting with the hose by herself, so I backed her up and took some of the weight. I heard Max on the radio inside the truck coordinating a large number of reinforcements that were only a few minutes out. We needed it. I was done, but it looked like the worst of it was over.

Then everything exploded.

I couldn't tell you what caused it, but thought maybe it was a spark from the damaged car. The crack in the propane tank widened like a mouth that vomited out a ball of fire that grew, and grew, and grew, and looked like it might never stop growing until it had consumed everything like a supernova. The truck and car vanished inside that ball, and I dropped the hose and snagged Rachael by the collar of her coat.

I hauled her around the truck and braced my back against the front wheel. There was a stiff wind in my face, the expanding explosion sucking up oxygen and creating a pillar of flame that I couldn't see from where I was, but I imagined was at least a hundred feet high. The shadow of the fire truck became sharply delineated against the pavement, the light taking on a queer orange-yellow tinge.

The shockwave hit us and it shoved the truck. More than forty thousand pounds of steel and eight enormous tires, and it moved sideways! I felt it go and I knew that if I tried to resist it would break my back, so I rolled with it. I came down on one shoulder and slid, my shirt torn to ribbons against the road. Rachael lay on top of me, the brim of her helmet digging into my cheek. A ferocious change in pressure caused my ears to pop, leaving me a little deaf and disoriented. Safety glass blew out from the windows in the fire truck and peppered us. A smoldering car door slammed down nearby. I saw the ambulance attendants shield their patient with their bodies.

In the following silence my ears were ringing, but underneath that I heard sirens, blessed sirens, headed this way.

Rachael's face was slack, her eyes rolled up to the whites. I reached under her face shield and rubbed her cheek. "Come on, Rachael. Stay with me."

Her eyes came around, and took a few moments to focus. She closed her mouth and blinked. "Wha? Where?" she swallowed and blinked again.

"Are you alright?"

"I'm," her focus wandered, then settled, "I think so. What about you?"

"Never better."

She gave me a weak smile.

I heard a groan and bits of safety glass tinkled almost musically as they fell to the road. Max lifted his head above the line of the blown out passenger window. Beads of glass stuck in his hair and his nose was bleeding. He looked around in confusion.

The fire truck had stalled, but the abandoned hose on the ground continued to belch water sluggishly. It flowed across the ground and soaked my back.

"You good to move?" I asked Rachael.

She nodded, but I thought a little uncertainly, so I rolled her gently off of me and sat up.

One of the EMTs came over and touched my shoulder. "Are you OK?" he shouted, but if he did so because he thought I was deaf or if he was deaf himself I didn't know.

I nodded, "OK!" I shouted back.

He reached out a latex-gloved hand and touched my cheek, then held it in front of me to show me the blood. I touched my own cheek and felt the hole. The new stitches had popped. That damned thing was never going to heal.

"Just give me a gauze pad," I said to him, enunciating each word carefully. "There are more cars on the far side of the accident you need to check out; it could be bad over there."

He dug around inside his jump bag and pulled out a couple of wrapped four-by-fours which he handed to me. Then he took off around the truck at a run. I peeled them open and held them to my cheek as I got to my feet.

Max, reassured that everyone seemed to be moving, had laid his head back against the headrest. He had his nose pinched and was making a report on the radio. I touched his shoulder and gave him a questioning look, and he nodded and waved me away.

I left him and staggered around the truck into a war zone. Thick, black smoke billowed into the sky. The road was scorched and scattered with pieces of both vehicles. Two huge oak trees had been blown down, leaves flying in little dervishes everywhere. There was a swamp nearby the road, and the cattails were burning. The propane tank had been peeled open like a banana. What was left of the truck and car was on fire. A crew from Milford had just arrived from the other side and was setting up hoses to fight it. Beyond them I could see a second ambulance way in the distance, the crew doing something I couldn't make out through the smoke and heat haze.

Rachael came unsteadily to my side and clung to me. "Oh my God," she said surveying the scene. "We could have, I mean, we really could have been," but she couldn't finish the thought. She pressed her face into my shoulder.

"It's OK." I said, putting one arm around her. Crews from Wilton and Amherst had arrived. A Pepperell tanker crept around the wreckage of our poor engine and then sped towards the fire. I stroked her hair. "It's over."

Twenty-Six

When you come through the doors into the emergency room, and the first words out of the receptionist's mouth are "You again?" you've probably been going to the ER too often. I sat on a gurney at St. Joes while Jeb Clampett again stitched up my cheek. He wore a disappointed frown as he worked, and I thought went stingy on the anesthetic and tugged a little harder on the stitching than necessary, perhaps to teach me a lesson about treating his previous efforts so poorly. Lesson learned. I thought it a kindness he had not reached for the stapler on the admitting desk when he saw me coming through the door.

My cheek seemed to be the worst of it. Otherwise, I had road rash, and plenty of it, but no serious injuries, at least none worse than I had started with. Rachael had come away in even better shape because she had used me as a sled. Max had a raging headache, but his nose bleed had stopped on its own. People on the far side of the accident had fared well. Most of them were in their cars when the explosion occurred. Protected by their vehicles, they had suffered little more than a handful of cuts and scratches from flying glass.

We had been staggeringly lucky, somewhere up near miracle status. If there had been less of a breeze, if we had arrived later, if Rachael had dispersed less vapor with the hose prior to the explosion, or if the topography of the land caused the propane, which is denser than air, to pool and concentrate instead of spread out, the headline in tomorrow's paper would have read, 'Dozens killed in propane explosion.'

When the propane truck had been towed away, the roadway underneath was melted, the asphalt crazed with cracks. Between that damage and the failure of the Main Street overpass in the spring flooding, the Dunboro road repair budget was going to be blown for the year, and it wasn't even August yet.

Rachael and Max waited for me in the appropriately named Waiting Room – my treatment took by far the longest – and we got a lift back to Dunboro in a Channel 9 news van in exchange for an interview on the way. A modest man, Max ummed and fidgeted his way through the interview, while Rachael and I made obscene gestures and funny faces at him from behind the camera. Who says we don't support our friends?

At the fire station we stood in the spot where Engine 2 would have been parked.

"She'll be back. She's a fine truck," Max said quietly.

"Sure," I said, but only because on top of everything else that had happened, the damage to Engine 2 seemed to have Max on the verge of tears. In truth we didn't know how badly off Engine 2 was, but after the explosion we couldn't manage to get her to start, and with five flat tires she had been hauled away humiliatingly on a flatbed trailer. She was currently resting comfortably at the same diesel shop where John worked as a mechanic, and it would be some time before she returned to the line, if ever. Together with the forestry truck we had lost in the same flooding that had washed away the overpass, the firehouse was getting thin on apparatus. We might have to hold a major fundraiser to buy more, and soon.

Max took a deep breath and let it out in a huff. "You two take care of yourselves. Jack, you might want to get some ice on your face."

"I will."

He shook our hands, a strangely formal gesture, and left the station.

"Let's get you home," I said to Rachael and led her out to my truck.

She was silent on the drive over to her place, watching the trees and houses and whatever flash by outside the window, though I tried several times to start a conversation. She was equally unresponsive as I led her inside and sat her down on the couch.

"Are you OK?" I asked squatting down in front of her, tilting my head back and forth, catching angles of light in her eyes and watching her pupils react as they tracked me, wondering if maybe the doctors had missed a concussion.

"I'm fine. It's just that..." she let the thought drift off.

"Just what?" I asked, taking her hand in mine, startled at how cold it was. When she didn't answer I said, "I'm going to make you some tea." I went into her kitchen and rummaged, familiarizing myself with where things were kept. "Green tea, lemon, honey, cayenne pepper, and cinnamon. An old family recipe." I found the kettle and filled it from the sink. "It'll set you right," I added as I put the kettle on the stove.

Saying 'It'll set you right,' reminded me of great grandma Fallon, who used to say the same thing just as she handed her special tea to me when I had had a cold as a child. I didn't mention that Nana also used to add a big slug of blackberry brandy from an old bottle made of smoky, gray glass. Eleven years old and maybe all of 70 pounds, I'd end up almost falling-down drunk.

I mixed the concoction sans brandy in a heavy white porcelain mug and sat down next to her on the couch. When I handed her the tea she didn't sip it, but instead just held it, rolling the cup slowly between her hands. She stared into its depths for a moment, and then her eyes came up to meet mine. She held the mug with one hand, reaching out and touching my damaged cheek with the other so softly that I almost didn't feel it. Maybe I still had some local anesthetic swirling around in my skin.

"Oh, Jack. Your face," she breathed sadly.

"It'll heal," I said, though I wasn't really sure that it would. Looking in a mirror at the emergency room I knew I was going to have at a minimum one doozy of a scar. Maybe I should join the body modification crowd and mount a hex nut or a big round washer in my cheek, though when I chewed food some would inevitably come shooting out the hole, which would probably be considered a pretty big social faux pas, right?

She let her hand drop from my face and her gaze back into the mug. "I don't think I can be a firefighter anymore. I just don't, that is, I can't." Tears began rolling down her cheeks.

She didn't have to say anything else. I knew exactly what she was thinking.

Ninety-five percent of firefighting, heck, ninety-nine percent, anyone in fair physical shape can do. Then comes that one call in a hundred: a burned body, or a drowning, or a mangled child at a car accident. You can't put it aside. The next call, the next car accident, all you can see is that child twisted up in the wreckage. You freeze. You blank. You can't do it. You can't work the accident. It's no reflection on the firefighter at all. It's just how they're wired. Whatever it is that would break them, whatever comprises their own personal nightmares, firefighting has shown it to them.

I was reminded of two EMTs I knew from the North Country, both twenty-plus-year veterans, and in those twenty-plus years they had seen it all: electrocutions, hunting accidents, suicides, beheadings, poisonings, animal attacks. One day they went to a call for two teenage sisters who had fallen overboard during a day of boating. The girls were recovered after only a few minutes in the water in full cardiac arrest. A family member had CPR training and began on one girl immediately, directing a second family member on how to do it on the other, while the boat traveled to shore at a high rate of speed. Those girls were in the ambulance less than ten minutes after they fell overboard. They were young and healthy. The odds were strongly in favor of their survival.

And they both died.

One of the EMTs filed his resignation papers at the hospital while the doctor was signing the death certificates. The other held on for another month or so, pawning off increasingly more of his shift time to others until he simply stopped showing up at all.

I ran into one of them at a department Christmas party a few years later. I didn't want to ask him about it, but the question that drove me was irresistible and I think he understood that. After all the awful things they had seen, all the horrible human tragedy, what did they see on that one call that had affected them so deeply? I had to know. I had to see if that potential for devastation lay somewhere within my own heart.

He wasn't surprised, though I think he was a little depressed people didn't seem to want to talk to him about anything else but that one call. "Jack," he said, his head tilted down and away so maybe he was looking at me with only half of one eye, "they both died."

I just stared at him waiting for more. I mean, that's the business, right? Surely in twenty years they had had lots of people die. It was inevitable. I didn't want to do anything as callous as shrugging, but my lack of reaction was kind of like a shrug in a way. Almost, but not quite as bad as if I had said, "Yeah, so?"

After a few moments of dispassionately observing the people partying around us, like some member of an alien race unable to comprehend their actions, he continued, "They were both in perfect health. They received good care almost immediately. The family said they knew how to swim for fuck's sake. So why?" his voice rose, though I'm not sure he realized it. "Tell me why? Why after the family did everything right, after we did everything right, did we still lose, not just one, but both of them?"

I shook my head. I didn't have an answer. When you lose a four hundred pound diabetic in their seventies to a heart attack, it doesn't surprise you. Heck, you were surprised when you kept them alive long enough to get to the hospital and die there. But those two...

He was way ahead of me. He had probably spent many sleepless nights with the same ideas surging through his brain, so he completed the thought for me. "When they're young, when everything goes right and still everything goes wrong. It was too random for me. Why the fuck bother? Why train and suffer and sweat, if God is just going to decide, 'Uh-uh, this one dies,' and flip a switch?"

Maybe for Rachael the truck explosion was her end, the moment she realized she didn't have faith in what she was doing anymore. The reality of firefighting is, beyond the jokes and the teamwork and the Band of Brothers stuff, people sometimes die despite your best efforts.

But I didn't want her to give up on herself so quickly, so soon after the accident. I wanted her to give time a chance to round off the sharpened edges of her doubt, and so I said, "Keep your pager. See how you feel the next time it goes off."

She nodded and swiped at the tears on her face, then

carefully put the mug down on the coffee table and leaned into my chest. Almost reflexively I put my arms around her, and in turn felt her arms wrap around me.

The kiss, when it happened, was entirely unexpected. Or maybe that's just a lie I tell myself in hindsight.

We held the kiss and pawed at each other, pulling clothing out of place. We found our way into her bedroom. After that, it didn't matter how many buttons I lost off of my shirt. It didn't matter if we made love slowly, savoring the sweetness and mystery of each other's bodies, or furiously, reaffirming our lives shortly after we had come so close to death. It didn't matter who was on top. It didn't matter what I thought of her orgasm face or she thought of mine.

What mattered, as I lay exhausted in an unfamiliar bed surrounded by our mingled scent, blood seeping past the fresh stitches in my face and staining her pillowcase pink, was the certainty that I had just destroyed my marriage.

Twenty-Seven

I left the next morning while Rachael was still asleep.

She was an extraordinarily deep sleeper, so much so that after I disentangled myself I spent some time watching her breathe, the throb of the pulse at her throat – a spot I was filled with longing to kiss – concerned that an undiagnosed concussion may have transitioned to something more serious. Comforted that she seemed to be resting normally, I grabbed my shoes and tiptoed out of her house, the perfect Hollywood movie cad, guilty about cheating on my wife and not man enough to wait until Rachael awoke and own up to using her as a one night stand. I realized I was being even more cad-ish, if in fact that is a word, standing outside next to my truck and remembering that Rachael's car was still parked down the street from Pogue's place, and the gentlemanly thing to do would be to give her a ride to it. I debated going back inside, cycled through how that scenario might play out in my mind, and ran for my very life.

Pursued by images of the slow, languorous, morning sex

that I had narrowly escaped, I drove to Norma's and had steak and eggs, an uncharacteristically large breakfast for me. Feeding a guilty conscience, or a last meal for the condemned? I asked Norma for a side order of self-loathing, which earned me a concerned frown. When it arrived, it had somehow become two slices of multigrain toast with homemade strawberry preserves. It tasted better than the self-loathing would have, and was high in fiber to boot. Norma takes such good care of me.

Knox was there having breakfast with the other town selectmen. He recognized me – he made it his business to know all the town personnel – and threw me a little wave. I had no idea if he was mocking me or knew of my knowledge of his previous involvement with the cult. Probably not, I decided, and so went with Plan B and waved back. If you're curious, Plan A had been to stab him repeatedly with the oversized knife that came with the steak and eggs breakfast.

It was mid-morning by the time I returned to the Fallon homestead and found that Valerie had already left. I experienced something like relief, but which I knew was as transitory as that felt by a student expecting to be creamed by a final exam who instead lucks into a snow day. Perhaps, I thought, my uncharacteristically large breakfast had been a delaying tactic on my part to give Valerie a chance to get out of the house before I came home. I can be so fucking transparent sometimes. Had I been less wrapped up in my own emotional state, I might have been curious where she was if not at home, or if maybe, like me, she had spent the night elsewhere, but at the time that capability seemed beyond me.

I showered, the scent of Rachael on my skin reawakened by the steam even as I rinsed her away. I dressed and played a little fetch with Tonk in the yard, keeping a baseball bat near at hand and a keen ear out for the throb of motorcycle engines as I did so. Afterwards I spent some time rereading Jonas' newspaper clippings and realized that I had a whole lotta nada in the way of fresh ideas, so I returned to my vigil at Pogue's house. It was the same thing as doing essentially nothing for an investigation that was completely spinning its wheels, and yet had the comforting veneer of productivity and progress about it.

When I parked I noticed that Rachael's car was gone, so somehow she had come and gotten it without my help; another unpleasant confrontation successfully avoided. On the whole it was looking like a good day for cads.

I rolled down my window and settled into my seat, the front of Pogue's house standing at about 11 o'clock in my field of view. The sun was high, and the air was warm, and I was full of steak and eggs. Not so much as a curtain twitched in any window. I wasn't even sure that Pogue was inside. I fell into a half sleep, my wandering and dwindling attention more or less centered on Pogue's front door, when Jonas opened my passenger door and climbed inside. He startled me out of my nap, and I cleared my throat and rubbed at my eyes as I tried to reorient myself. My fresh road rash stuck uncomfortably to the back of my shirt.

"Wake you?"

"A little," I admitted, stifling a yawn. It was then that I noticed he had brought an ancient rifle with him that he held between his knees pointed straight up. "What is that?"

"This," he said, turning it sideways and admiring the finish on the walnut stock, "is a Marine Corps issue Springfield M1903-A4 sniper rifle with an Unertl eight power scope."

"A Springfield A4 what?"

"You can call her Nadine," he said with a smile. He ran a hand lovingly down the forehand grip. "We saw a lot of action during the war, her and me. Got me out of a lot of close scrapes."

"You're just walking around town carrying a sniper rifle?"

"This is America; I got the right. Besides, after what the

bikers did to you, I figured I could use a little firepower. You're young; you can still take a beating. They would probably kill me. Sooo," he said, drawing the word out and giving a little shrug, "I brought Nadine."

I didn't consider taking a beating as one of my better skills; it wasn't on my resume. Perhaps I should consider arming myself as well. Or I could go full Mad Max and mount a machinegun on a tripod in my pickup bed. Overreact much?

"Anyway," Jonas continued, "I went by the police department and asked Dawkins what he was going to do about Pogue. He told me that Pogue had done his time and was a free citizen as far as he was concerned, but that you were up here watching him. I think he thinks you're crazy, by the way."

"Popular sentiment," I commented. Bobby thought I was crazy. Valerie thought I was crazy. The cop in Lowell likely thought I was off my rocker. I wondered what Rachael really thought of my activities.

"Not with me," Jonas replied. "I think he and his cult are still murdering people. Have you seen anything?"

"Not today," I said, and didn't add, nor yesterday, nor the day before that. Whatever was going to happen was sure taking its sweet time getting going.

"Heard you had some excitement yesterday."

"Yeah. Hell of a call."

So I told him about the propane truck explosion, asking his opinion here and there, curious if he would have done anything differently. He told me about a propane tank explosion in Massachusetts in the eighties where shrapnel from the tank had cut down two firefighters instantly and seriously injured four others.

"I ever tell you about my first fire as Fire Chief? A nasty

basement fire; took a turn for the worst."

"Yeah, I remember it."

He nodded. "I thought I had."

It was a good story; he had probably entertained a lot of people with it.

We settled into an easy silence as the sun worked its way towards the horizon. I checked my phone to see if I had missed a call or text from either Valerie or Rachael. No dice. I drummed my fingers on my steering wheel.

"Something on your mind?" Jonas asked.

I considered divulging what was going on between Valerie, Rachael, and I. Jonas was a guy who had been around a bit, and his advice might be helpful. Still, even in light of all the secrets and confessions he had shared with me, I was for the most part a closed guy not interested in sharing my feelings.

"No, not really," I replied.

Though he knew I wasn't being wholly truthful, he didn't press, and we fell back into our easy silence.

At seven, according to the clock on the dash, Jonas and I split a sandwich and a bag of chips I had packed into a cooler that morning.

"How long you figure on doing this?" Jonas asked between bites of sandwich.

"I don't know. I've got nothing better to do just now. Maybe something will happen. Maybe I'll come up with a better idea." Maybe, I didn't add, I didn't know what the hell I was doing, and if Jonas was in real danger, he was most likely screwed if he was counting on me to get him out of it.

Jonas frowned. Perhaps he had had the same thought as the one I hadn't voiced. "I didn't mean in the grand scheme of things. I meant tonight."

"Oh, let's give it another couple of hours. You can go if you like. I'll even break the stakeout and drive you home."

"No. No. I'm fine here."

We watched and waited as the sun set. Lights came on in Pogue's place, but that didn't mean anything; maybe he had a couple of those automatic modules to run them. Time passed slowly, and I found myself almost more fascinated by the glacial pace of the dashboard clock than the absolutely static scene outside.

I was minutes from calling it quits for the night when a glow appeared at the end of the block and the air shivered with the sound of throaty engines with minimal mufflers. The glow resolved into half a dozen separate headlights that jumped and jittered on the stiff suspension of heavy road bikes. The pack had returned.

Jonas and I ducked down below the dashboard with just our eyes peeking over as they rolled to a stop in front of Pogue's house. In the wash of the headlights I recognized the same guy who had hit me. He and another man got off their bikes while the rest of the pack waited. They swaggered up the walkway to the door, I imagined with much creaking of leather and the jingling of chains, but if so, those sounds were lost in the idling of the motorcycles, a low, predatory, and threatening sound.

The leader pounded on the door hard, a sound I heard even over the engines, and called out Pogue's name. After waiting a few moments, he drew the gun from his belt and pounded on the door again with the butt.

"Should we call the cops?" Jonas whispered harshly, his knuckles white on the stock of his rifle.

"They'll never get here in time." Besides, lights had gone on in several of the neighboring houses and I was sure someone else was already doing it.

"I'm not prepared to shoot it out with a bunch of automatic weapons. Not at this range."

"We're not going to shoot it out with anybody." I had been about to add 'Not over Pogue,' as uncharitable as that sounds, when the front door opened and Pogue stood there framed by the light in his front hall.

The second biker reached out and grabbed Pogue by the collar, lifting him up onto his toes. He shook Pogue and yelled something unintelligible into his face at very close range. Pogue yelled something back. I only caught the word "Paul."

Was the second man Paul Rhodes, fresh from Lowell, most recently in residence at the Concord prison and killer of Alice Lahey? If so, my mind insisted, working furiously, all the pieces of the cult were back in place. Pogue, Rhodes, Knox, Laura Banks, maybe Bobby Dawkins, John Pederson, and Emmy Farmer for all I knew. Here comes the other shoe.

Rhodes passed Pogue to the other biker who held him by the scruff of his neck as he muscled him down the walkway and onto one of the bikes. Rhodes followed. The front door of the house was left open, the rectangle of light falling on the front walk looking abandoned and forlorn. They revved up their engines and pulled a U-turn, headed back up the road the way they had come. I started the truck and tailed them with my headlights off.

"Where are they taking him?"

"I don't know," I replied, though I thought I did know, and a short while later my deduction was rewarded as they steered off of Route 13 and onto the Bartlett Trail.

Twenty-Eight

I pulled past the parking area for the trailhead and drove the truck off the road and into the low bushes on the shoulder. Convinced that it was sufficiently camouflaged, Jonas and I got out and made our way back. Jonas carried his rifle slung over his shoulder by its padded canvas strap, the barrel pointed at the heavens. The sky was clear and there was a lot of moonlight, the edge of every leaf and blade of grass limned in shimmering silver.

We stood at the edge of the woods, the trail a dark tunnel in front of us. On their bikes, the path in good condition, the bikers could have been all the way to the mansion already.

"Now we call the cops?" Jonas asked.

"Way ahead of you," I replied, punching the direct line for the Dunboro police into my phone even as I started moving down the trail.

I got their answering machine.

I know this may sound weird to people who live in the big city, but Dunboro's police department actually closes at night. After a short recorded message about their business hours and a long series of clicks, the call was transferred to the State Police.

With dread I remembered being first on the scene of a three-car accident on Route 93 on a rainy night a few years earlier. There were injured people scattered around, one of them lying in the road where he had landed after getting thrown from his vehicle. Cars, unable to really see or understand the twisted wreckage in the dark and the rain, had been whizzing by at 75 miles per hour in serious danger of adding to the carnage. I had stood in the road with a pathetic two D-cell Maglite trying to keep drivers from running into either them or myself as I called the Staties. It had taken more than twenty minutes for the first cop to show up. This isn't a knock on the quality of the State Police, but the simple reality of New Hampshire being spread out and the State Police substations spread thin.

I tried to figure out where the units would be responding from and how long would it take them to get to the church. I concluded too far and too long.

Exasperated, I hung up the phone.

From where he trotted beside me, Jonas shot me a questioning glance.

"Staties," I said simply, and he nodded. Through his experiences on the fire department, he had been on the wrong side of the same unfortunate timeline on more than one occasion.

I started going through my contact list for the number of Bobby's cell when we heard the first gunshot. This was followed rapidly by two more. I went into full spaz mode, dropping my phone, and hurling myself awkwardly off the trail and into the bushes. Jonas, a guy who had probably been shot at before and who more importantly could tell just from the sound when a bullet wasn't aimed at him, got down on one knee and scanned ahead of him through the rifle scope.

When no more shots followed, I belly-crawled out of the rough to Jonas' side. He still had his rifle up. "Handgun. Large caliber. Maybe half a mile ahead. Probably at the fence," he said through the side of his mouth.

I was reminded of scenes from the old Lone Ranger TV series of Tonto putting his ear against the ground and pronouncing how many men were coming and on how many horses. "Good work, Tonto," I muttered.

Jonas kept his rifle up and continued moving forward, now in a sort of crouched fast walk that they had probably taught him in infantry school sixty years earlier. After a little hunting around I found my cell phone and followed him. Uninterrupted by gunfire, I located Bobby in my contact list and dialed. The line rang and then dropped me to his voicemail. Figures. If someone had called him and he had gone up to Pogue's place, he might be either inside the house or talking to the neighbors, his cell phone lying in his car or in the charger at home.

I left a message: "The bikers who grabbed Pogue are at the church. Jonas and I are on the way there now. We've heard gunshots. Join the party. Bring firepower. "

"We're on our own," Jonas said when I hung up the phone.

"For the time being, but Bobby will come running as soon as he gets the message."

We kept moving down the trail. When we reached the fence, we found the cause of the gunshots. The locked gate had caught them by surprise so they shot off the lock, which lay in a shattered pile on the ground along with its chain. The gate was swung open, the ground through the gap churned by the passage of all the motorcycles.

We were not that far behind now. Jonas and I exchanged a

look, and then he, the guy with the gun, went through the gate first. I followed.

The road was just turning over from gravel to cobblestones when we heard the shriek. At first I wasn't sure it was human. It rocketed up and down in pitch like someone was torturing a coyote, and it went on and on, far longer than I thought a human could support. I was certain that lung volume would become a factor, but the scream somehow persisted. It dwindled off into a moan that raised goosebumps on my arms and legs despite the warm temperature, and then soared, without pause, back up the scales.

Jonas broke into a pretty good approximation of a run.

"Jonas!" I called after him, though I was pretty sure he didn't hear me over the yelling. Just as I was losing sight of him around the corner, I took off after him. My approximation of a run was probably worse than his was.

Beyond the bend in the road I couldn't see Jonas anywhere. I slowed as I approached the wrought iron entry. The right hand gate was open. I could see the bikers gathered near the fountain. As I crept forward Jonas reached out of the darkness and snagged the cuff of my jeans. Whatever sound of surprise I made was lost in the shrieking, which had become hoarse and was broken by sobbing. I crouched down next to Jonas who was lying just off the road on his stomach, the rifle propped in a vee between two rocks he had positioned for that purpose.

In the bright moonlight, I could see everything very clearly. The bulk of the bikers stood in a clump leaning against or straddling their bikes. Two of them, I thought Rhodes and the leader, stood in front of Pogue who was on his knees. One of them was sawing at Pogue's fingers with some kind of a small saw or large knife. It was hard to tell from this distance, but at least a few fingers were already missing. Pogue was rapidly approaching beyond caring, probably in shock, just wavering on his knees moaning.

The man stopped sawing as the two men exchanged words, too low for me to hear. The one holding Pogue's hand shook it which caused Pogue's head to snap up. He spoke to Pogue, rattling his hand to make sure he had his attention. Then he let go of the hand and Pogue hunched over it, cradling it in his other, breathing deeply.

"What's it going to be?" one of the men standing over Pogue asked.

Pogue straightening up, his wavering stopped. "Fuck you, Paul."

The man I thought was Paul Rhodes turned away. He rubbed his hand along his jaw for a moment. "No, Martin," he said. "Fuck you." He turned back and drew a gun from his waistband and pointed it at Pogue's head. I held a steadying hand on Jonas' shoulder – this was a firefight that would go badly for us if it started – as Rhodes pulled the trigger. I felt Jonas tense, but thankfully he didn't shoot. Pogue flopped onto his back and was still.

The other man with Rhodes flew into a rage. He grabbed Rhodes and shook him. "What are we going to do now with Pogue dead? Where's my money?"

Rhodes shoved the other man away from him, and came close to but didn't quite point his gun at him, "I've got it under control. There are others who will talk even if Martin wouldn't." He shoved the gun back into his waistband and made for the bikes. "Saddle up!" he announced, "We're done for the night."

The other man stood and seethed for a moment before joining the others. I lay as flat as possible and buried my face in the broad leaves of a hosta. They started up their bikes and circled the fountain before accelerating back up the road. Jonas kept them in his crosshairs the whole way, and I felt only reluctantly let the last one slip away without firing a shot.

Once the sound of the motorcycles had faded to a distant

droning, Jonas and I got up and scampered to where Martin Pogue lay. They had cut off all the fingers on his right hand and two on his left. It had been a butchering, done with something jagged and toothy and not particularly sharp, the skin more shredded than cut, pieces of tendon and muscle flapping from the ends, the bones broken off like sticks. A single hole was slightly off center in Pogue's forehead.

"What did he know? What secret did he keep even as they tortured him?" Jonas' voice was thick, but with grief or anger or long held vengeance finally released, I couldn't tell.

"Good questions. Come on," I headed for the gate, the trail and my truck, "As soon as Bobby gets my message this place is going to be saturated by State Police. They'll want to detain us for questioning, and I have something else I want to check out first."

Twenty-Nine

We found the front door to Pogue's house closed and locked. That meant that Bobby had been there, checked the place out, and locked it, and was probably on his way to the mansion.

"What are we doing here? We should be talking to the police!" Jonas whispered frantically as he moved beside me in a surprisingly silent and agile crouch.

When did the voice of reason in my life start speaking to me through Jonas, and when did I become so steadfast in my determination to ignore it?

I reminded myself that I was here, leading Jonas around the side of Pogue's house, because I had to find out one thing, one single thing, and then we could go to the police. The moment the police knew that Pogue was dead, this house would be sealed to me, and I would never find the answer I needed. That thought was followed by the realization that there always seemed to be just one more thing, one more piece of the puzzle, one more person I needed to talk to, one more opportunity to risk my life and damage my marriage, one more stone on the road to hell that I was carefully and conscientiously paving with the best of intentions.

We reached the back door. It was built into a little bump out on one corner of the house and probably opened into a mud room, from there into either the kitchen or living room.

"This is crazy," Jonas insisted. "What if Bobby finds Pogue shot and comes back up here, or what if he has already sent one of his deputies this way to guard the house?"

I held up a hand for silence and mercifully Jonas gave it to me.

From some boggy area back in the woods behind the house a colony of peepers were really making a ruckus, and it drowned out nearly all other sounds. I couldn't see any lights from the neighboring houses, but not every insomniac who stands in the kitchen window watching people break into the house next door turns on a light to do so.

"I bet a neighbor is calling the cops right now," Jonas whispered harshly, echoing my own fears back at me.

I gave him a frustrated expression and held up both hands to quiet him. Then I turned and tried the back door. Dunboro is a small town, and most people still do not lock their doors at night. Pogue had felt that he had something to fear, rightly so it had turned out, and his house was locked up tight.

Firefighting has taught me many ways to open a locked door, but not how to do so quietly, and often very little of the door remains in the aftermath. I was hoping to use some finesse. I took two paperclips from my pocket that I had found in the center console of my truck. I unwound them and crouched down, inserting them into the lock.

"You know how to pick locks?" Jonas asked.

"Sure," I replied lightly, "doesn't everyone?"

As a graduate student I had read something called the MIT Guide to Lock Picking, a web page which showed the basic construction of locks and how they worked, and how some of them can be picked. In my dorm room I had toyed with many simple locks; a padlock, a desk drawer, the door to the room itself. On paper it looks like a ludicrously simple process, one which very quickly runs up against the reality of sticky pins and balky cylinder springs. Still, like juggling, which is another skill I have, it was just a matter of practice before I became pretty good at it.

"Pretty good" of course meant picking a lock in a brightly lit room without my heart thudding in my chest or sweat stinging my eyes or an old man yammering behind me. I ignored those distractions as best I could and focused in the dim moonlight, trying also to ignore the insects buzzing around my face and a knotting pain building in my ankle, hoping to sort of Zen myself inside the lock mechanism and feel it out.

It was a cheap lock, one with big, obvious pins and only a few of them. There was a lot of catch room in the cylinder and I was able to set each pin firmly and move on. It probably took me no more than five minutes to get it open.

Jonas leaned down and whispered right in my ear, "What if he's got a burglar alarm?" just as I gave the knob a twist. I held my breath as the door swung away from me. I stood up slowly and waited thirty seconds, then sixty, then another thirty just for good measure. If he had an alarm system, it was a silent one.

"He might have one of those silent ones that notifies the cops directly," Jonas said.

"Would you please give it a rest?" I replied sharply as I shoved the door open a little more with my shoulder and went inside. Jonas followed me.

The room was, as I had surmised, a mud room. There was no alarm panel on the wall next to the door. There was a great deal of garbage piled up neatly bound in big black plastic bags in the tiny space. Dunboro is far too small for a commercial company to come in and set up shop to collect the trash. The citizens have to bring it to the village transfer station themselves if they want to get rid of it. For most people this represents no great hardship, and in some ways the transfer station has become a minor hub of social activity where news and gossip, along with small appliances, tools, and books are exchanged. Had Pogue tried to go he would have been immediately mobbed, so he had been stuck stockpiling it. As a short term plan it seemed OK, but I wondered what he might have been planning to do in the long run, not that it mattered now.

Skirting the pile of bags, I turned on a small penlight and moved into the next room, which turned out to be the dining room. The beam reflected off the hardwood flooring and illuminated a big oval table that could seat six. Overhead was a chandelier that held hundreds of teardrop crystals. Prime digs for a recently-released convict.

"Jack," Jonas whispered, "what do we do if the bikers show up?"

I was just about to tell him to be quiet again when what he

had said penetrated my brain and froze my heart solid. If there was something they wanted out of Pogue, something he didn't give them, it only made sense they would come look for it here. Sure, they had left the mansion first and should have beaten us here easily, but maybe they were slow thinkers. Maybe they had stopped for a beer first; torturing and then shooting a man is thirsty business.

It seemed stupid to me now, having insisted that Jonas leave Nadine in the truck. At the time I figured that I had witnessed enough jovial gunplay for one day, but would have felt much more secure had he been carrying it.

"We move fast," I told him. "We'll be gone before they get here." My voice sounded to my own ears as if I almost believed it.

With two doorways to choose from I picked the one that led more towards the rear of the house. I was looking for the kitchen, and figured the view of the street would be from the living room. Greeted by a wood-grained Formica countertop, the kind that is supposed to look like butcher block but fails entirely, and white Maple cabinetry, I knew I had chosen correctly.

My flashlight beam traveling across the counter picked out every modern kitchen convenience. I saw a toaster oven and microwave, a coffee maker and a small television. There was even a bread machine. But I didn't see what I was searching for. I moved from the doorway into the room to get a better look.

"What are we doing in the kitchen? What are you hoping to find?" Jonas asked me.

Just as I was about to answer him, I found it. It had been tucked back into a corner between the microwave and the toaster oven. The distinctive handles were instantly familiar, the edges of each knife gleaming at me from their respective slots. It was a Wusthof Icon chef's knife set. Two knives were missing from the block.

I'll give you three guesses which ones, and as the saying goes, the first two don't count.

Thirty

After our unsanctioned perusal of Pogue's house, Jonas and I had returned to the mansion. We were instantly scooped up and whisked off in a squad car, lights blazing and sirens blaring, to the State Police barracks in Concord, and there into a big rectangular conference room inside. Guarded by two burly Staties who made sure we didn't wander off, we remained there drinking cups of the worse coffee in creation, until dawn arrived and others began filing in.

By 8 AM the big rectangular conference table in the middle of that big rectangular conference room was stacked two spectators deep, at least on their side. They had stolen all the spare chairs from our side of the table, which held only Jonas and me.

There was a state homicide investigator whose name tag read Doherty. He was apparently a chief with enough cheese to have an assistant: a young zaftig blonde named Brittany who packed herself into a secretarial outfit in a way that made me think, perhaps unkindly, that it was not the skills listed on her resume that had gotten her the job. There was a liaison from the Governor's office and a guy from the State Attorney General, or maybe it was the State Attorney General himself; I never could remember what his name was or what he looked like. He was flanked by a whole posse: paper carriers, water bearers, suits, and handlers. I noticed, not without some amusement, that the suits all carried identical briefcases, likely a yearend bonus gift at the office, and gave off a vibe very much like a precision drill team in the metered way they opened and closed them and passed papers back and forth. There were two people from the state forensics lab, a balding and intense looking older man and an equally serious younger woman, both in lab coats. There were also five or six cops who perhaps were involved in some tangential way, or maybe were just there seeking some entertainment to go with their morning donut and coffee. The crowd was rounded out by a stenographer and a guy running a video camera. I hoped he was getting my good side, the one with the horrifically inflamed stitches.

Bobby Dawkins sat at one end of the table, a place psychologically similar to Switzerland. Whose side he was on, where his allegiances lay, I couldn't guess.

Our story took a long time in the telling, and Jonas seemed perfectly willing to let me tell all of it. In fact, everyone in the room, and it wasn't a small room, and as I've pointed out there were lots of people in it, seemed willing to let me keep on talking without interruption until I either passed out from lack of oxygen or talked myself into a jail cell.

I tried to stick to just the facts, like Harry Morgan used to ask for on Dragnet. I was pretty sure that conjecture or supposition on my part was only going to feed someone enough rope with which to hang me. Our discovery of the missing knives, linked as they were to an illegal entering even if no breaking had occurred, I conveniently left out. Besides, Wusthof was like the number four manufacturer of knives worldwide. They probably sold two million knives every year, over five thousand every day, so what did that really prove? I also couldn't help but feel that the people in this room were the guys actually being fucking paid to investigate this stuff, so let them do their job and connect a few dots on their own. I wasn't going to sweat and bleed just so I could spoon feed them all the answers. I also left Nadine out of the conversation, whose presence I felt would prove a needless complication. But other than those two small omissions, I pretty much stuck to the truth.

As I laid it all out, the first time I had told the whole story out loud in one piece, it kind of didn't seem to me that the murders were directly linked to one another. Sure, Alice Lahey stabbed Kevin Anderson and was in turned stabbed by Paul Rhodes; I thought the knives proved that even if I didn't say so out loud. Then Rhodes turned up with the same biker gang that attacked me and they shot and killed Martin Pogue. That was a pretty solid chain of events. But Fred Teeg, the Milford plumber and rapist of Alice Lahey, had been shot, not stabbed with a Wusthof knife. So did I chalk his murder up to Alice, or the bikers? The death of Ellis Banks, he of the steep stairway, likewise lacked a solid anchor point in the story. Althelia Temple? Edward Knox? Emmy Farmer and the missing piece of the town model? Ernie Banks and his books? It was an unhinged mess, unless you believed that somehow something about the cult tied it all together. Then the pieces looked, if not exactly like a chain of islands, at least like a clump of islands all in the same region of the ocean. Geography metaphors were never my strong suit.

When I finished talking it took a few moments for the silence to register on the other side of the table. The suits kept passing papers, the liaison had his nose to his Blackberry, Brittany was fiddling with the top button of her blouse, the guy from the forensics lab held rapt by her fiddling, his tongue practically hanging out of his mouth. They all froze at once, forming a tableau that I hoped the guy with the camera was capturing for posterity. A still image could be hung in the statehouse with the title "Your Government in Action!"

Doherty sat, as he had throughout my monologue, all closed off, arms tightly crossed, I was pretty sure legs crossed at the ankle under the table though I hadn't ducked down to check, Mr. Frowny Face. He took a moment to untangle himself and leaned forward, the first to speak.

"Mr. Fallon, can you positively identify Paul Rhodes as the man who shot Martin Pogue?"

I had to admit, I admired the method and speed with which his mind had cut through all the extraneous facts to try and come down on the most recent murder, the one he could maybe put someone in prison for, even as I was frustrated that he wasn't seeing the bigger picture.

"No. Pogue identified him only as Paul."

"Inadmissible," one of the suits chimed in.

Doherty looked at him, chewing on the inside of his lip until he won the staring contest and the suit, flustered, buried himself in something of suddenly great importance in his briefcase. Doherty turned back to us. "What about you Mr. Gault? You knew Paul Rhodes in the past."

Jonas shook his head. The stenographer asked him to give a verbal response, so Jonas said "No."

"Can either of you positively identify or give identifying characteristics of any of the other assailants?"

"No," we both replied, in stereo.

"Then what are we doing here?" he asked over his shoulder, addressing the crowd behind him.

The guy from the Attorney General spoke up. "Mr. Fallon, is it your insinuation that all of this," he made a sort of all-encompassing gesture with his arms, "is related to the activities of the now-disbanded Disciples of the True Path?" He said this with careful precision and just the barest hint of disbelief, as if we were in front of a jury and he was the prosecutor pointing out that my carefully constructed defense, perhaps posted on a cork board using index cards with pieces of yarn linking them together, constituted nothing more than a fabricated rat's nest of misdirection.

"I'm not insinuating anything."

"But what do you think, Mr. Fallon?" he shot back pointedly.

I had been Mirandized and offered a lawyer earlier which I had rejected. I was starting to regret that decision now. His question was fraught with so many dangerous side effects that it should have come with an FDA warning label. 'May cause increased risk of heart attack. Do not operate heavy machinery or serious injury may result.'

"I think," I began, then paused. I wanted to be very careful here. "I think that, maybe buried under an avalanche of coincidence, something very dangerous is going on and it is related to the cult.

He was clearly disappointed at all my equivocations, like a provider of cold medication who says 'may provide temporary occasional relief of some cold symptoms in a certain percentage of patients.' Before he could ask a follow up question to try and pin me down further, Doherty had another one.

"When the biker mentioned money to the man you believe was Paul Rhodes, what money do you think he was referring to?"

"I don't know," was all the answer I gave him.

And I didn't know, but while it was feasible that Rhodes was paying the biker gang as some kind of freelance mercenary army, I had the growing suspicion that the cult had had some money stashed away, perhaps even at the mansion. This was the money he planned to split with the bikers when they managed to torture its location out of someone. That thought led to other ones. Who was left who might know where that money was or even if it existed? Who were the 'others' that Rhodes had felt could be convinced to talk? Like a good poker player I kept all those cards exceedingly close to my vest. It was all conjecture on my part, and I could never recall Harry Morgan saying, "Just the conjecture, ma'am."

There seemed to be some debate going on as to who would ask the next question. The camera caught a lot of silent glances, lifted eyebrows, and knowing nods like some kind of British farce. I followed this covert message as it made its rounds, and was only a little surprised when it stopped at the guy from the Governor's office who lifted his nose from his Blackberry with the expression of someone who has no clue of what is going on around him, though I had the feeling he had not missed a single word spoken in the room.

"Gentlemen," he addressed Jonas and I, "we believe what you witnessed yesterday was the unfortunate outcome of a very longstanding grudge between two felons who frankly never should have been released from the prison system. We thank you for your diligence, and at such time as Mr. Pogue's killer is caught, you will of course be expected to testify in court. Until then, you are free to go." He said this last bit with his steely gaze fixed upon Doherty, who looked as though he was being made to swallow a double-handful of something unpleasant in one big gulp.

Jonas stood and stretched. I stayed in my seat and turned lazily to Doherty. "You OK with that, Detective Doherty?"

Wisps of steam appeared at his ears. "Sheriff Dawkins will drive you back to Dunboro," he said flatly.

"Gotcha."

The room was filled with the sound of chairs scraping back from the table and the coordinated closing of all the identical briefcases. Bobby, Jonas, and I left first, traversing a confusing maze of corridors past briefing rooms and locker rooms and equipment storage closets and out into the bright sunshine. It was another beautiful day in New Hampshire, perhaps all the more beautiful because Pogue was no longer in it. If I waited long enough, if everyone killed everyone else, this thing would end on its own without my help. If only I could think of some way to keep Jonas safe, somewhere to stash him, until then. I wondered if he had ever seen Bermuda.

When we reached Bobby's cruiser, he got behind the wheel and Jonas got in back. I climbed into the front passenger seat, which earned me a look from Bobby though he didn't actually object. Everyone belted in and we hit the road back to town.

Bobby seemed to be content playing the role of the silent chauffer, but I wasn't going to let him get off so easily.

"Jonas and I are being hung out to dry. You know that, right? The State figures it's safer to stay on the sidelines and let this thing burn out on its own, even if Jonas and I are killed in the process, than create another Ruby Ridge or Branch Davidian compound. Can't upset the summer tourist season, don'tcha know?"

"The State's position is that these deaths all represent unrelated acts of violence. The cult no longer exists and is not involved, and you and Jonas are in no danger."

"Bullshit," I said heatedly, turning my head and giving him the stitched side of my face to consider. "Doherty certainly doesn't believe that."

"Doherty's got more than eighteen years in on a twenty year pension. He believes what the Attorney General tells him to believe."

"What about you?" I pressed. "What do you believe?"

He sighed, a sound laden with self-deprecation, the

acceptance that solving crimes of this complexity was just beyond him, along perhaps with the grudging admission that I, for reasons that were a mystery to both of us, seemed to be better at than he was. The sigh bore down on me, freighting me and me alone with the responsibility for solving this mess, and I became suddenly conscious that I had not gotten to sleep last night, complete exhaustion waiting in the wings to pounce Phantom of the Opera-style. I noticed Jonas had undone his seatbelt, stretched out across the back seat, and was snoring softly with a forearm over his eyes.

"I don't know, Jack," Bobby finally said. "The pieces make no sense. Is this somehow all about money? Did the cult even have any money?"

I found it interesting that, unprompted by me, Bobby was starting to raise the same questions I was. "If so, Jonas doesn't know anything about it. What does your Uncle say?"

He gave me a surprised look, wondering how I knew about his Uncle's involvement. The pause before his response was a long one, and I thought he was going to try and deny it or spin out some tale. Instead he frowned and blew a breath out through his nose. "Not exactly Uncle Bobby's shining moment, was it? And I'm not going to make any excuses for him. He was there, but whatever he's got locked inside his head today, he refuses to talk about it; I've asked. However, I think if there were buried treasure at the church, he would have told me."

"Well, the cult had money somewhere. They owned the building and the land. They ran the community outreach programs and whatnot. They housed and fed people. They didn't do all of that by passing the collection plate and doing a little gardening. Plus Pogue got out of prison and immediately bought himself a house."

"He didn't buy that house. He rented it. The house is one of dozens Knox owns around town."

"Wait a second, are you saying that Pogue was renting that

house from Selectman Edward Knox?"

"Knox probably did it as a favor to the State Parole Board. Pogue had to go somewhere."

Maybe Knox had done it as a favor, or maybe he had had another reason. If the knives that Alice Lahey used to kill Anderson, try and kill Rhodes, and with which she herself was killed came from that house, as I believed they did, that linked Knox with Alice and Anderson and the attempt on Rhode's life. Then Alice died and Pogue moved in. And now Pogue was dead. A web was forming between pieces that seemed previously unconnected, and Knox appeared to be at the center of it. The most powerful man in town and one who had serious pull at the State level as well, and all I had so far were unsubstantiated accusations. Super.

"What?" Bobby asked, casting me sidelong glances as he drove. "What did you just figure out?"

"You have a pension with the State, right?"

"So? What does that have to do with anything?"

"Believe me," I said, "I don't think you want to know."

Thirty-One

Bobby dropped us off at my truck. "Keep your heads down," he told us through the window as he prepared to drive off.

"What a meaninglessly pleasant platitude," I replied snidely. "Should we also watch our backs, look before we leap, and make hay while the sun shines?"

"I get it," he said. "I'm sorry. I'm doing everything I can. Be careful." He drove off without another word.

"You didn't have to be such a bastard to him," Jonas scolded me, "It doesn't help anything."

"I know. He's just the closest target to vent on." I realized that if I were still alive after all of this was over, I was going to have to spend some time repairing all of these bridges I was so furiously burning.

After a little discussion, Jonas and I opted to go back to my place.

Valerie wasn't at home and neither was Tonk. Had she actually gone so far as to move out? I checked to see if there was clothing missing from her closet, but she's such a clothes horse that it was hard to tell for certain. How many pairs of shoes does one woman need?

"Where's Valerie?" Jonas asked as I made us herbal tea to try and alleviate our night of endless high-octane coffee.

"Please," I replied, "one mystery at a time." I turned on the television.

If the State Police were trying to keep secrets about the circumstances of Martin Pogue's death out of the news, they were doing a crappy job of it. Either, that, or the Governor's office was leaking like a sieve. The morning news shows were chock full of it. Highlighted by a flashy banner and preceded by a warning to have children leave the room, the anchor launched into a graphic description of Pogue getting his fingers hacked off with a serious expression on her face but the happy sparkle of breaking news in her eyes.

We sat down at the kitchen counter and watched it all unfold. One morning show went so far as to have a doctor, I think the man was actually a gynecologist, come on and describe the pain involved in having ones fingers cut off in that manner. He even had anatomic models to assist him. Try sawing into your breakfast sausage with that on the screen.

"It's got to be about money, right?" I said to Jonas or maybe no one in particular, "It's the only thing that makes sense."

"I never saw any money or heard anyone talk about it while I was there, and it wouldn't be easy to hide a big bundle of cash, even in a building that large. Everyone knew everyone else's business; we didn't keep any secrets from one another."

Well, his friends had been keeping a whopper of a secret from him in that they likely kept going to the church after he had quit. Althelia and Ellis visiting Pogue in prison proved that. Instead of opening that old wound, I said "I don't think we're talking about cash. Maybe they had a painting. Maybe stolen Nazi diamonds for all I know, but something of value, something that a biker could relate to."

"What about drugs?"

I shook my head. "The Sheriff, whatever you may think of him, was a member. Do you think he would have let that go on in his town if he knew about it? And Althelia and Ellis?"

"OK, money," Jonas agreed. "So who knew about it?"

"There are actually two questions there if you stop to think about it. Who knew about the money, and who knows where it is now? This is where we have to do some guesswork. Let's say a lot of people knew about it. Anderson, Rhodes, Althelia, Ellis. Maybe it wasn't much of a secret at all among the true believers." In my head I wondered about Knox, and if he knew. It clarified his motive for letting Pogue crash at his place nicely.

"And where is it now?"

"Ah," I held up an index finger, "that's the real secret. That's the one that for the sake of argument we'll guess Pogue kept to himself. Everyone knows he knows, but he hasn't told anyone. Until recently. Until he was getting out of prison. He would need that money to rebuild his dream of the church, or flee to Guatemala, but he knew he couldn't retrieve it himself; he would be watched and followed. He needed someone else, someone he could trust to get it for him."

"Althelia," Jonas added in, "or Ellis."

"Probably both, and Teeg as well. Each one visited Pogue in prison and he told them where it was. Anderson learned about it, or his biker buddies in the prison did." I paused there,

recalling the inmate mopping the hallway while I spoke to
Pogue. I continued, "They told more biker buddies outside of
prison, and they went by and asked some questions. We've been
witnesses to their interrogation techniques. In trying to get their
answers, they killed them all." Had Althelia's body had all its
digits when it was discovered? What about Teeg? Had the
Milford police managed to keep that little fact secret? His wife
had been unwilling to talk to Valerie and me before. How would
she feel if I asked if her husband had had his fingers chopped off
before he died? It might explain the look of terror in her eyes
when we tried to talk to her, her belief that whoever had done it
might come back and do it to her or her daughter.

"That ties up everything, doesn't it?"

I gave a cynical bark of laughter. "Not even close. It
doesn't explain Ellis' death, unless you think Laura is somehow
in league with Rhodes and the bikers. The connection between
visiting Pogue in prison, and getting murdered over money we
can't even prove exists is all vapor. And how did Alice end up
with knives from one of Knox's houses?"

"Knox gave them to her," Jonas said angrily, "Alice wanted
revenge for what they had done to her. Knox met her at some
homeless shelter or mission where he was volunteering and used
her as an opportunity to eliminate competition for the money."

I ran that through in my head a few times. It actually fit in
the theory pretty well.

"That's not a bad idea," I told him.

"But as you said, it's a lot of guesswork. How can we
prove it?"

"There's a dangling thread here to grab. Someone still
knows about the money, or at least Anderson believes someone
does."

"Who? Knox?"

"If Knox knew, he would have retrieved the money years ago." I rubbed at my forehead, carefully avoiding the stitches. "Maybe Rhodes is wrong. Maybe there is no one left, but he thinks there is."

"Like me?" Jonas pointed at himself.

"If they thought you knew, you'd probably be dead already."

Jonas' eyes widened, "What about you? You visited Pogue in prison."

I felt my stomach fall into my knees and again recalled the halo of the inmate mopping the hallway. Their first visit had been a warning, their assumption being that I was getting involved in something that was none of my business. Perhaps now desperate for anyone who Pogue might have told where the money was, they would reassess their previous assumption and come back with more questions. They could hack off all my fingers and my toes as well; I had nothing to tell them. And they knew where I lived, while Jonas and I were standing around in my kitchen schmoozing about it. The feeling of events closing in on me, that I was in the jaws of a trap waiting to spring closed, was suffocating.

I splashed the dregs of my tea into the sink. "Let's go."

"Go where?"

"I think we're running out of time to solve this thing." I headed for the front door. "We've got to find someone who knows where that money is."

"Who?"

We went out to my truck, and I climbed in behind the wheel. Before turning the key I stopped to think about that. In the dwindling list of players, there were damned few people left. "Laura Banks," I said at last.

"Laura?" Jonas said incredulously.

"Maybe Ellis told her. I don't know. We're running out of options here." I felt something rising in the back of my throat that felt dangerously like panic and turned the key with way more force than was necessary. I was lucky it didn't snap off.

"OK," Jonas said, skeptical but just as desperate as I was, "Laura it is."

Thirty-Two

I never really understood why Laura and Ellis decided to move their two sons into their own house. Even the elder, Steven, was incapable of supporting himself, and his younger brother David really required the kind of long-term dedicated care that necessitated either permanent hospitalization in a state facility or a private nursing staff which would cost a fortune, surely more than Ellis, a dump truck driver, and Laura, an elementary school teacher, could have amassed in their lifetime. Perhaps they had done it as a kind of experiment, an attempt to give Steven more responsibility, a more normal lifestyle, and see how he did with it.

If so, they had met with mixed results.

They had selected as their lab a mid-seventies split-level on Farm Road, not far from their own place, and arranged a stock worker position for Steven at Shaw's in Milford. He had managed to keep the job, but it left the younger brother at home alone for most of the day, an arrangement that would lead to certain disaster in time. The house fell into considerable disrepair which became even worse when Ellis' failing health left him unable to keep up the maintenance. I could understand Laura not being interested in living in the house where her husband had died, but where she was living now was in a sad state.

"That roof is going to leak come next spring," Jonas commented as he got out of my truck in front of their house.

The roof was the worst of it, or at least the part in most critical need of repair. Once the roof is gone, water gets in, and once that happens there will be rot, mold, and mildew. The floors will warp, and the sheetrock will crumble, and the framing will check and twist. The siding however wasn't far behind the roof, and the chimney had lost so much mortar it looked like a nearly random stack of bricks that might blow over in the next storm. More sadly this tumbledown house stood in the middle of a nicely tended and freshly mowed lawn, a metaphor perhaps for damaged minds living inside otherwise healthy bodies.

"Maybe I can get some of the other firefighters together to come out here and do something about that," I replied as we went up the walk and rang the bell. It was likely a moot point as whatever state and federal aid they received would probably not be enough to let the sons keep it after their parents were gone, though the sale of the house on Main Street, in far better condition, might bring in enough money to delay that outcome for a few years.

Steven answered the door and led us into the living room, then left us to get Laura. Jonas leaned Nadine against the wall next to the couch after making certain the safety was on.

"This has been very hard on Laura, Jack. Go easy on her."

"I have to ask her some hard questions, Jonas."

"I know," he said unhappily. "Just…" he trailed off.

216

"Just what?"

"Go easy on her," he said again, then turned away to look out the front windows onto the perfect lawn.

Laura was wheeled in by her son David. Of the pair, it was David who drew the eye first. He looked almost perfectly normal dressed in jeans and a blue button work shirt, but there was something about him, the slack expression on his face or his strangely rounded posture normally seen in a much older man, that told you there was something very much wrong with him. Laura by contrast looked almost too put together. Her hair was done as was her makeup, and because she could not have known we were coming and hadn't kept us waiting long enough to do all that primping, it must have been how she just hung around the house. It might have been a regimen she enforced on herself after the death of her husband, a small piece of normalcy that she could control in a life suddenly missing its anchor.

Jonas went to her, took one of her hands gently in his own. "Are you OK, Laura? Is there anything I can do for you?"

She took her hand back and shooed him away. "Like I told you at the funeral, I'm fine. Losing Ellis has been hard, but I have my boys to take care of me."

I thought it was likely the other way around, but being needed was probably the best thing for her right now.

Jonas moved around the coffee table and sat down slowly on the couch across from her. "Laura, Jack and I have some questions, maybe uncomfortable questions, about what happened to Ellis. I want you to know that we're only asking them to try and protect you."

"Protect me? Is this about the church again?"

I noticed that she called it a church. Everyone else called it a cult. Except for Pogue, he called it a church too.

217

"It's different now," Jonas insisted, "others have died."

She gave an exasperated shake of her head and looked at me, "What about you, Jack? Has Jonas got you buying into his conspiracy theory too?"

I sat next to Jonas on the couch. "Jonas is right, Laura. Something very dangerous is going on."

"Martin Pogue is dead," Jonas blurted out.

"I know that," she said, "it's all the news is talking about. But what makes you think it has anything to do with his church? He spent forty years in prison; you don't think he might have made a few enemies there?"

"I think he was killed by Paul Rhodes," I added.

"Who?" She asked.

"He was at the church. Don't you remember, Laura?" Jonas beseeched.

"I'm sorry, Jonas, I don't."

"What about a woman named Alice Lahey? Do you remember her?" I asked.

She turned to me, already shaking her head, "No. Was she at the church too?"

"She was, and now she's dead, murdered."

"Oh, Jack, I don't know who these people are. It was so long ago, and I haven't spoken to any of them in years."

She sounded as confused as I felt, and I was starting to doubt the chain of events I had been starting to forge. And yet, I had one piece of evidence that could not be so easily dismissed.

"Laura, when was the last time you saw Martin Pogue?"

She looked to Jonas for the answer, "When was it, Jonas? You were there the night we left the church."

I didn't give Jonas a chance to answer her, and instead pushed ahead with, "What about Ellis?"

"It would have been the same time. We were all there."

I shook my head, "Ellis visited Pogue at the prison one week before he died."

"That's not possible. Someone must have gone there claiming to be my husband."

"It couldn't happen. Too many layers of security, too many people checking IDs. It was your husband."

She sat there looking from Jonas to me and back again. "Then I don't know what to say. He never said anything to me about it, and I can't imagine-"

"I think he went," I spoke over her, "because Pogue hid something of value. He told your husband where it is, and that was why he was killed."

She was shaking her head more vehemently. "No. No. My husband wasn't killed. He fell down some stairs. Why, Jonas?" she pleaded with him, "Why won't you believe that?"

Jonas regarded her sadly, "Because we think your husband told you."

"Do I look like someone who knows where a pile of money is buried?" Laura exclaimed, gesturing at her sad surroundings. "I can't play this sick game with you anymore, Jonas," tears tracked down her cheeks. "My husband is dead, and all those other people, I haven't had any contact with them in years. Whatever you think is going on doesn't involve me. Please just leave, and let the past stay buried in the past."

Jonas looked at me, devastated. What had we done, his look asked me, what have we accomplished?

I didn't have any answers for him. I didn't have any answers for anyone. If the money existed, and I was a long way from being sure that it did, there was no one left who knew anything, except Rhodes. If he came to cut off my fingers maybe I would ask him about it. There was a comforting thought.

I got up from the couch. "Laura, I know this all seems outlandish to you, but I want you to know that there is this gang of bikers led by Paul Rhodes-"

She cut me off, "Enough, Jack. I've heard enough."

I considered trying to warn her again. Whether or not she knew anything didn't matter if Rhodes thought she did. But she wasn't going to listen to me. I would tell Bobby my theory and see if he wanted to do anything about it, put a deputy on watch at their house, something.

"Come on, Jonas. Let's go."

Jonas picked up Nadine by her strap and we headed out. Steven stayed close behind us as we walked out of the living room and into the front hall towards the door, kind of too close, as though he was rushing us out.

I turned back suddenly causing him to almost bump into me and then back up a few steps. I asked a question while facing him but directed it at Jonas. "Jonas, I thought you told me that Ellis didn't drive anymore."

"He didn't," Jonas replied, "he and I both gave up our licenses when we felt we were becoming hazards on the road. Ellis chucked his in the trash on his ninetieth birthday."

"Then how did he get to the Concord prison?"

Jonas didn't have an answer for that, and I hadn't expected him to. I was watching Steven's eyes which had suddenly begun darting everywhere.

"Steven," I said, forcing his eyes to mine, "you drove your father to the Concord Prison to visit Martin Pogue, didn't you?"

A flush stained Steven's cheeks and his breath started coming out in little huffs. Quite a poker face he had there. "Mom!" he said loudly, "He knows! He knows everything!"

Laura wheeled herself into the front hall a moment later. Her tears were all dried up and her confused old lady routine was neatly tucked away. This Laura was completely in control, and frankly a little scary. "Of course he does, dear." She patted his hand in a calming gesture, and then turned her attention to me. "You're a very smart man, aren't you Jack? There's no hiding anything from you, is there?"

I thought both questions rhetorical so gave her no answer, though she seemed to wait some time for me to supply one. Then she sighed. "You might as well come back and sit down. This is going to take a while."

Jonas put Nadine incongruously into the umbrella stand by the door, his features hardened at having been lied to and fooled so easily by a woman he thought of as his friend. "No more lies this time, Laura."

"No, Jonas," she said, her eyes tired, "no more lies."

Thirty-Three

Laura had her sons serve tea. It was a task they completed with great precision, a process that had the flavor of a ceremony about it. When David stutteringly offered sugar I asked him for two lumps, but the number two was apparently beyond him because he added six or seven before handing the cup to me. The cups were translucent bone china, so thin and delicate that I was almost afraid to handle mine.

Jonas seemed impatient to get some answers, but I knew there were secrets here, dark secrets, and they could not be forced. They would come out in their own way and in their own time, but they would come out. I wasn't going to leave there until I knew them all.

I sat with the saucer balanced on my knee, stirring the sugary slurry. I was sure it was undrinkable, but it made a pleasingly silky friction against the spoon.

David prepared a cup for his mother without her direction.

I figured he was making her usual. He then passed it to her and sat on the floor by her chair. She rested a hand on top of his head and absently stroked his hair. Her treatment of him, like some kind of dog, gave me an uncomfortable feeling in the pit of my stomach. Steven leaned in the archway to the front hall.

She took a sip with her pinky extended, cultured. Settling down to a little high tea and murder. "Martin Pogue was a generous and caring person," she said sadly, "a true man of God."

Jonas made a snorting sound, a swallowed fragment of cynical laughter. I silenced him with a look. Still, I couldn't be too critical of him; had I been holding a mouthful of tea, her comment probably would have made me spew it all over her coffee table.

Laura pretended as though she hadn't heard him. She lifted the cup and then took another drink, like she was making a toast in Pogue's memory. "He was on a great spiritual mission," she continued. "Every day the world sinks deeper into filth and depravity. He was doing the Lord's work, until he was beset upon by evil men."

"Rhodes," Jonas said.

"Knox," I added.

Jonas looked at me with surprise.

Laura nodded. "Both men are devils in their own ways."

Confused, Jonas said "What does Knox have to do with the church beyond being a member?"

"Do you know?" Laura asked me.

"I think I do," I replied.

"Then tell me, Jack. Tell me what you think you know."

"I know that Knox funded the church. He bought the building at the end of the Bartlett trail. I suspect he paid for all the furniture and whatever it cost to heat it."

She nodded for me to continue.

"And I think, though I can't prove it, that he was doing it all to launder money from his construction business. When the church went belly up, his business almost did too. I think their finances were inextricably linked."

"You are a smart one," she said.

I blushed a little at that. It felt like getting a gold star on my homework from my second grade teacher.

"There was a river of dirty money flowing through that church," Laura confirmed. "Knox had friends in Boston and Concord who funneled money to him. He would donate it and take the tax write off, then use the money to build homes for his friends. He would pay his construction company to do work at the church at ten times what it cost. He maintained the building, put in the cobble stone street, and that ridiculous fountain."

"Why didn't Martin put a stop to it?" I asked.

Laura looked at me as if she was thinking of picking that gold star off my homework with a fingernail like a scab. "Because the church needed the money. Martin was running a religious school. He was housing homeless people and feeding them at the church. He was taking in runaways. Knox was always generous."

He could afford to be, I thought. He was saving a fortune in state and federal taxes.

Jonas dropped his cup onto the coffee table where it rattled but didn't break. "I can't listen to this," he said angrily, and got up to look out the front windows. "Pogue was a madman who raped and murdered little girls."

"No, Jonas," Laura said, her voice pleading. "That was all Rhodes. Martin tried to stop it."

"Let her tell it, Jonas," I insisted.

Jonas was silent, but he didn't sit down. He remained by the windows.

Laura finished her tea, and then leaned forward and placed her cup down gently. She bunched one fist against her mouth, and her eyes misted. It took some time for her to collect herself, and I waited patiently while she did so.

"The church was a beautiful thing, a sacred thing, and then one day Rhodes showed up. I never knew where he came from or why Martin let him stay. Perhaps Martin was afraid of him. Or maybe Martin believed that Rhodes could be saved. He was like that. Always trying to see the good in people. When girls started disappearing, at first we thought nothing of it. Runaways came and went all the time, rarely telling anyone why they were leaving or where they were going."

"But it was Rhodes," I said softly.

"And Anderson. And Teeg. When Martin figured it out, it destroyed him. All he had worked for, all the evil he was trying to prevent, it was going on under his own roof. The church was lost to him; he knew that, but he wanted to salvage something. Like Noah and the ark, he planned for the future, for the day when the Lord's wrath would wash the evil away and he could rebuild the church again."

"What did he do?"

"He took Knox's money. He emptied the church bank accounts and he buried the cash. Then he called Bobby Dawkins and told him to arrest Rhodes, Anderson, and Teeg."

"Wait a second," Jonas said turning from the windows and advancing on Laura. "What about the naked girl who went to the police station?"

"It never happened," Laura said simply, looking up at him. "That was a story Bobby Dawkins and Martin made up after the fact. Bobby came because Martin called him, and Rhodes and his men barricaded the front gate. Then the FBI showed up, and you know the story after that. They all went to prison, Martin included. Everyone was so ready to believe that he was involved, he never had a chance," she said sadly. "And maybe he felt he didn't deserve one; it had been his church, and prison was where he belonged for what had happened there."

The pieces were coming together for me very quickly now, but the picture they were forming was different from the one I had been expecting. Pogue wasn't the bad guy here. On the contrary, he appeared to be one of the very few innocent people.

"Martin started the fire, didn't he?" I asked.

"Yes. He was afraid the others wouldn't go peacefully. You've seen the mansion, so much like a fortress. If it had become a standoff, no telling how many FBI agents and others might have been killed to get them out. So Martin set the fire to force them out, to prevent more deaths."

Exasperated, Jonas said, "None of this makes any sense. Who killed Althelia? Why did your husband die?"

"It makes perfect sense," I said, "You thought it was about the cult, but it was really about the money. Pogue knew where it was, and Rhodes wanted to find out. When Althelia visited him in prison, Martin told her. Rhodes got some of his biker friends to force the location out of her, but they must have gotten too rough and killed her." I paused as Pogue's inhuman screams echoed in my head. "Then he told your husband, and they killed him too. Finally, when he got out of prison, they killed Pogue himself."

Laura regarded me for a moment with silent, inscrutable eyes. She went to pour more tea for herself, but found the small pot empty. She held it out to her son. "Steven, would you be a dear and get us some more tea, please?"

He stepped forward quickly and took the pot from her and headed off for the kitchen like a shot, rapturous just to be serving his mother.

She folded her hands in her lap and sighed, as if the telling was exhausting her. "Martin would have never put Althelia in that position, Jack. He never told her about the money, and no one killed her. She just died."

"What do you mean, 'she just died?'" Jonas asked.

Turning to Jonas, her gaze softened, "I mean that she just died. She was old, and she died. Look at us, Jonas. I'm old. You're old. Old people eventually die. It's what we do."

"But she died within a week of visiting Pogue in prison. That can't be a coincidence," I said.

"It's no coincidence, Jack. Althelia was certain to die within a week of visiting Martin."

"I don't understand."

"She had visited Martin every week. She had been doing so for the past forty years."

Jonas, almost in spite of himself, became interested in the story she was telling. He left the windows and slowly crossed the room to sit down on the couch across from her. "Why?"

"They were in love," she said simply.

"Love," I repeated in wonder, my opinion of Martin Pogue changing by the second. I looked down into the sludge in my tea cup. If I had a piece of string I could have been well on my way to making rock candy. I occurred to me that Steven was taking a very long time coming back with the tea.

"That's ridiculous," Jonas exclaimed.

"They were in love," Laura insisted. "Why do you find that so hard to believe? Althelia was a beautiful, intelligent woman. She was kind and well-liked. Didn't you ever wonder why she never married, or even dated? The firefighters certainly tried hard enough."

"I never thought…" Jonas began.

"No, you never did," she cut him off, though not cruelly. "Althelia and Martin were in love, and they promised each other that there would never be anyone else in their lives, and there wasn't. And now they're dead," she concluded sadly.

"What about your husband?" Jonas asked, somewhat skeptically. "Did he just die?"

I looked up from my consideration of my cup when Steven came back into the room. He wasn't carrying the tea pot. Instead he had a big black revolver held in both hands in front of him pointed at me. Nadine's green canvas strap was over one shoulder, the rifle slung on his back.

"That," Laura sighed, "is where things get complicated."

Thirty-Four

"Laura, what is this?" Jonas asked as he stood up slowly from the couch, anger and alarm in his voice.

"I'm sorry, Jonas. I'm deeply sorry that it had to turn out like this."

"Steven killed your husband, didn't he Laura?" I asked.

"No, Mr. Fallon," she replied with great conviction, "The cancer killed my husband. He and Steven fought, and he fell. The cancer had left his spine so brittle that he broke his neck."

She said this incredibly monstrous statement in a very matter of fact way. When Jonas had first told me about the cult and the deaths while sitting on a park bench in the town common, what seemed like eons ago, the whole thing had sounded wildly implausible. I thought the only way Ellis Banks could have been killed with his wife at home was if she was somehow involved in it, what I had then perceived as an absolute impossibility. Fuck me, but it had turned out to be true. Laura Banks and her sons had conspired in Ellis' murder. And for what, money? My soul demanded that it couldn't possibly be as simple as that; there had to be some other factor that drove a woman to murder her husband of more than fifty years. I had to ask. "They fought over the money?"

She nodded, more simple yet monstrous truths, "Martin told my husband where the money was and told him that it was time to rebuild the church, but my husband had lost his faith in the face of his illness. I told him to pray with me, that whatever the disease did to him, his soul would still bask in the light of the Lord. He didn't believe. He thought the money had to be returned to Knox; his rightful place in heaven required it."

"But you wanted that money for yourself," I said. "Isn't greed one of the deadly sins?"

She glared at me. I was pissing her off. Did I want to do that? Was there any advantage to be gained? She lectured to me, biting off each word, her voice high and thin and reedy. "With Martin dead the dream of his church has died with him, and the world will be less for it. Mr. Fallon, my sons are gentle souls and our society is not kind. They will need that money to shelter them from life's storms."

Her continual use of my last name, when earlier I had been Jack, was giving me the willies. I remember reading somewhere that killers often dehumanized their victims; it made them easier to kill. I was probably thirty seconds away from being referred to as 'hey you.'

Jonas beat me to the next question. "If you knew where the money was, why didn't you just go get it?"

"We don't know where the money is. Ellis never told us."

"And now Martin is dead as well," I pointed out. "The church is a huge building on a big piece of land. You have quite a treasure hunt ahead of you."

"We, Mr. Fallon. We have a large treasure hunt ahead of us. We have to find the money. I'm sure Martin hid it in that building, and since he set the fire he must have known it was somewhere safe. You know fire, and you know construction, and you're going to use that big brain of yours find it."

"What if I refuse?"

With surprising agility and speed Steven leapt forward and struck Jonas on the forehead with the butt of the gun. Jonas reeled and the coffee table caught him in the back of the knees. He landed on it, upending the tea service, sugar cubes scattered across the tabletop like dice, the cream pitcher sluggishly spilling its contents into an oozing puddle. David curled himself into a ball and began emitting a low moaning sound.

Jonas put a hand to his forehead and squeezed his eyes closed, his free hand clenched into a shaking fist. He managed to contain the pain and opened his eyes, but the effort left him gasping. I helped him back to his feet on which he swayed unsteadily. When he found his voice, he said to Steven, "Try that again, boy, and I'll shove that gun up your ass."

"You shut the hell up!" Steven said angrily, looking as if he might strike Jonas again, and I placed myself in his path. The blow Steven delivered had been solid, and I was worried Jonas' skull couldn't take another one, that some serious damage might be done if it hadn't already. If Steven tried to take a swing at me, I was planning to do a little bob and weave and make a play for the gun, but the blow never came.

"Steven," Laura chastised him, "Watch your language."

"Sorry, mom," Steven said, lowering his head without taking his eyes off me or letting the barrel of the gun drop so much as a millimeter.

"OK," I said, my hands held up, palms out in what I hoped was a calming gesture, "I'll go find your money, and I'll bring it back here."

"Oh, no, Mr. Fallon. We shall all go," Laura said.

"But you're in a wheelchair," I said.

"And you have a very large truck. God always giveth; his gifts are in plentitude."

She said that as if God worked for Ford.

Steven waved us towards the front door with the gun.

Outside it was a quiet, lazy day in Dunboro, and my hopes of a passerby seeing us came to nothing as Jonas and I were marched at gunpoint and loaded into the truck. I drove with Laura in the passenger seat, her wheelchair strapped down in the bed. Jonas was in back sandwiched between the brothers. No one said a word as I maneuvered up Route 13 and then nosed off of that road and down the Bartlett trail.

The trees were thick and lush, and their branches and leaves brushed against the side mirrors. I checked Jonas in the rearview. A trickle of blood oozed from a small cut in his skin high up on his forehead, but his color was good and he seemed to have recovered well from the blow.

The sun dappling her face through the windshield Laura mused, "It used to lift my spirits just to drive down this road, knowing that Father Pogue was at the end, his love and guidance a beacon in those troubled times."

"Amen," said Steven softly from the seat behind her.

Heaven help me, there is no nutjob as dangerous as a religious nutjob.

I slowed to a stop when we reached the gate. The State Police had replaced the shattered padlock and chain with one of their own. A strip of police warning tape fluttered from the fencing. "We'll have to go on foot from here," I said. Jonas didn't have a key to this lock, but I thought I could break it with a tire iron.

"Nonsense," Laura said, "Just drive through it."

The gate was far too narrow for my truck. I looked at the chain link fence. Sure, it was rusty, but the galvanized posts, likely set in concrete plugs, were in great shape. I wasn't sure my truck could make it through.

Steven tapped me on the back of my head with the barrel of the gun, hard, and I felt my eyes cross and tear up a little at the pain. "You heard her. Drive."

I leaned against the steering wheel until the pain became manageable, then straightened up in my seat and put a hand on the shift selector. If I shifted into reverse, I could back up some and get a run at the fence. The impact would probably deploy the airbags, and might kill Laura outright. To the elderly, the force of an inflating airbag is often almost as bad as hitting the dashboard itself. In the confusion maybe Steven would lose his gun, and it might land somewhere near where I could get to it first. Jonas, almost certainly not belted in, would launch between the two front seats and out through the windshield. I had seen that outcome enough at accident scenes to not want to send him on that flight.

I shifted instead into drive and eased the truck forward until the front bumper rested against the two support posts on either side of the gate. Then I pressed down on the gas just a little, the engine revving, the bumper dancing against the posts. I gave her some more gas and the front wheels spun in fits and jerks, stones and pebbles rattling around inside the wheel wells.

When the gas pedal was just about to the floor, the bumper collapsed on one side and the truck lurched forward and to the left, the pole slamming into and crumpling the hood, the headlight on that side disappearing in a crunch of glass. The front end climbed the poles, which started to bend. Restraining straps on the fencing snapped off. One flew way up in the air and landed on the hood with a pinging noise, an oddly clear and crystalline sound. The chain link curled back on itself.

Off the ground, the front wheels spun uselessly and I switched into four-wheel low. The differential locked up with a clang that shuddered through the vehicle and the rear wheels bit in ferociously. The poles bent over farther still, the nose of the truck raised higher, the tops of trees visible through the windshield. I pictured the concrete plugs levering out of the earth underneath us.

There was as sudden metallic crack, one of the posts breaking off near ground level, and the truck front end dropped down with a suddenness that had us all rocking in our seats. We moved forward, all four wheels lurching and scrabbling. There came an awful squeal of metal on metal, the remaining post or perhaps the broken off end raking the undercarriage of my truck. Whatever was going on down there, it sounded expensive. I would have been more concerned, had I not thought I had little probability of surviving long enough to worry about getting it repaired.

We jounced and rocked from side to side, and finally cleared the fence. David made an enthusiastic whooping noise while Steven yelled "Yeehaw!" The Dukes of Hazard were alive and well and riding in my truck.

We climbed the hill and made the corner, and the road turned to cobblestone, the tires squeaking and shimmying against them.

The check oil light lit on the dash and the gauge dropped to nothing. The oil as well as most of the oil pan was probably lying back in the wreckage of the gate. I thought about pointing it out to Steven, though I doubted he would care that the engine was eating itself. He would likely have cared more had I pointed out to him the truck wouldn't get them back out the way we had come, but I was going to let that be a surprise.

It was not a secret the truck kept to itself for long. Black smoke began billowing out from under the hood just as we cleared the gate to the mansion, and the pistons shrieked and froze up solid at the near corner of the fountain, the suspension swaying as we came to a fitful halt.

"Looks like we're going to need another truck to get out of here," Steven said happily. What had my truck ever done to him?

"The Lord will giveth," Laura said simply. I

thought it must be wonderful to have such an effortless philosophy in life.

"Out," Steven tapped me on the skull with the gun, the same spot at before. It hurt about fifty times worse, but I didn't give him the pleasure of groaning out loud.

I got out, taking my keys with me. Force of habit, I supposed. It wasn't as though anyone was going to be stealing the truck without a crane. My poor girl was at the end of her road. In fifty years she would look no better than her cousin quietly resting on its rims and rusting across the parking area.

Steven waved Jonas out with the gun and had him stand beside me. David lifted the wheelchair from the bed and helped get his mother settled into it. He struggled, the chair sliding and swimming badly on the uneven cobblestones, as he rolled it around the truck to our side.

"So, Mr. Fallon. Where do you think the money is?" she asked as she rolled to a stop.

I looked at the building. How the hell was I supposed to know? There were, as a conservative estimate, a hundred thousand places that money could be hidden. If kept in some secret room behind a false stone wall there was no reason to think it would not have survived the fire. It could also be under some loose stone in the floor somewhere. For all I knew the mansion might have a rabbit warren of tunnels underneath it. I was also uncertain of her logic: why did the money have to be in the building and not buried somewhere on the property?

"Beats me," I said. "I've never even been inside. You've been inside a hundred times. Where do you think the money is?"

"That's your idea?" Steven asked angrily, "To ask her?"

"I'm just saying that I don't really have anything to go on. I can't even make an educated guess without more information."

Steven thumbed back the hammer on the gun and pressed it against Jonas' skull. "Try harder."

"All right. Ease off," I said. "Any idea how much money we're talking about here?"

"More than a million," Laura said confidently, "maybe as much as two."

It had to be in cash, I reasoned. Pogue had gotten the money out of a bank. I didn't think he would have had the resources to convert it into something more portable like gold or diamonds. So we were talking about a fair stack of cash, several cubic feet worth. I recalled that the FBI had dug half the place up looking for bodies; they might have located the money had it been buried, and Pogue had to have known they would dig and wouldn't have wanted it discovered. Perhaps Laura was right about the money being in the mansion. So, secret room, hidey hole, or tunnel? They all seemed like equally plausible options.

While I pondered, Steven held the gun against Jonas' head, and his impatience was increasing by the second. He might decide to shoot Jonas just to let me know how serious he was. Believe me, I would have told him if I knew. I also knew that their plans for getting out of here probably didn't include Jonas or me.

I stalled as long as possible, as much as I dared, hoping an opportunity would present itself, but the tableau didn't change. David stood behind his mother looking at some bushes in the distance, or maybe some butterflies. Steven held his spot, the gun didn't waver. We could have been a photograph except for the hum of insects and the song of birds.

The quiet of the day was suddenly shattered by a familiar bone jarring sound. Motorcycles roared into the turnaround. Steven spun to point his gun at this new threat, but delayed fatal seconds trying to decide which one to shoot. One of the bikers raced by and struck his gun hand with a baseball bat. Fingers broke and the gun flew far away and Steven crumpled to the ground, balling up his body protectively around his injured hand. The rifle slipped off his shoulder and landed on the ground next to him; Jonas' eyes focused on it.

The motorcycles circled the fountain several times, like a conquering army on parade, displaying their might. None of the bikers had any guns out, but most held some makeshift weapon like a club or length of heavy chain that they swung overhead, and the butts of guns were visible at every waistband, a few with a second firearm in a shoulder holster. One guy had a shotgun in a custom rack welded to his motorcycle frame.

When they finally stopped, Rhodes got off the bike on which he had been riding tandem and casually strolled over to Laura. He spoke, his voice deep and drawling. "Laura Banks. Why, you haven't changed a single iota since I last saw you, except for turning into a shriveled up old bitch. Have you found my money yet?"

"Martin never wanted you to have that money," she said, her chin held disdainfully high. "That money was meant for the church."

Rhodes gestured to the burned out building, "Dear Laura, the world has moved on. The church is gone. Pogue is dead. That money is mine now, so I suggest you tell me where it is. Or do I tell my boys to shoot your sons."

I noticed Jonas to my left take a tiny shuffle step towards the rifle on the ground. I tried to catch his attention with my eyes, communicate to him that was a very bad idea, but he was completely focused on his rifle and didn't see me.

"I don't know where the money is," Laura said. "He was going to find it for me." She helpfully pointed me out for Rhodes' benefit.

He turned his attention to me, his eyes gleaming. His gaze was uncomfortable and undeniably malevolent, like he was trying to decide how best to hurt me if it happened to come to that, and he was quite frankly hoping it would. "Mr. Fallon, I have heard a great deal about you. Do you know where my money is?"

"Maybe."

He barked a laugh, a single humorless explosion of air. "You better come up with more than maybe or I'm going to let my boys take another crack at you. Better yet, I'm going to start by killing your friends."

I thought about telling him Laura and her sons were not my friends, but that would have singled out Jonas for early elimination.

Rhodes pointed past my shoulder at the building. "Fetch."

I tried again to make eye contact with Jonas who was still completely focused on his rifle. Failing that, I turned and walked towards the black rectangle of the doorway. I moved at a measured pace, trying to give myself as much time as possible to examine the situation from all angles. I was certain that whether or not I came out with the money, Jonas and I were dead. I was equally certain that Rhodes was not going to wait outside for hours while I searched for the money. Once I crossed the threshold I figured I had ten, maybe fifteen minutes tops to come back out. It was not enough time to sneak out some rear window, if one existed, and make my way back to town and return with help.

As I approached, the doorway became larger, but no light penetrated the interior. It was pitch black in there, without shadows or discernible features, like I was about to step through a portal into deepest space.

I looked back one more time to see if there was any way out for Jonas and me. It would have been nice if the Lord saw fit to giveth me Bobby's cruiser coming up the road at that moment with his blue lights flashing. I must not have been among the Lord's favorites, because He wasn't giveth-ing me shit. There were nine guys behind me with guns. Ten if Rhodes had one, though I didn't see it, but of course he could borrow one from his pals. I had no idea where Steven's gun had gone. All eyes were on me and the building, its hidden treasure of at least a million dollars. I did notice that Jonas slowly, stealthily had moved until his feet were right next to his rifle.

What happened next looked like a stunt from an action movie.

Jonas hooked his toe through the strap of the rifle and kicked. Instantly, almost magically, the weapon leapt off the ground and into his hands. He didn't even raise it; he just fired from the hip at the nearest biker.

The rifle made a noise like an explosion, a deafening slap in the face. I reflexively put my hands over my ears; I saw many others do the same. The sound pealed back and forth throughout the parking area, ricocheting off of the stone building, the metal of the gate, the trucks, the cobblestones under our feet, every hard object it could find. It thumped me in the chest and shivered through my bones. It was so loud that the noise of the dead biker flipping back over his ride, the bike crashing onto its side, and two other bikers going down in a heap when he landed on them was nothing in comparison.

In the stunned silence that followed the only sound to be heard was the slapping of Jonas' shoes as he ran for the mansion entrance. My reaction was sluggish, and he passed me and was through the door before I had taken a single step. It had been even louder for the bikers because the gun had been pointed in their direction when Jonas fired, and not one of them thought to get off a single shot before we were both inside.

Once they recovered their wits, however, they opened up on us with a vengeance.

Thirty-Five

As my eyes adjusted, the blackness took on some texturing. There were vague shapes of things that were slightly darker shades of black, and others that brightened up all the way to a color I would call charcoal. We scrambled ahead through the darkness, climbing over wreckage that might have been pieces of broken furniture or building debris. I tripped on something hard that didn't yield, maybe one of the stone blocks that made up the floor, one thrust upwards as though from a geologic upheaval. I became airborne and expected to hit the floor and hit it hard, but landed instead on something like a discarded mattress that smelled foul, so foul that I was kind of glad I couldn't see it, but was thankfully soft.

As I regained my feet I looked back at the doorway to the outside which was distinguishable as no more than a blinding rectangle of light that actually hurt to look at. The shape of a man stepped into the light and I felt more than saw Jonas turn around and point the rifle, its barrel I was sure quite close to my face. I managed to get my eyes closed a fraction of a second before he fired. The shockwave of sound at this range was more like a punch than a slap, and I stumbled back several steps, becoming even more disoriented than I had been. I didn't know if he had hit the man he was shooting at, but the rectangle of light was once again clear.

I followed Jonas and we climbed a stone staircase, some kind of big, sweeping, circular affair. At the top there was light coming through an archway ahead, and we crossed into a room in which two narrow windows looked down into the turnaround.

While Jonas and I had been making our way upstairs, the bikers had fanned out and taken cover. Three took refuge behind the fountain, and two more behind my truck. Two others had scuttled to the guard shack, Rhodes with them. The one that Jonas had shot just lay there with his blood and brains dribbling between the cobblestones of the turnaround. I looked down at an extreme angle and I could just see the edge of a denim clad leg that ended in a worn black leather boot. Jonas had hit and killed the man in the doorway.

Laura and her sons remained where they had been, frozen in place, uncertain where to go. I suspected that was their best course of action; any movement on their part would likely get them shot. Of course, staying where they were wasn't all that safe either.

One of the bikers spotted us and pointed out our position to his buddies, and they opened up on us, a bone-jarring cacophony of handgun and machinegun fire that peppered the front of the mansion. The spray of bullets was impressive, but only a few found their way through the narrow windows. They hit the far wall of the room where they struck sparks against the stonework but did little damage to the building and none at all to either Jonas or myself. Nonetheless, they scared the shit out of me.

I cowered below the windowsill, trying to fold into the smallest possible ball, attempting to channel a swami I had seen on television when I was a kid. Over a period of about ten minutes the man had contorted his tall, gangly frame into a small Plexiglas box. Give me that box today, I thought, and I'd cram myself inside in nothing flat.

Lying beneath and to one side of the next window over, Jonas looked patient, almost bored, his rifle across his chest and his thumb caressing the stock lovingly. The gunfire came in one continuous roar, though occasionally there was a slight cessation as a few bikers paused to reload, and Jonas used the next one that came along to act. He calmly rolled into a kneeling position in front of the window, the rifle propped on his hand resting on the stone sill. He took a single shot, a loud, sharp and thunderous clap compared to the reports of the other weapons. Over the ringing of my ears I barely heard the muted crash of one of the motorcycles falling over. Jonas rolled back to his initial position, the entire movement completed in less than a second.

The gunfire stopped nearly as suddenly as it had begun. I took the opportunity to get a darting glance out the window and saw that one of the bikers who had been hiding behind the fountain must not have kept his head down far enough, because Jonas had blown off most of it, or at least most of it above his eyes. The body had been thrown back by the impact into one of the motorcycles which fell onto its side. Blood dripped from the wound onto the chrome of the exhaust pipe which was still hot from the engine, and it vaporized when it hit into little gouts of steam.

"Come out now, or we kill Laura and her sons," Rhodes bellowed.

"We go out there, you know we're both dead, right?" I asked Jonas.

"He'll kill them if we don't," Jonas said.

"I don't think so. He's running out of people who might know where this money is to just keep killing them. We're staying put." Even as I said it, I had no idea if it were true. Rhodes didn't strike me as a guy who spent a lot of time pondering the ramifications of his actions, especially his murderous ones. Though I had made it quickly, the decision had been a wrenching one. I believed in the concept of justice administered by the court; Laura and her sons didn't deserve to be shot by Rhodes and his merry band of bikers for killing Ellis. If Rhodes' next action was to shoot one of them, I wasn't sure how I would live with myself. I waited.

Jonas also waited, though he didn't seem any happier about it than I was.

There were some low voices as Rhodes spoke to others outside. Then he yelled, "If you come out now, I promise I'll shoot you in the head, make it quick and painless."

Jonas let out the breath he had been holding in a relieved sigh. "That's funny," he shouted back, "I was about to make you the same offer."

From his position behind the guard shack, Rhodes made some gestures to the others, and then opened fire, the others joining in.

"He's sending some guys around the building to come at us from the rear," I told Jonas.

"Well, at least he's not a complete idiot," he replied.

Jonas worked the bolt on the rifle and the empty cartridge kicked out of the eject port while a new one slammed home. He rolled into the window, but this time he stayed there, sighting down the barrel, heedless of the gunfire directed at him.

I crept up the wall until about a quarter of my head was visible through the window, just enough to see out with one eye. The two remaining men behind the fountain got up together and ran for the side of the building using the gunfire as cover. Jonas shot one of them through the knee, and the joint disintegrated. The man fell, shrieking, the gristle that held his leg together twisting as he went down so that his foot was facing the wrong way. When he hit the ground he either knocked himself unconscious or passed out from shock because he went silent immediately.

The other man skidded to a halt and tried to dive back behind cover, but Jonas calmly jacked in another round and shot him through the neck before he made it. He veered off course and fell dead into the lowest bowl of the fountain.

I felt a bullet whiz by my head, like someone had run a finger through my hair, and I ducked down.

Jonas rolled away from the window onto his back and worked the bolt again. "We having fun yet?" he said with a grim smile.

The gunfire died off, slowly this time instead of all at once. I wondered if the bikers were losing their nerve. I know I would have. Almost half of them were dead, and we had yet to suffer so much as a scratch.

I also wondered if at some point the police would show up. This was wilderness area, and kids hung out plinking cans and bottles with twenty-twos all the time, but even at a distance it had to sound like a war was going on out here. I tried figuring out how long it would take for Bobby to respond in my head. Someone who wasn't indoors running an air conditioner would have to hear the shots, recognize them for what they were, and call him. Given what had been going on, Bobby would probably drop everything and drive right over, I assumed with lights and siren going just to be optimistic. His cruiser could get most of the way down the trail, but probably couldn't clear the fence even after my truck had knocked it over. Call it, I told myself, six minutes of driving and another couple on foot. It could take, I concluded unhappily, as much as ten minutes for help to arrive at a minimum, and it would probably take even longer. Most gunfights didn't last ten minutes, did they?

Jonas pulled the clip out of the rifle. It was empty and he tossed it aside, and then dug another one from his jacket pocket. He rattled it and tapped it against the floor a couple of times, and slammed it home. "Stupid kids," he muttered, "holding their guns sideways like it's cool. My gunnery sergeant would have cracked their heads together like castanets."

"Are you seriously complaining that they're not shooting well enough?" I asked incredulously.

"I guess I am," he replied. He yelled out the window, "I shot a German General once with this rifle at four hundred yards. The furthest of you ain't but a hundred feet away. Like shooting monkeys in a barrel."

There was no reply and I peeked out the window. It was all quiet outside, and as near as I could tell everyone was staying put.

"Jack," Jonas said, "down the bottom of the stairs to the left is a door leading out back to a trail that heads due north. It's probably overgrown with grass, but you should be able to follow it to the power lines and run them back to Route 13. When I start shooting I want you to take off and bring back the Sheriff."

"I'm not going to leave you, Jonas." I watched as Rhodes gave the others a new plan using a complicated set of hand

247

signals. I didn't like the looks of it.

"You have a gun on you?" Jonas asked.

"No."

"You know how to shoot this one if something happens to me?"

I shook my head. I knew where he was going with this.

"Then the best thing you can do is go and get the cavalry."

I started to object, but he spoke over me, "Jack, this building may look like a medieval castle, but the guys outside aren't the Huns, and they're not going to lay siege and starve us out. At some point if they have any brains in their heads they'll rush us with whatever numbers they have left, and I probably won't be able to shoot them all. I'll keep the pressure on and make them think twice about it, and you should be able to get back here in plenty of time. Believe me; I got through worse scrapes than this in the war. These punks aren't going to win."

He rolled up and took aim out the window and put a bullet through Rhodes' hand. It was hard to tell from this distance, but I think he took off three fingers. One of the bikers poked his head up above the truck window line and tried to say something, but no one would ever hear what because Jonas put a bullet through the windshield that also shattered the side window, hit him in the mouth, and blew out the back of his neck, killing him instantly.

"Go, Jack!" Jonas shouted at me. "And tell the Sheriff to hurry his ass back here, or I won't leave anyone alive for him to arrest."

"I'm going," I told him.

I moved away from the window to the room doorway, and then looked back at Jonas kneeling in the window. The gunfire had started up again, but he waited patiently, sighting, assessing, and picking his targets with great care.

I ran down the stairs and out the back door as fast as my legs could carry me.

Thirty-Six

The day was sweltering, the fabric of my class A dress shirt sticking to my back in a line from the base of my neck all the way down to the crack of my ass.

I was far from alone. There were hundreds, possibly edging up near a thousand other firefighters around me, a great shifting mass of blue that filled the cemetery, bursting outside of the picket fencing in places to crowd the adjacent roads. Fire departments from every town in New Hampshire had at least one member present. The same was true of Massachusetts and Vermont, and most of Maine, and a few from Connecticut, and there was a company down from Canada. A crew of firefighters had even shown up from West Virginia, a group of more or less professional firefighter funeral attendees. That strikes me as heartwarming; the idea that the brotherhood of firefighting extends beyond your town and your department, a fabric that stretches across the entire country.

Milford and Hollis came with their tower trucks gleaming, freshly washed and waxed. Parked on either side of Main Street at the northernmost tip of the cemetery, they extended their ladders fully, a hundred and twenty five feet of polished aluminum, to form an arch over the roadway. An American flag seventy feet long was draped between them. Dunboro Engine 3 drove beneath this arch, under that flag. A pair of boots, bunker pants, jacket, and helmet had been ingeniously wired to the front bumper of the engine in a neat stack. The upper hose bed had been emptied of hose.

Jonas' coffin resided there.

When the truck stopped, I and the other pall bearers stepped forward and lifted the casket. There was a flurry of activity like the releasing of a flock of doves as nearly a thousand white-gloved hands rose to salute. An aisle opened in the crowd between the truck and the open grave. It was edged by firefighters packed in so tightly, that their elbows were jammed into each other's ears. Tank was on the handle opposite mine, and I was doing all I could to shuffle forward on my weak ankle and keep the coffin on some semblance of level. By the time we reached the grave I was trembling, fat beads of sweat clinging to my cheeks and dangling from the end of my nose. Once relieved of our burden I dabbed them away with the sleeve of my jacket, careful to avoid the stitches.

The priest stepped up and did his thing, and then Jonas' niece had some words to say. John Pederson spoke for a while.

I honestly didn't hear any of it. I was too busy playing the 'what if' game. What if I had never started digging into the cult? What if I had called Bobby with my suspicions before going over to talk with Laura Banks and her sons? What if I had stayed with Jonas instead of going to get help?

I was especially troubled about that last what if. Would things have turned out differently if I had stayed? I had really thought Jonas was going to be able to hold the bikers off until I returned with the cavalry. Had that been naïve on my part? Jonas occupied the high ground, had good cover, and he was a crack shot. What he hadn't told me was that he didn't have much ammunition. He had brought the rifle with him with just one spare clip, ten shots in all. He hadn't expected to march into Little Bighorn against Rhodes and nine deadly bikers.

With those ten bullets Jonas had killed eight men, possibly some kind of marksmanship record. He had critically wounded a ninth with a serious hit to the femoral artery. It was only through a heroic measure, self-applying a bandana as a tourniquet, that the man was going to survive at all, and he was going to lose the leg below the knee. Score one for the good guys.

Rhodes had come into the building, no doubt elated that Jonas had killed all of his partners; he wouldn't have to split the money ten ways. Out of ammunition, Jonas had drawn some old combat knife and charged, driving the blade through Rhodes' throat. Possibly in his death spasm, Rhodes' machinegun had discharged, and in the spray Jonas had been hit six times. At least that was one scenario consistent with the placement and condition of the bodies. All I knew for certain was that when I had returned with help, everyone with the exception of one biker was dead, including Laura and both of her sons, who had been shot a dozen times each. When that had happened or even why, I couldn't say. Perhaps with some ballistics work it could be figured out, as if it mattered.

What if I had stayed? Would Jonas have died? Or would this be my funeral as well? Every time I examined that question I liked the answer less.

Sometime during my ruminations the funeral had ended. The crowd was streaming away from the cemetery and up Main Street, a metallic ringing of hundreds of pairs of hard-soled shoes crossing the steel plates on the bridge. I stood and stared numbly at the tombstone; Jonas was being buried next to his wife Elizabeth. With a silent goodbye to both of them, I finally left the cemetery as well.

Back at the fire department people packed into the meeting

room. The trucks had been pulled out of the garages, and both the upper and lower equipment bays were filled with folding tables, chairs, and firefighters. The reception spilled out into the grassy field behind the station house and into the street in front, which was blocked off by Bobby's cruiser at one end and his deputy's car at the other.

I circulated, shaking a lot of hands and hearing a lot of old firefighting tales about Jonas, some of which I had heard before and some of which were new to me. I talked about the shootout at the mansion at least a hundred times, and told the story of Martin Pogue and the cult.

At some point I found myself in a quiet corner of the building back by the department offices. Edward Knox came out of nowhere and manhandled me with surprising force into the chief's office, closing the door behind us. I spun around and he showed me a face likely no voter in town had ever seen, his eyes narrowed in deadly menace.

"Well," he said, "you're quite the hero, aren't you?"

"Not the way I see it," I replied, "or Jonas and I would be having a drink at your funeral."

"Do you have any idea all the good I've done for the people of this town? All the sacrifices I've made?"

"That's it? That's your whole excuse? You sponsor the little league scoreboard and that entitles you to arrange a few murders?"

"Can you prove that, smart guy? Because unless you can prove it," he said, "you'd better watch what you say." He poked me in the chest with his finger emphasizing those last words. I recalled some cop movie where a bad guy had poked the hero in the chest like that, and the hero had reached out, grabbed the offending finger, and snapped it like a twig. I came sorely close to doing just that.

"I have a reputation in this town. People love me." He stepped in even closer, so close someone walking into the room at that moment might have thought we were kissing. "But you? You're starting to look like a real troublemaker. I'm not going to have any trouble with you, am I?" he whispered softly but menacingly to me.

I clamped down on the rage boiling inside me and looked him in the eye. "One way or another, for Jonas and Alice Lahey, you can count on it."

At the mention of Alice's name a look that might have been fear crept into his eyes, but he quickly battered it down with more anger. He opened his mouth to say something, but I gave him no chance. I shouldered my way past him, like a hockey player checking an opposing player into the boards. He stumbled against the wall, knocking several pictures down in the process before regaining his balance. I threw the door open and let it bang hard against it stop.

"Jack! Jack!" he called to my back. "We're not done here! Jack?"

I ignored him and forged ahead, certain that if I went back into that office I was going to do violence, possibly quite a lot of it. I went outside and circled the building a few times, trying to get my blood pressure down a few notches. There was no question in my mind that Knox had sent Alice Lahey to kill Rhodes and Anderson; the knives from the kitchen in Knox's rental house convinced me of that. Of course, convincing myself and getting a conviction in court were two entirely different things, and on that second goal there were no threads left to pull. Everyone was dead.

It galled me that Knox looked untouchable for the murders, and probably for everything else he had done over the years. The bribery, the contract kickbacks, he had been doing that stuff for decades. If no investigative reporter had managed to punch his ticket yet, there wasn't anything I was going to be able to do.

But for Jonas, I was going to try.

Everywhere I went in the fire station, I looked for Valerie. I hadn't seen her at the cemetery, and now I couldn't find her at the reception. Whatever the problems between us, I couldn't understand her skipping Jonas' funeral. I wandered down the street to where Bobby leaned against his cruiser. Lurch hung his huge black head out the passenger window, lolling his tongue, spilling copious amounts of saliva across the town seal on the door panel.

"Quite a turnout," he said as I approached.

"Jonas touched a lot of lives," I replied.

Bobby nodded, then frowned, "Listen, I want to say that I'm sorry. Maybe if I had taken Jonas more seriously when he came to me or been less concerned with my uncle's past, pushed his idea to the State Police, things might have ended differently."

"When he came to me I honestly didn't think there was anything there either. I only looked into it because Jonas was a friend. And if I hadn't started digging, Jonas would still be alive," I said bitterly.

"Don't beat yourself up about it," he said.

"It's all such a fucking mess," I continued, getting heated, "All the people who have died, and no one is going to prison for it. Is that fair? Is that justice? I don't even have any idea who killed Teeg or why. But Jonas is dead and a bunch of bikers are dead and a whole slew of elderly guys mixed up with that fucking cult are dead. I did a fantastic job, didn't I?"

Bobby looked away at the throngs of firefighters who talked and milled and ate standing in the street while balancing plates of spaghetti and open cans of soda in their hands. He said nothing.

"But I shouldn't beat myself up about it," I finished

sarcastically, the 'what if' game rattling around in my skull, making my head throb.

"I don't know what to say," Bobby said, reestablishing eye contact.

"I don't think there's anything left to say," I told him.

The sun was sinking low and the golden light was slanting down the street, winking sharply off of uniform badges and polished brass buttons. I felt melancholy, frustration, and a tremendous sense of loss and waste. I pressed a hand to my forehead, felt the line of stitches there. They were finally healing, and if I could keep people from hitting me in the face, I would be getting them out in a week or two.

"You haven't seen my wife, have you?" I asked.

"She's not somewhere in there?" he gestured towards the firehouse.

"She probably is," I replied, thinking to myself that she probably wasn't, and that the distance between Valerie and I had widened to a chasm that was threatening to swallow our marriage whole. "I just haven't managed to find her yet."

"Speaking of missing," Bobby said, "Just as a heads up, one of the lifeguards at Baxter Beach, a sixteen year old girl, finished her shift at two this afternoon and left to walk home. No one has seen her since."

"Did you talk to her friends?"

"Her parents are making some phone calls now."

"She have a boyfriend?"

Bobby nodded. "Twenty-two. Works in a bar in Manchester. I have Manchester PD looking for him."

"A sixteen year old girl with a twenty two year old boyfriend, last seen wearing a bikini at the beach three or four hours ago? She'll turn up."

"Probably," he agreed. "But just in case she doesn't," he added, "could you maybe ask some of the guys to ease up on the booze? If I need a search party later, I'd prefer it to be sober."

"I'll pass the word," I told him.

"Thanks."

I turned to go, but Bobby called out "Jack" and I turned back to him.

"I'm sure you did the best you could," he said.

I didn't have an answer to that. I likely had done the best I could. That was what I found so damned depressing.

I returned to the station house, went up to the meeting room, and picked up my own plate of spaghetti. The wives of the firefighters had been up since dawn cooking the sauce, boiling pasta in ten-gallon batches, and cutting up salad fixings by the bushel.

A crowd in the corner of the room was getting a little rowdy. There was a baseball game between the Red Sox and their arch-nemesis Yankees on the television. Jonas wouldn't have minded; he had been a diehard Sox fan for his entire life.

I considered joining them, losing myself in the game, but then decided that I'd rather be alone, torturing myself with a few more rounds of 'what if.' It looked like the Sox were going to lose anyway, and on the whole I've never been a big baseball fan.

Rachael came in through the door from the lower bays, spied me, and came over. She hugged me lightly, a momentary contact that created an unfathomable churn of conflicting emotions inside. When she released me, she stepped back and cupped my face in her hands. I gathered her hands in my own and pushed them down, but didn't let them go.

"We have to talk," I told her.

She gave a sad smile, "I know."

"I want," I began, but someone across the room called out to me excitedly.

"Jack! Jack! Your wife is on television!"

I released Rachael without another word and shouldered my way to the front of the group. They opened a spot for me near the screen which showed a local news channel, a 'breaking news' banner flashed across the bottom. Valerie, Melissa Teeg, and a man I didn't know stood behind a podium on a small stage. They were flanked by officers of the Milford PD and I recognized the woodwork of the Milford town hall. The gentleman looked composed, Valerie solemn. Melissa Teeg looked like a wreck: pale, haggard, her hair in disarray, with enormous dark circles under her eyes.

"That's the Milford town hall," a voice said from somewhere behind me and to my right.

"What is your wife doing on television?" Tom Schmitt asked from my left.

Good question, I thought.

Someone shushed them both, while someone else reached forward and hit the volume button. A little green bar extended across the bottom of the screen as the sound increased.

The man was speaking, "My client is confessing to the murder of Frederick Teeg in March."

"Who did Valerie murder?" Tom asked.

"Shhh!" I hissed.

A reporter had yelled out a question that I hadn't caught. The man was answering, "She takes full responsibility for the murder, and wants it made clear that her daughter played no role in his death. She is voluntarily..." there was a moment of bedlam, several shouted questions at once. Something bumped the camera which swung up to the ceiling and recovered, coming back down to the podium, several seconds later. Melissa Teeg had broken down in tears. She clutched at Valerie who put her arms around Melissa protectively.

The man continued more forcefully, "Melissa Teeg is voluntarily surrendering to police at this time."

The officers moved in to take Melissa. Someone from off frame jostled Valerie from behind and she stumbled into one of the cops who shoved her away roughly. I had an urge to claw my way through the screen to her side.

Melissa Teeg was put in handcuffs.

The scene devolved into chaos. Some people got up to leave the room. Others tried to push their way in at the same time. A mass of bodies surged and swirled in front of the stage. A question was yelled out, louder than the background noise. "Why did she do it? Why did she kill her husband?"

The man leaned into the microphone, "I won't be discussing the details of her defense here. I will say that there is much more to this case than meets the eye. Melissa and her daughter are the victims here, the tragic victims of a crime stretching back more than forty years with its origins in a violent cult in Dunboro."

The townspeople were going to love that. That cult was the gift that kept on giving.

As Melissa was led away, Valerie was harassed by reporters who shouted questions at her. The firefighters around me did the same to me as I pushed my way through them out of the station to my rental car.

When I arrived in Milford I found a snarl of police cars and news vans. I couldn't get close, not in the stupid rental. I have never missed having my big truck with its lights and siren more than I did at that moment. Parking in the lot of a supermarket half a mile away, I made my way back, only to be told once I had bulled into the town hall that Valerie had left for the police station.

The police department was worse, its front walk crowded with reporters doing stand ups, its front door clogged with print reporters clutching notebooks and tape recorders. If I had yelled out that I was Valerie's husband, I might have gotten through. I also might have been mobbed on the spot.

With no better plan in mind, I remained outside, waiting to see if Valerie would come out, gathering any information I could. The rumors flew fast and thick. Tenuous parallels were drawn between the shootings that had happened at the mansion last week and Melissa Teeg's surrender today. Teeg had been a member of the biker gang. Teeg had laundered money for the bikers through his plumbing business. Teeg was running an offshoot of the cult out of his house in Milford, a white supremacist thing and the bikers had all been members. The police were said to be getting a court order to dig up Teeg's backyard looking for bodies.

One of the reporters had managed to find a copy of Elmer Branch's book. Elmer had apparently been wrong; the one I had in my possession was not the last one. The reporter stood on camera with the book open, showing the picture of Frederick Teeg as he had been arrested forty years ago.

Were any of the rumors true? Was it all connected back to the cult? I had been right in the middle of it all, and I didn't have the slightest idea what the hell was going on.

One news crew decided to do a live feed from outside the

mansion, and that started something of a stampede into Dunboro. I called Bobby and warned him what was headed his way.

Afterwards, when the crowds had thinned, I made my way into the police station. The guy behind the front desk told me that Valerie had left some time ago out the back door.

Exhausted and dejected, I thanked him and walked back to the car.

Thirty-Seven

I returned home to a dark house. When I opened the front door, Tonk came over and twined around my ankles like a huge cat. Overcome by the moment I bent over to pick him up, planning to rub noses with him. When I tried to do so I recalled that, contrary to what his size would make you believe, Tonk weighed close to sixty pounds. I managed, barely, to scoop him off the ground awkwardly and hold him in my arms. He didn't enjoy it, and pin wheeled his short legs in the air until I put him down and he dashed off into the kitchen.

I followed him, stripping off my tie, opening my jacket, and undoing the top two buttons of my shirt as I went. I threw the wad of tie onto the breakfast bar and reached for the light switch.

"Leave it off," Valerie said from the darkness.

"OK," I replied.

As my eyes adjusted I detected her outline against the soft

blurred blue-green light from the numerals of the clock on the microwave.

"What are you doing sitting in the dark?"

She shrugged, and then I heard more than saw her pick up a cup from the counter, drink, and put it back down. My first thought, coffee, was swept away in a waft of something from south of the border. Valerie and tequila, not a good mix.

I moved over to her slowly, like approaching a wild animal, uncertain if it will bolt for the woods or go for your throat. I took a seat on the stool next to hers.

"I saw you on the news," I told her.

This earned me another shrug, and her another drink.

"When did you go back and talk with Melissa Teeg?"

"The day after you and I went there," she said tiredly. "And the day after that. And the day after that too."

"Why?"

"She wanted to talk, Jack. I saw that the first time I laid eyes on her. She needed to tell someone what she had done. Killing her own husband, she couldn't keep it inside; it was destroying her."

"But why? Why did she kill him?"

She picked up the cup and drained it all the way, her head tilted back, the shadows of her eyelids closed. I didn't know how much had been left in the cup, but I heard her gasp as she put it back down. "He was raping her," she rasped, her throat scraped raw by the alcohol.

"Who? Melissa?"

"Their own daughter!" she shouted. She dragged both hands through her hair and then buried her face in her palms. "Their own daughter," she repeated sadly, softly. "She turned thirteen years old, the same age as those poor girls in the cult, and that sick fuck started raping her."

My heart wrenched at the thought of Valerie and Melissa talking, the story slowly coming out over days, the abuse of a daughter Valerie would never have. She would have shot Teeg herself if it came to that. I would have. The world was a better place without such monsters. The pain Valerie had gone through, that I had put her through with my continual snooping, made me feel as through my heart was being squeezed in a large fist.

I reached out tentatively and put a hand on her shoulder. She turned to me and we leaned into one another. I put my arms around her, and her hands, like timid creatures, moved across my back to clasp loosely around my neck. Burying my face in her hair, strands of it snagging in the stitches on my face, I inhaled deeply of her scent, a yearning for her blooming in my chest so strong that it hurt.

We stayed like that for a long time, and when we finally parted I saw a glimmer of the light from the microwave reflected in the tracks of tears on her cheeks. I took her face in my hands and leaned forward to kiss her. At the last instant she pulled back and turned aside, my intended kiss glancing off the armor of her jawbone.

"I've," she began, and then took a deep breath, let it out, enveloping me in a tequila breeze. "I've been having an affair."

I stopped then, stopped everything. Breathing, thinking. My heart froze solid in my chest. All I did was ache, a rush of feelings too complex, a Gordian knot of love and hate and anger and fear and hurt that made it hard to swallow. And guilt, an overwhelming burden of guilt. At Rachael and I. At what my choices, my pursuit of Batman-esque justice, had done to my life and my marriage and those I love. It seemed that we all kept dirty little secrets hidden deeply within our hearts. They festered and rotted and putrefied, but they never went away. And they always worked their way to the surface, eventually.

I reached out and grasped her hastily, forcefully, pulling her to me, wanting desperately to meld us together. Valerie struggled weakly, shaking her head, a soft keening sound in her throat. I put my lips to her ear, took a shaky breath, felt as though my spirit was melting, burning in a nuclear fire to cold, dead slag.

"Me too," I scarcely whispered.

Valerie stopped struggling and sagged against me. The stillness of our house surrounded us, a silence as delicate as a ball of the thinnest blown glass. My heart began tentatively beating again. I was totally and completely there, hugging my wife. I thought that we would hug for a while. We would hug, and then we would cry, and then we would talk.

Instead my pager went off and the moment was shattered.

The voice of the dispatcher followed. "Tone is for the Dunboro fire department, Dunboro police, and EMS units. Respond to Baxter's beach to form search parties. The subject is a sixteen year old girl, last seen wearing a blue swimsuit and baseball cap at approximately 2PM. All units respond code one."

She hadn't turned up.

My first instinct, to rush out the door, to play the hero, I quickly attempted to quash. Not apparently quickly enough to pass unnoticed by Valerie, and she pushed me away.

"Go," she said.

She said it angrily, heatedly, at the realization that other people's problems always came before our own.

"Valerie, it's a sixteen old girl," I pleaded with her in response to the accusation she hadn't made.

"Go," she said again.

This time she said it sadly, in resignation to the understanding that her needs, our needs, somehow constantly came last.

"She's missing," I added.

"Go," she said, numbly, finally. The sacrifices we made would never end; there would always be another call, another emergency.

I looked from her to the front door, and then back to her again. Valerie's tears had dried; her eyes were closed. The decision that lay before me twisted my insides, dislodging and destroying things precious to me.

The stillness of the house was palpable, the hush of a rapt audience awaiting the dénouement.

I went.

Afterword

As before, I have drawn on my firefighting experiences in the creation of this novel. The call about the family on the front lawn of their house afraid that their electric oven was about to explode is completely true. While I have been to several accidents involving propane trucks, never has one exploded, and although I have not researched the issue, I suspect safety systems would keep that from happening in all but the most catastrophic of events. The story that Jonas tells Jack about the propane tank fire that killed several firefighters is sadly true. Finally, the story about the two veteran EMTs who retired immediately following an awful call is true, though I have altered the specifics of the call to make it difficult to identify them. They deserve to attend Christmas parties in peace.

Here's where I announce that I'm looking for firefighter stories to weave into the books. If you've got a good one, please send it along to psoletsky@gmail.com. If I use it, I'll give you credit, and ship an autographed copy your way. Such a deal! For those who wish to contact me for any other reason, that email address is good for that too.

Now turn the page for a special preview of *Little Girl Lost* the fourth Jack Fallon mystery.

One

The firefighters were arranged in a ragged line that stretched over three hundred feet across, the dark woods lit with the bobbing and weaving of our flashlight beams, the air filled with the echoes of crackling branches and the crunching of leaves underfoot. We were exhausted and dejected, reeking of sweat and insect repellant, thoroughly covered with mosquito bites where the former had washed off the latter. The beam of the flashlight clipped to my jacket bounced and skittered across rocks and sticks, tangles of mountain laurel and patches of lichen and moss. The coming dawn was a thin line of pink that I caught occasional glimpses of here and there through the trees.

Ten feet to my left I could hear the jingling of Winston's

key ring which sounded like spurs in a spaghetti Western. Tank ten feet my right breathed heavily but in a controlled fashion, deeps ins and outs like an enormous bellows stoking a fire. He was bulky and muscular, hence the nickname Tank, but bulky and muscular were not exactly the optimum adjectives for a search on foot in dense woods at night.

We kept a strong pace, an urgent pace. Sixteen-year-old Tracy Crawford had last been seen yesterday afternoon when she left her job as a lifeguard at Baxter's Pond. The longer she stayed missing, every minute that passed, her odds of returning home safely decreased.

The call had come in near the end of the funeral for Jonas Gault, a retired Dunboro, New Hampshire firefighter. Firefighters from other towns who had been attending the funeral had joined us in searching the mile of abandoned railroad bed which ran between the pond and Tracy's home. Hundreds of men and women were combing the woods in dress blues and patent leather shoes. Sheriff Bobby Dawkins had handed out white plastic garbage bags and encouraged us to pick up every scrap of manmade anything we came across should the worst turn out to be true, that Tracy had not vanished on her own. We fanned out into the forest surrounding the trail, first fifty yards off, then a hundred, then a hundred and fifty, as if there was any chance she had become lost or disoriented and wandered so far off course. There was no sign of her.

We had collected beer cans, fast food wrappers and bags, empty ketchup packets and sodden napkins, and crumpled sheets of yellowed newspaper.

My flashlight picked out a glint among the leaves and dirt. I dug in and came up with an empty Moxie bottle. Jack Fallon, New England garbage collector. I added it to my bag which already held a child's blue flip flop, a toddler's size, much too small for a teenage girl, and a single weathered playing card, the four of diamonds, missing a corner. The playing card had the enticing feeling of an exotic clue, perhaps from a Sherlock Holmes novel, but in all likelihood was just another piece of garbage.

We kept moving, and my portion of the line broke out into the open in the Crawford's backyard. The house was completely lit up as though for a party. As I stepped onto the grass, the glare of the big rear floodlights made me shield my eyes. They cast sharp shadows from a soccer net stretched over a metal frame, the railing from the rear deck painting a stark bar pattern on the ground. The morning dew sparkled, as though someone had scattered diamonds on the lawn.

Tank closed the gap with me and the two of us huffed up the small rise to the house and climbed the steps onto the deck. Winston stayed on his course which took him past the house and out to the street where he would cross into the neighbor's yard and keep going into the woods beyond.

Somewhere in the distance I heard a dog howl.

Sam, one of the town Deputies, sat on a lounge chair on the deck. He wore latex gloves as he pawed through the garbage bags, smoothing out pieces of newspaper, turning the scraps of fuzzy, bleached paper this way and that under the floodlights looking for writing. We added our bags to the pile in front of him.

"Find anything?" he asked as he lifted a rusted Altoids tin out of a bag, rattled it, opened it, found it empty, and tossed it aside.

"Lotta garbage," Tank replied. "The rail trail probably hasn't been this clean in years."

We picked up fresh bags intending to rejoin the line.

"Jack," Sam said to me, "Bobby wants to talk to you. I think he's in the living room."

"OK."

Tank and I went into the house through a sliding glass door. The kitchen was full of people, neighbors, local relatives, whoever. They spoke in low voices, picking at food on paper plates with plastic utensils. Ziti, Swedish meatballs, mac and cheese, taco dip – foods that could be assembled quickly and reheated often without becoming totally inedible. Electric casserole dishes and crock pots covered the counter; a single outlet split a dozen different ways to power them all. Nice fire hazard there.

Everyone looked to us as we came inside, our fire department jackets and helmets immediately identifying us as searchers. A man I recognized as Tracy's father, his name was David, asked me a question with his eyes. I shook my head minutely in reply. His jaw tightened and his gaze turned down. The man standing next to him put a hand on his shoulder.

Tank fished two plastic bottles of water out of the sink which had been filled with ice and drinks. He handed me one.

We went through a swinging door into the dining room. Five women sat around the table with cell phones, still working the phone tree at 6AM, getting the word out about Tracy. I heard her mother say "This is Naomi Crawford. I'm sorry to wake you at this hour, but I'm calling about Tracy. Has your daughter seen or heard from her?" A pause. "I know it's early, but could you wake her up and ask her please?" There was a plaintive, pleading tone in her voice that scraped ominously across my nerves, a premonition of a tragedy just getting rolling, the first rattling pebbles preceding an avalanche.

Past the dining room Tank split off to the right, went through the front hall and out the front door to rejoin the search as if the house hadn't stood in his way at all. The line would shift and readjust to cover my absence without missing so much as a gum wrapper.

I entered the living room, which looked like a brass convention: seventeen fire chiefs from various towns all in Class A's, spit and polished from the funeral. They had maps and radios spread out on the coffee table and the couches, coordinating hundreds of firefighters as the search widened and grew, concentric rings like the rippling of a pond. Bobby Dawkins stood among them, six inches taller than any other man, half again as wide. He looked like he was suffering the worst day of his life.

Fresh off a major shootout in his jurisdiction that had resulted in Jonas' death, the town was overrun by reporters trying to out maneuver one another for the most exclusive angle, the burned and abandoned stone mansion that had been the operating base for a violent cult forty years earlier forming a cinematic backdrop for dozens of newscasts in the past week. So far it was only local stations, but the story had proven to have legs and was threatening to go national. The only hotel in town – really it was more of a bed and breakfast – was booked solid. There were so many questions left unanswered about both the cult and the shooting, and new revelations and allegations were surfacing hourly. Could Tracy's disappearance be related?

Bobby's face lightened just the tiniest fraction when he caught sight of me, allowing himself the faintest hope that I would find the answers, and bring Tracy home, and make everything work out alright.

Oh Boy, here I go again.

Made in the USA
Middletown, DE
25 March 2015